D1148666

For all my family and friends, especially
my Mum for encouraging me to write.

LONDON BOROUGH OF HACKNEY LIBRARIES	
HK12002224	
Bertrams	11/03/2015
GEN	£8.99
	31/03/2015

1

Dear Lucinda,

I haven't got a boyfriend and all my friends do. On
Valentines' Day I didn't get any cards. I think everyone is
laughing at me. I don't want to go into school anymore
because of it and I don't go to the school parties now. I
am always the one left on my own. It makes me feel really
ugly. Sometimes I wish I was dead. My Dad says I'm really
pretty but I know I'm not. I'm too fat. I'm 14. Can you
tell me what to do?

Katy.

PS. I know you say you might print the letters you get. If
you print mine, please leave my address out. I hope that's
alright. I get *Misty* every week but so do my friends. If
they recognised me it would make things worse.

Dear Katy,

Growing up is a difficult process for all of us. Believe it or
not, almost all women have felt like you do at one time,
including a good few of the team here at *Misty*.

The trick is to concentrate on your good points. If you are
good at dancing, for example, put your efforts into that.
You'll soon find you meet other people with the same
talents who you get along well with – among them boys.

If your Dad says you're pretty then you probably are. Listen to the good things people have to say and not just the bad, which are often the result of jealousy or unhappiness on the part of those saying them. You'll soon find things get better.

Good luck,
Lucinda.

Mystic Misty

Pisces
Week beginning 3rd March

The past few weeks have seen a lot of upheaval for Pisceans. Even for those born under one of the calmest signs in the zodiac, the fall-out has been hard to handle. The good news is that a period of happiness is on its way. It promises to be a good time for cementing that burgeoning relationship. Single Pisceans will find members of the opposite sex irresistibly drawn to them. Love is in the air, breathe deeply.

Misty in Love
Tip of the week

Sex should be fun for both parties. But it should also be safe and that means using a condom. Using a sheath needn't spoil the pleasure for either partner. Make putting on a condom part of the love making process. Why not ask your partner if you can put it on for him? Some women use their mouths to do this – fine as long as your teeth aren't too sharp. However you do it, take time and enjoy. You'll soon find a condom can actually enhance sex, not detract from it.

Clearing the Mist

Poor old Geri Halliwell. The spice has really gone out of her love life since she decided to carve out a solo career. Judging by this photograph of her it's no wonder she's alone in more ways than one. That stomach looks as if it's ready to burst. Come to think of it, darts is something you can do on your own, Geri.

Misty Makes-up

Unprotected skin ages faster. Fine lines and dry patches are just two of the seven visible signs of ageing. Clarins' moisturising base with UV protection is a non-greasy formulation which will protect your skin from the withering effects of sun and pollution while also giving your face a healthy, natural glow. At just £15.00 it's also very reasonable. *Misty* is giving away free samples of Clarins' Moisture Glow to the first 25 readers who write in to tell us why Moisture Glow is the base for them. Remember to put your name and address on your letter. Offer closes Friday, 15 March, 2002.

Millhouse Farm,
Craigie,
Scotland

6th March, 2002

Dear Misty Makes-up,

My name is Katy and my address is above. I would love to
win a free sample of Clarins' Moisture Glow because my
skin is really dry but a bit spotty too and I need to cover
it up. Also, I don't have much make-up and it has to be
natural looking. If it isn't, my Dad will notice and give me
a hard time.

Katy Clemmy.

Misty House,
Tedford Tower,
Hammersmith Road,
London W6 3PQ

19 March, 2002

Dear Katy Clemmy,

Misty is delighted to inform you that you have won a free
jar of Clarins' Moisture Glow. We hope you will enjoy
using this quality product. You will find Clarins stockists
all over the country. We have enclosed a history of Clarins
and a colour guide to their products, and where to find
them, with your prize.

Thank you for reading *Misty*.

Jacqui Goodie
Misty Beauty Editor.

March 14th, 2002

Dear Lucinda,

I wrote to you last month and I hope you don't mind me writing again. You told me to do things I was good at and that I'd meet boys that way. I'm not very good at dancing but I can play some instruments so I went to the school orchestra. (I'm also going to audition for the junior choir because most of the third year girls in the orchestra are in that as well.) Now I'm playing piano, and sometimes violin, at assembly every day. The teacher who takes the orchestra is quite young and I'm 15 now. I really like him a lot. I can't stop thinking about him. I am going to his house for a lesson because he thinks I could sit Grade Six piano if I started practising again. (I stopped lessons when I was 12.) I'd really like to go out with him but I know that's wrong and my Dad would be angry. I still feel really ugly all the time but when I'm with this music teacher I feel better because he's nice to me. What should I do?

Katy.

PS My lesson with my teacher is two weeks today so if you can write to me direct again, or email me, I would really appreciate it. My email address is at the top of the page. I don't mind if you print my letter later too (but please don't put my real name or address in).

Katy Clemmy
Literature Ink Exercise

Discuss the part of fate in *Romeo and Juliet*.

"Romeo and Juliet" is a sad play in which fate plays a big hand. They are "star-crossed" lovers who are meant to be together. But while fate brings them together it also keeps them apart. Everything that could go wrong does.

Romeo goes and kills Tybalt when he's just trying to sort out a fight. Tybalt is a Capulet so Romeo ends up getting banished for this. He's secretly married to Juliet by this point so being banished is a bit of a problem if he wants to be with her. The Friar suggests to Juliet that she pretends to be dead so, amongst other things, Romeo can meet up with her in the vault and they can be together. He sends a message to Romeo so he knows what's up but in the end Romeo just hears that Juliet is dead and ends up killing himself over her dead body (although she's not really dead of course, just drugged). Then Juliet wakes up, sees what's happened and can't stand it so she kills herself. Really, it couldn't get any worse.

In conclusion, if Romeo hadn't killed Tybalt, if the Friar's message had got to Romeo okay, if Juliet had wakened up a bit earlier and if they hadn't been from two families at war with each other everything would have been fine. (It might also have been better if the Friar had come up with a better idea than Juliet pretending to be dead.) Romeo and Juliet were ill-fated lovers and that's the tragedy.

2

3B ENTERED the classroom at the end of the corridor on the third floor of Craigie Academy like a pack of steaming animals. The buffaloes entered first, boys who scraped chairs away from desks as they fought to reach the seats furthest away from the teacher. They bumped each other deliberately, kicked each other on the shins. Their faces shone with a mixture of exhilaration and aggression. Eyes alight, hair wet, spots glowing, they went for the kill and when they had claimed their prize, sat on it as if it was nothing to them. They didn't want to be here anyway. English was for girls and Miss Ellingham had the contemptible scent of weakness about her.

Next came the hyenas, giggling girls with their arms folded across their recently grown bosoms, hair hanging round their faces in untidy ropes you would never have guessed they had spent hours arranging. They kept their heads down, feigned awareness of no-one except themselves. But the strong scent of perfumes, soaps, deodorants and hair preparations revealed to the watchful Miss Ellingham who stood like a gamekeeper at the edge of the savannah that these were animals on heat, dizzy from the proximity of testosterone, who could tell by instinct alone which boys were sitting where and what they were wearing.

After the hyenas came the gazelles, graceful and long limbed, quivering with nervous beauty. Of these, Katy Clemmy was the last to cross the room, dropping into a seat in front of Miss Ellingham's desk with a flustered quickness which betrayed her self consciousness. Wide-eyed and watchful, she sat forwards and kept her blazer on, as if anticipating a need to run from danger at any moment.

The gazelles were closely followed by those who had somehow missed the point of evolution. Girls like Madeleine McCutcheon who wore thick glasses, and shoes she allowed a comparatively elderly mother to buy for her from Damart. Boys like Kevin McCarra who excelled at everything but could only talk to himself. These pupils, like the gazelles, deliberately took seats close to the teacher's desk and pulled out their jotters as if they were hymn books. Then, eyes lowered, they meditated above them, looking as if they expected their teacher to say, "Let us pray."

"Ink exercises down to the front," was what, in fact, she did say, and there was the rumble of conversation and another scraping of chairs on the black and white linoleum tiles as the buffaloes slapped their ink exercise jotters down on their desks.

"Pass them down then," Miss Ellingham said and the buffaloes took the opportunity to slap the hyenas on their backs and necks with the yellow exercise books. Soon the hyenas were giggling and rolling their eyes, attempting to hide their excitement beneath feigned indifference.

Miss Ellingham was by now rolling her eyes too, for among the things she hated most about a job she hated was the sheer juvenility of the pupils. Outside, she observed, it was fine spring day in which cauliflower clouds were coursing across a bright blue sky. The trees that ran round the perimeter of the nearby park looked less black and spidery than they had done a week ago when she had last taken 3B for literature. Craigie, the Godforsaken cultural backwater she had reluctantly taken a job in seven years ago, telling herself it was only for a year (something 'stable' that would utilise her 'talents', as her mother put it) looked almost picture-postcard pretty.

But time out for reflection was time she could ill afford. Turning her eyes back to the classroom she saw that the jotters had now made their way down to the wounded and gormless.

Madeleine McCutcheon had piled the jotters neatly on top of each other so that they formed an erect skyscraper but somehow a paper airplane had lodged itself in her bushy brown hair without her realising it and the sight of its nose emerging from just above her left ear was causing mirth in the desks behind her. Elise MacDonald who sat behind Kevin McCarra was making a show of dropping the jotters she had collected onto his desk one by one. She threw each from a slightly different angle so that Kevin, whose life would have been much easier if he had simply turned round and collected the jotters as a job lot, jumped nervously at the arrival of every one. Next to him, Katy Clemmy was faring little better. Her elfin face fixed on the window, blue eyes wide with panic, she was pretending not to notice as Billy Neill flicked rolled up balls of paper at her with his ruler from five desks back. As Miss Ellingham could have predicted, the ink exercise jotters were meanwhile lying on her desk in such a higgledy-piggledy fashion that they were starting to fall onto the floor.

"Katy..."

"...Clemmy's got big tits," said a voice that sounded suspiciously like Billy Neill's.

Miss Ellingham felt a sudden burst of pity for the girl just a foot away from her whose delicate face had flushed red and who appeared to be trying hard to fight back tears.

"I'll just pick those up, will I?" she said, bending down to scoop up the jotters lying at the girl's feet.

But as she gathered them, her fingers running across a film of dirt and dust the cleaners had failed to observe, sympathy turned to confusion. Katy Clemmy, recovered from the embarrassment of Billy Neill's comment, was watching her, along with most of her classmates. Watching her and, in Billy's case at least, smirking. *"Check that bum." "Lost a contact, miss?"* Miss Ellingham rose to her feet and stared out the window at the web of trees in the distance. All of a sudden she wanted to cry too. But I am too old to cry like Katy Clemmy, she thought, which made her want to cry all the more.

3

MY NAME is Corinne and I'm an alcoholic. I don't remember when I had my first drink. At eighteen maybe. 1975 or so. I was shy, wouldn't say boo to a goose. Drink made me talk, helped me flirt. I can't say I'm always glad to be here. But that's what we say when we get together in recovery, isn't it? Glad to be here. Glad to be sober.

4

Mystic Misty

Pisces
Week beginning 17th March

Dreamy Pisceans had better wake up and smell the coffee. Someone you've long admired is taking an interest in you at last. With all your planetary aspects indicating romance, there is no better time to make the most of this opportunity.

Millhouse Farm,
Craigie,
Ayrshire

20th March

Dear Gran,

Dad says I should begin by apologising for taking so long to write and thank you for my birthday money. I am sorry for taking so long to write and thank you.

I have been very busy at school. We have exams after Easter and a lot of reading to do. We are doing Romeo and Juliet by Mr William Shakespeare in English and the aftermath of the Napoleonic Wars in history. I think I am doing okay in them except that Miss Ellingham the English teacher says my literature essays need to be more mature. I don't know what more to say in them but she says they should be longer. Kevin McCarra who is top in everything writes twice as much but I don't know what he says. I am still very bad at maths.

I am taking Grade Six piano this summer if I get good enough. I have a new teacher, Mr Turner, who is a music teacher at school. He lives in a flat in Ayr and I am going there next Thursday for my first lesson.

I go jogging round the field behind the milking barn every morning now.

Mum isn't well today. She's in bed so I'm going to go and make the tea. Thank you again for the money. I am going to buy new trainers with it.

Love,
Katy.

20th March

Dear Lucinda,

I sent you a letter last week but I don't know if you got it or not. Anyway, I thought I'd email you in case you hadn't because the problem I have is to do with something that's happening really soon. A week tomorrow I have a piano lesson with my music teacher at his house and I'm in love with him. I know my Dad would be angry but I think he'd like him if he got to know him. I can't stop thinking about him and I think he likes me. I'm really excited about seeing him on my own. Do you think it's wrong of me?

Katy.

Wednesday list

Write thank you letter to Gran. Done.
Practise piano.
Make tea.
Phone the number in Misty.

5

SHE DID at least like her house. As she opened the front door every night after returning home from work it gave her pleasure just to see the brass plate reading "Jane Ellingham". Not Miss Ellingham, the unmarried English teacher of much-disputed age in the class at the end of the third floor corridor in Craigie Academy. "You know, the pretty redhead who's supposed to have had an affair with Mr Beetham the art teacher before he dumped her and married Miss Pickett the home economics teacher." And not Jane, the dutiful daughter. "She's teaching near Ayr now, in a good school. A permanent contract. No, not married. Well, she's not had much luck in that department. But as I tell her myself, she's better off on her own than with a man like that last one. The artist. More of a playboy if you ask me."

She watched the reflection of her briefcase grow bigger in the brass name plate as she approached the door. Jane Ellingham didn't have much of a chance to breathe anywhere else except inside this cottage, she thought, dropping the briefcase on the porch floor to put the key in the lock.

Inside, the sun from the back of the house came forward to greet her. She saw dust motes darting like tiny fish and felt the stuffy warmth of a house which hadn't been aired all day. The grandfather clock on the landing upstairs ticked, the fridge hummed like a familiar member of her family, Rocky the cat curled round her left leg like tourniquet. She felt as if she had left dry land and was floating in a warm sea. As if leaning back to let the tide do its work, she sunk down on the wickerwork chair next to the telephone and closed her eyes. The grandfather clock struck four. Eight hours and then a broken night's sleep until she was washed back to Craigie Academy.

6

TALKING about my feelings, especially when it is in front of other people, doesn't come very easily to me, but I'll try to be as honest as I can. The trouble is, I don't really know what the truth is. I thought, used to think, that if I was true to my heart then nothing else mattered. I suppose I *was* true to my heart and nothing else did matter. I tended it like a sick plant. Every day I watered it. Well actually, I wined it. Wined and dined it, no expense spared. It got the best Shiraz to begin with. It had expensive tastes my heart. But at the end it had to make do with whatever I could afford, whatever I could sneak into the house without my husband knowing, whatever would do the job quickly. Carlsberg Special Brew, White Lightning, Buckfast. Quick anaesthesia. You see, I think I indulged my heart too much. I grew to hate its moaning, its constant pain, the way it was always nagging at me. I wanted it shut up. I wanted it assassinated. I'd have paid a hit man good money. When he phoned me up to tell me it was done, I'd have sat back and laughed. Maybe I'd also have lit a cheroot, like Clint Eastwood, and bedded a local youth. God, the release from having no heart.

7

All third year pupils are requested to pass on the attached letter to their parents.

22nd March, 2002

Dear Parent,

As intimated in the school's most recent newsletter, Craigie Academy will be holding a parents' evening for anyone with a child in the third year on Thursday 28th March at 7.30pm.

Parents are requested to assemble at the school hall, which is marked on the accompanying map. There will be sixth year pupils on hand to guide you to your child's teachers. Tea and biscuits will be served in the school hall between 9pm and 10pm when parents will have a chance to mingle less formally with school staff.

Yours sincerely,

Malcolm Dick.
Headmaster

34, Seaforth Street, Ayr.
Tel 62490
22/3/02

Katy,

Looking forward to seeing you at 5.00pm on the 28th.
Mrs Simpson is taking the orchestra next week because
I'm on a course, and I forgot to remind you to bring your
copy of the Pathétique and any scale books you have.
(Seem to have lost my own copies of the Pathétique.)
If there's anything else you are playing just now I'd like
to hear that too. My address and telephone number are
above. Just ring if you have any problems.

Ron Turner.

PS. Hope this reaches you okay. I see you're in Miss
Ellingham's guidance group so I thought she could deliver
my note for me.

8

"KATY Clemmy – girl in your guidance group," Ron Turner said to Jane in the staff room. "Can you give this note to her?"

The music teacher bundled an envelope into her hands and immediately turned his back on her. "Craigie RFC is on a downward slide, Pete my man," she heard him say with bonhomie to the cauliflower-eared P.E. teacher, Peter Bryce, who was standing near by. He slapped the lumbering former prop forward on the arm and laughed loudly.

Jane looked down at Turner's "note". The way it had been handed to her proclaimed disinterest. *You, Miss Ellingham, and what I have just passed you, are of no consequence to me.* But now, as she turned the envelope over, it struck her that it was made of paper that was rather too thick and creamy to have been lying around in a school cupboard. What's more, the writing on the front of it was studied and neat, executed in the type of fibre tipped pen she herself reserved for Christmas cards, or letters to aged aunts.

Jane looked up and found herself still faced with a rear view of Turner. The back of his neck was inflamed with several angry boils. Under the arms of his pale blue shirt, two patches of sweat spread like ink stains. There's something untrustworthy about him, she thought, and then immediately scolded herself for being so judgemental. But her unease returned as she noticed Pete "my man" Bryce staring down in bemusement at the arm Turner had just given a matey slap. Without giving the music teacher so much as a glance, Bryce wandered off to join a group of noisy male maths teachers at the far side of the room.

If only there was someone she could talk to, *really* talk to, thought Jane. Close by, a group of female teachers were discussing cups. "My mug simply disappeared," Ellie Littlejohn from P.E. told Jeanette Wilkins from Biology as they fussed over jars of Nescafe and Coffee Complement. "Poof! Evaporated. Just like that." She flung up her hands like a magician. Jeanette Wilkins laughed a hard, clipped laugh which died on her lips: "Terrible. But I tell you what's worse. That creep Eric from the library helping himself to your mug and not even washing it afterwards. Have you *seen* the state of him? I had to throw that cup out!"

What was the point, thought Jane. All around her there was chatter and clatter, men prizing open Tupperware boxes to peer at the sandwiches their wives had made for them that morning, women on mobiles instructing teenage children where to find the soup they were to defrost for lunch. *"No, below the ice-cream... there's a label... lentil..."* The truth was she did not fit in here. She had never fitted in here, even when she was going out with Jim.

Perhaps if we had married... But that way madness lay. Jim had lost interest in her when she told him she wanted children. Pity she hadn't had the Home Economics' teacher's guile and marched him into matrimony – and paternity – before he'd had time to notice what was happening. Too honest for my own bloody good, she thought. She turned her back on the hubbub of the staff-room at interval and looked out the window. She wanted colour but was greeted by grey. Grey concrete. Grey uniforms. Grey sky. She bit her lip and tried to fight off the urge to cry which had been with her since her lesson with 3B on Wednesday. *Ron Turner. Katy Clemmy. Who cares?* It's not as if anyone had cared much about her when she was Katy's age. She walked to the staff-room door and half kicked, half pushed it open. She had made the mistake of allowing the bloody, throbbing pulp of her inner life into the workplace. It had to stop.

When she handed Turner's letter to Katy during 3B's second English lesson of the week later that morning she concentrated her mind on the face which had looked at her as she picked the jotters off the floor the previous day. She hadn't imagined it. Katy Clemmy barely saw her and what she did see was not a human being. Miss Ellingham was just a teacher, a woman old enough to be her mother. It was according to the natural order of things that she pick up her fallen jotters for her.

Katy looked puzzled at the envelope. Then her face flushed red. She took a swift look round to see if any of the rest of the class had noticed it. But Kevin McCarra was mumbling to himself and Madeleine McCutcheon two desks along was polishing her glasses in a fierce way which suggested to Miss Ellingham she was doing her utmost to appear indifferent to the existence of the rest of the class. Only the troubled Billy Neill had seen anything. "Hey, Miss Ellingham's passing dirty letters to Katy," he yelled. But as the rest of the class, including Katy, ignored him, he soon shut up and took to pinging one of the hyenas' bra straps instead.

"*Romeo and Juliet* today again," said Miss Ellingham. "Open up at Act Two."

As the shuffling and noise which accompanied the act of book opening started up, she took her opportunity to read out a notice which had been passed to her by Malcolm Dick.

"You'll be interested to know..."

"You'll be interested to know," said a parrot, which sounded suspiciously like Billy Neill speaking in received pronunciation.

"That..."

"Thet..."

"Billy Neill, if there's one more word from you, you can go and report to Mr Dick right now."

Proceedings appeared to pause for a moment. In what could have been no longer than two minutes, Miss Ellingham saw her whole class as if freeze framed on video. Her eyes bore through the hyenas' make-up to their delicate faces and clear eyes and on into their hearts. She felt them beating and was panicked to feel her own beat in time. She saw Billy Neill staring down at the blue-eyed, Nordic beauty that was Katy Clemmy with the gaze of a boy who already knew there were going to be a lot of things in life he would never get. And she saw Katy Clemmy herself, distracted, self-obsessed but vulnerable as an alpine flower that had somehow found its way into a hothouse.

"The school show this year is going to be *West Side Story*, which for those of you that don't know is a modern take on, guess what?"

"South Park," said a giggling hyena.

"Buffy," said Billy Neill, never one to miss an opportunity to attempt endearing himself to a hyena.

The silence had lit up too much of the adolescent nether world. Why should she bear witness to all their pain? Hadn't she enough of her own to carry? She felt her lips thin and tighten. To communicate with the pupils at the level of one human being to another was impossible anyway. She'd seen others try, by wearing Simpsons' t-shirts and inviting sixth formers round to their homes for video and pizza nights, or by letting their classes call them by their first name. Miss Ellingham shuddered at the very thought. It was her lifeline that Jane Ellingham remained unknown to all in Craigie Academy. Well, almost all.

"Actually it's based on *Romeo and Juliet*," she said, relieved to find her firm, no-nonsense voice again.

"Romeo, Romeo..." said a hyena called Shirley Stapleton who had dyed platinum blonde hair and an hour-glass figure she painted her school uniform on to each morning.

"That's right, Shirley. Glad to see you're learning your quotes. And perhaps you'll want to become a real actress by going for an audition."

There was a murmur of interest.

"They take place on Thursday 18th of April in the school hall. Four o'clock onwards. And if you want to see what you're auditioning for, Mr Turner is showing the film of *West Side Story* on Tuesday 16th at the same time. The production team, it says here, is looking for dancers, singers and actors. If you're all three in one, even better."

9

THEY say there's an alcoholic personality, that you're born a drunk and the actual drinking is just a way of medicating a nest of nasty traits like selfishness, pride and wilfulness. Certainly, I exhibited a lot of what the likes of you in this room would call 'alcohol*ism*' long before I found the corkscrew.

Take selfishness. God knows, it's not my only character defect but it's probably one of my worst. Anyway, I came across a photograph of me with my husband – e*x* husband – the other day. It was taken in 1997, twelve years after we were married. We're standing at the front door of our farmhouse and there are baskets of flowers hanging above us. The sun is shining. My then husband has his arm round me. He is looking at me as if I'm all that matters to him in the world.

Look more closely, though, at the woman so beloved of that devoted man and you will see an impatience in her expression. The truth is I had long begun to resent what many other women would have been grateful for. The way I saw it, I'd been cheated out of a life of glamour and passion, and cast into one that consisted of little more than muddy fields and home baking fairs. The fact that I had a man who cared about me and was prepared to love me through the most awful of trials meant nothing to me back then.

About a year after that photograph was taken I met an old school friend who appeared to agree my discontentedness was justified. "Corinne MacBeth," I heard someone call to me on Craigie High Street. I turned round and saw a tall woman with bronze-coloured hair. Her green eyes flashed with all sorts of mischief. She was wearing thigh-high leather boots over tight fitting jeans, a sheepskin waistcoat over a black jumper. An Amazonian princess. So un-Craigie. I stared at her for a long time, like I would a plate in a fashion magazine, before she nudged me out of my stupor.

"Corinne... it's Susan, Susan Flockhart. Remember? Sixth year art class at Craigie Academy? I'd been expelled from Campsie Girls' in Ayr... But I probably didn't tell you that – mother's orders.

Anyway, all that's ages ago now."

You could say meeting Susan again was like pulling at a loose thread. Before long, I'd unravelled most of what I had become and was left with who I really was. And it wasn't a farmer's wife. The farmer had wanted a wife but I – I began to convince myself all the more – hadn't wanted him.

Soon I had also convinced myself I needed a holiday (on my own, of course) so I booked myself into a hotel in Deja, Majorca, for a fortnight. I spotted it in a magazine and with Susan to encourage me, it seemed only fair.

"Tell Alan you need a break," Susan said. "For God's sake, Corinne, it's 1998, not 1898. When did you last have a holiday? Sounds like you've been stuck on that God forsaken dump of a farm since the day you got married."

Fuelled by Susan's sense of outrage, my indignation grew with every day. "What happened to the Corinne I knew – Corinne MacBeth?" my old school friend asked me once. "Didn't you once go to a school fancy dress party dressed in a Vivienne Westwood t-shirt, a black PVC miniskirt and canary yellow tights, telling everyone you were Malvolio? And look at you now – in your wellies and cardigan – cleaning out barns."

In Deja, watching an emerald sea from a beachside cafe, I bumped into Ruaridh again and thought I had my answer to Susan's question. My college sweetheart was what had happened to me – and what hadn't happened to me.

"I still love you, never stopped," we said to each other in as many words before the fortnight was up, my husband of 13 years suddenly no more real than if he had been a character in a quickly read novel.

See what I mean? The selfishness of the alcoholic. I had it in abundance and I had not really begun to drink – or at least, not like a true professional.

10

2002 Astrological Chart
for Katy Clemmy,
born 1st March, 1987

Love Omens:

An older man will have a big effect on you. But you will have obstacles to overcome before true love is to be realised. Beware of a person who seems to be a friend but isn't. A period of turbulence will be followed by a time of true serenity. You will find out things about yourself in the summer months which you never knew. What happens in the first six months of this year could have big implications in the coming years. Listen and learn.

Misty Body Gauge

If you tend to put weight on the bust then you are an endomorph. Believe it or not Naomi Campbell is an endomorph too. Make the most of this type of figure by wearing low, rounded necklines and A-line skirts. Well-cut jackets are good too. A well-fitting bra is essential. If you're not sure what size you are, go to our guide on page 23. Remember, if your cup overfloweth it's not necessarily a good thing.

De-Mistyfying Your Cup Size

To find out your cup size you'll need an old-fashioned measuring tape. Bras sizes are still measured in inches. First measure yourself round the biggest part of your chest – across the nipple line. Then measure below the bust. Add four if the number is an even one, five if it is odd. Subtract this figure from the first measurement. If the difference is zero, you're an A cup. If it's 2 then you're a B cup. If it's 3 you're a C cup and so on. The second figure also tells you what size of bra to buy – a 30, 32, 34 etc.

"This is a message for Katy Clemmy from House of Fraser in High Street, Ayr. You phoned to ask about 30DD bras with clear straps. I'm afraid we don't do that type of bra in a 30DD. I'm sorry we can't help."

Secret Venus

Underwear for the Bigger Woman

Our products are aimed at real women who want to enjoy their femininity. Cup sizes D to GG. All hip sizes. Excite those you love with your full potential. Send for our free catalogue today.

Classified Misty

Shape Your Future

The Rosewood Clinic is one of Harley Street's longest established cosmetic surgeries. We specialise in fat removal and breast surgery. Only one initial appointment necessary. Speak to our specialised staff in full confidence. Prices start at £1,000.

Special Discount Offer

Why not let Rosewood enhance *your* life by taking advantage of our Easter Offer? Contact us before April 5, 2002 and win a free initial consultation plus a 50% discount on any subsequent treatment.*

*Terms and conditions apply.

11

JANE had seen Ron Turner passing her door once already. He had looked in with a smile she feared was a pretext to something. After all, what would the young music teacher be doing in the English corridor at 1pm on a Friday afternoon? He didn't even work in this building, music being tucked away, along with technical drawing and art, in the part of the school known as the Old Tech.

Turner's second saunter past her door took place less than five minutes later and was heralded by some operatic humming. The light trill was so unusual that it prompted Jane to look up from her desk. To her annoyance she failed to drop her head quite quickly enough and found herself making eye contact with Turner.

"Hi," she said, and looked back down at the essay on *Romeo and Juliet* she was in the middle of correcting. She had just reached Katy Clemmy's summation of Romeo and Juliet's plight. "Really it couldn't get any worse." Little did she know, thought Jane.

She felt Turner hovering, like a wasp she'd attempted, but failed, to swat out the window.

"Marking?"

Miss Ellingham raised her head slowly and stared at him. Despite the sweaty armpits, a premature thinning of the hair and a small paunch, he had a boyish confidence that probably made him more attractive to the opposite sex than she appreciated. He was talented too, from what she heard – a first class degree from the Guildhall and a bursary to study piano at a Conservatoire in Austria.

Turner cleared his throat and looked round the classroom.

"Nice room."

She would have dismissed this as just another example of Turner's smooth confidence had it not been for the fact that it *was* a nice room. Unusually so. She had made a big effort when she had first begun working at Craigie Academy and much of it had been directed at this room. ("This job's a fresh start," her mother had told her. "And you'll be using your brains at long last. At least try to give it a go.")

Jane felt a wave of sadness wash over her. Her room, she had to admit, only remained 'nice' because of those first few months at Craigie. The posters for productions at the Barbican that lined the back wall were years old now and faded. The prints of actors who had appeared at the RSC in Stratford in the 1950s – Paul Robson, Peggy Aschroft, Laurence Olivier – were torn at the corners from constant re-pinning. Even the plants and flowers that cluttered the space between the window and her desk – a Christmas cactus, a yucca, two pale pink orchids and several geraniums – were a poor remnant of a collection which had once stretched all the way along one wall of the classroom.

"So, what can I do for you, Ron?"

Ron Turner stopped looking at a poster for *Chicago* and stared at his Camper trainers.

"Oh, I was just, you know, heading up to… having a bit of a break. That Old Tech we teach in is so stuffy."

He looked around the classroom again. He had small, regular features set in a fleshy face. His pale blue eyes seemed to darken when he was thinking.

"It's nice and bright in here."

The word "bright" surprised Miss Ellingham. She would never have associated it with Craigie Academy in general, or her place in it in particular.

"Well, even the dying need a little beauty in their lives."

Ron Turner's eyes opened wide. He looked alarmed. Miss Ellingham suppressed a chuckle.

"Katy Clemmy…" said Turner after a pause.

"I gave her your letter in English this morning."

"That was to remind her about her piano lesson."

Oh, for heaven's sake, thought Jane. She had Advanced Higher draft dissertations to look over by the end of the day, not to mention the remainder of 3B's literature essays to mark. If Ron Turner had an agenda, which she was sure he did, she wished he would get to it.

"I just thought I should let you know that if Katy seems upset, well, I think there's, you know, trouble at home. I'm going to be teaching her piano, you see, as you know, and she's in the orchestra so I see quite a lot of her."

Miss Ellingham watched Ron Turner closely. His face flushed a little as he spoke and he avoided looking at her directly.

"It's just your name is down as her guidance teacher," he added, inspecting his shoes again. "I just thought in case there were any problems or anything... or you were wondering why I gave her a note... I'm just trying to help out. Her mum was teaching her piano but seems to have stopped and it's a shame for her not to progress when she's so good..."

Teacher's embarrassment leads to upset. Upset teacher is embarrassed. Miss Ellingham felt there was a clue lurking in her classroom but was unable to decide what it might be, or whether, indeed, it was important. She would, perhaps, think about it later, after she had dealt with the more urgent tasks awaiting her that afternoon, namely her marking and a request to meet Jim Beetham in the art department.

"Okay, well, thanks. I'll bear it in mind. Trouble at home," she said.

"Yes."

"What's the problem then?" she asked, reluctantly.

"Her mother," Ron Turner said, raising his eyes at last. "I think she's really unwell."

"And it's upsetting Katy."

"Yes," said Ron Turner. "She won't say much but it seems she's doing everything at home, the washing, the cleaning, cooking, that sort of thing. I don't think she's getting on all that well with her father at the moment either. She was in a state about a row they'd had the other day."

"A row about the cleaning?"

Turner gave her an incredulous look. "What? No. Well, maybe – I don't know. The point is the girl's coping with a lot. The situation can't be good for her."

"No, I can see that," replied Miss Ellingham.

Ron Turner looked at her for a moment, opened his mouth

to speak again, then appeared to think better of it and left. When he shut the door, Miss Ellingham had the same sensation of relief she did when she closed her front door behind her on arriving home after work. Ron Turner was trouble. Teacher upset by embarrassment, she decided.

12

I DON'T have a photograph of Rhuaridh and me together in our art college days but if I did it's unlikely you would see him looking at me with the same loving devotion as my husband Alan once did.

"What are you thinking about?" I asked him once when we were in the union bar. He'd just told me how much he loved me, how we "made sense". It was 1975 and we'd only known each other a few months.

He turned back to look at me and laughed. "You, of course," he said, and kissed me on the cheek. It was only then that I noticed a pretty fresher staring over at us. She was standing in the direct line of where his gaze had been two minutes before.

If it wasn't a fresher it was an attractive mother pushing a buggy, or a gorgeous tutor in the college library. Ruaridh had what they call "a wandering eye". But for some reason I ignored this. If I thought about it at all I took it as sign that I was honoured in some way. This was a man who worshipped beauty, who intended to make his name painting it, and I was the muse who had captivated him more than any other.

Girlish nonsense when I look back on it now. Naturally, I was to be disillusioned. A year after we left college, he met the woman who eventually became his wife. In phraseology that sounded as if it had been plucked from an article in a women's magazine he told me that his "needs had changed" and mine would too, if they had not already done so. Unfortunately, he was wrong.

Oh, there were other boyfriends, of course, but none who I cared for in the way I had for my first love. There was a passion between Ruaridh and me in those college days that nothing else could match. Even today I can remember the constant yearning to be together, the unspoken connection as we worked in the studio.

Friends began to marry and have children. "When are you going to settle down, Corinne?" they would ask me. "You can be too fussy, you know." Perhaps that's why, five years after splitting up with Ruaridh, I said "yes" when a quiet farmer's son proposed to me. Passion had ended in heartache. Flamboyance was not to be trusted. I threw in my lot with a man I knew to be steady and kind.

And of course, if I hadn't married, I wouldn't have had children. First Katy, nervous and anxious from the moment she arrived, and five years later, Ben, the little boy we called "the angel" on account of his sweet countenance and easy-to-please nature.

I can't deny that both of them brought me happiness but it wasn't long until my daughter's watchful, tortured eyes began to unsettle me. Katy cried when she was shouted at. If there was a loud noise she jumped. While other children relished the prospect of holidays away with school Katy refused to go. When she was forced she wrote a letter home every day and, to her teachers' dismay, cried herself to sleep each night.

I carried on – polishing school shoes, making packed lunches, feeding chickens – but sometimes when my life as a farmer's wife was at its most strained I would think about Ruaridh and the passion we had shared all these years ago. By the time I met him again in Deja my sense of rage at what life had dealt me was so great I felt the universe owed me a little happiness. If that was to be at the expense of my husband and his wife what did I care?

13

Misty Problems

Dear Reader,

Thank you for your letter. Feelings for older men are very normal for girls of your age but you shouldn't confuse what they are – just a crush – with love. You'll find boys of your own age will start becoming interested in you soon enough, and you in them. Meanwhile, enjoy your piano lessons.

Lucinda.

Misty Position of the Week

Doggy

Growl. This position is for those of you who like a bit of bite in your sex. It leaves your partner's hands free for clitoral stimulation. And if he doesn't know where to look, then you can lend him a hand yourself. Both of you will find there's something about the doggy which brings out the animal in you. Do use: when you're extra horny. Don't use: if you've got a knee injury. Reading on the Richter Scale: 8. (This one could bring the house down so be careful if your parents are around.)

For March 28th

Pathétique:
LH too heavy. No sirens. Hold back in opening chords.

Chopin Prelude 15:
Steady build up. No thumping.

Scales:
Slow, with metronome.

```
I  c  u  big  boobs  I
want 2 do it with u
```

"You have one new message. First new message: 'Hello. Is that Katy Clemmy? The one with big tits and fanny? Well, I just want you to know I want to screw you.' You have no more new messages."

Marks and Spencer Minimiser Bra

This bra has been specially designed to create a smooth line for the bigger woman. Your minimiser bra can be machine washed but for best results, hand wash in lukewarm water. For full care instructions see inside label.

Misty's Easter Special Guide to Star Quality

She may be your Dad's age but Kylie's eternally youthful looks ensures she's a hit with any man. What's her secret? A super-fit body, tiny clothes and, phew, that sexy dancing. Give yourself a Kylie make-over with the help of Misty stylist Mandy Brazil and ensure your Easter really sizzles.

Step One: Bright red lips with shimmer will give you Kylie kiss-ability. We used Boots Pillar-box Attack with a little Clinique clear gloss to create the perfect Kylie mouth. A touch of glitter around the eyes will complete the look. Don't blink too fast or you might cause a pile up.

Step Two: No-nonsense pigtails will give you Kylie schoolgirl sex appeal. If your hair isn't long enough, indulge in extensions. St Trinian's girls never had it better.

Step Three: Lately Kylie's been wearing Madonna t-shirts but who wants to advertise that old bag? We suggest a sequined off-the-shoulder top like the one she's wearing in this photograph, taken at last year's Brit Awards. We like the emphasis on "Babe" rather than "Madge". Round off with platform trainers and hip-hugging flairs and make sure your belly button ring has a touch of glitz to it.

Now you are ready to pull them in like Kylie. You should be so lucky.

Dear Ms Clemmy,

Thank you for making an appointment for Friday 29th March at 3.45pm with Dr Nanjani to discuss breast reduction surgery.

Here at the Rosewood Clinic in Harley Street we have performed thousands of such procedures in the past five years. Our satisfied customers live the length and breadth of the country, and abroad.

The Rosewood Clinic is one of Harley Street's best established clinics specialising in cosmetic surgery. We have enclosed a full colour brochure, outlining the procedures we perform and containing testimonies from some of our many clients. Many of our clients return again and again to build upon the visible improvements we have brought into their lives.

A separate price list is attached to this letter.

Yours sincerely,

Marlene Davis

Manageress, The Rosewood Clinic.

To Do – Weekend

Foundation.
Powder.
Blusher.
Mascara.
Body glitter.
New bra.
Pathétique.
Chopin. Nocturne?
Tell Dad going to Mad's Thurs.
Perfume?

14

JIM Beetham's hands were covered in clay and to Jane Ellingham it seemed for a moment as if time had stopped still. Six years ago, in this very room, she had taken one of Jim's clay-covered hands in her own and traced the clearly etched lines on his palms with an index finger.

"I see great things," she had giggled.

"Like what?" he'd laughed back, grabbing her face between his hands and squeezing it as if she were a child. "Naughty sculptures of a gorgeous, red-haired English teacher? Fired from passion."

The memory almost made her smile but she stopped herself just in time.

She closed the classroom door quietly and stood with her hands behind her back, one gripped round the door handle.

The classroom still reminded her of a family garden shed, full of oddments nobody wanted anymore. Straight ahead, beneath three enormous windows that looked onto the park, ran a long bench. Busts, logs, old shoes, a broken typewriter, failed attempts at pots and jugs which had cracked in the kiln, all cluttered its surface. Beneath were pots of emulsion with drips running down the side of them, cardboard boxes with "First Year Christmas projects" or "Higher folios" scrawled on them in felt-tip pen. The air was permeated with the smell of paint and turpentine. The walls were covered in drawings and paintings mounted on black card, the best of what Craigie Academy had to offer the artistic world, going back at least a couple of years.

Jim Beetham was looking out the window, with his back to her. His sleeves were rolled up and Jane noticed now that the drying clay covered not only his hands, but his wrists. She noticed too that his sandy coloured hair was thinner than it had been and that there was a patch close to bald around his crown. Staring at that and the striped shirt, which was similar to one he often wore six years ago, Jane felt herself weighed down with an immobilising sadness. Everything is futile, she thought suddenly and if she had been able, she would have turned on her heel and left.

But Jim had become aware of her presence. He turned round in the sunlight like a lion, golden hair glinting, his stocky frame alert and assessing. He took a few seconds to decide how to react and in those moments Jane felt for all the world like a defenceless child. For it was as it ever had been, he would make the decision and from there on her fate would be set.

I have spent years growing away from you, she wanted to say. I am mature, independent, not the person you think. And yet here she was immobile, all the books on living alone and recovering from a broken heart rendered useless. Jim would have laughed at them. "American psychobabble," he'd have said before tossing them away. But then Jim didn't need help, didn't need to grasp at badly written books by people with names like Elton Goldstein, MD, PhD, "world renown expert on communication from the heart". Jim was the king of the jungle. Alpha male. Craigie Academy's James Bond. He both hated and thrived on the scent of weakness. He saw what he needed and hunted it down. When he'd finished with it he felt no remorse. Metaphysics was for the birds.

"Jane," was what he eventually said.

He feigned surprise to make the air lighter, dispel any suggestion that his request to see her had stemmed from personal need. You've chosen to come and see me, he implied, with his usual ability to turn reality on its head.

"I got your note," Jane said, her grip on the truth of the situation already loosening.

"Hm," responded Jim.

He *had* sent her a note, she told herself. It had been in her pigeon hole waiting for her when she'd gone into the staffroom that morning. The very reason she was standing here now was because of that note.

"What was it?" she asked.

"Hm?"

"What was it you wanted to speak to me about? Your note said you wanted to see me."

Jim inspected his hands.

"Oh that."

Jane stared out the window. The blossom trees were in full bloom. As their heavy branches wavered in the faint breeze speckles of sunlight shifted across the classroom walls. It was so quiet that she could hear the screams from the playground on the other side of the building, the sound of a small child crying in the park. Early spring leant a fresh brightness to Jim's normally dank classroom. He never switched the radiators on – art is physical, he told his pupils, give it your best and you'll soon warm up.

"Do you want a coffee? The kettle's on."

Jane turned the doorknob with her right hand.

"I've got marking," she said.

He stared at her for a moment, as if observing something new about her, and moved towards a row of sinks at the far end of the room. Beside the one nearest the window the kettle was reaching boiling point. He took a jar of Nescafe down from a shelf and put a spoonful into a blue and white striped mug.

"Sure?" he asked, nodding at the coffee jar.

Jane clutched the doorknob more tightly and nodded.

He walked back from the sink nursing his mug of black coffee, pulled up a stool and sat it next to the bench. Then he sat down and placed his mug next to a sheep's skull.

"Oh, sorry," he said, after a moment or two had passed and stood up again. He walked over to a Formica table in the centre of the room, not far from where Jane was standing, and pulled out one of the orange, plastic chairs pushed underneath it. He dragged it back to where his stool was placed.

"Have a seat," he said.

And I would sit beneath you, she thought, observing the diminutive height of the plastic chair compared with that of the stool. I wouldn't even be able to see out of the window, but you would have it that way, my horizons constrained.

Six years ago she had lain on her back naked on the floor of this room as Jim Beetham had made love to her. Later, she had crept down the corridor, her underwear damp, her back sore from the wood, bruises that resembled squashed soft fruit already beginning to form on her white flesh where Jim had half-bitten, half-kissed her. She had bumped into the cleaner and told herself her disapproving look was that of a woman who had no love-life of her own. She had told herself this was passion, raw and unconstrained, something which could not be held back. In reality, she thought now, it had been sex for Jim and the hope of love for her.

Jim was shifting the sheep's skull on its axis, looking at it from each angle. But Jane knew this was just a distraction, that aesthetics were the last thing on his mind.

"Sicko Dicko has asked me to do the scenery for the school play," he said, looking out of the window.

"*West Side Story*," said Jane.

"Yes. *West Side Story*."

"It could be good fun."

"It's hard to refuse."

"You just say 'no.'"

"Not if you want..."

"Promotion?"

Jim pushed the skull away from him and turned round on his stool to look at Jane straight on.

"I suppose you'll be directing."

"I haven't been asked," she said, choosing her words carefully.

"But you would, if you were."

"Right now that's academic."

Jim stood up and looked back down at the sinks.

"Sure you don't want a coffee?"

Jim's awkwardness was beginning to make Jane feel rather powerful.

"Ron Turner's putting in for the assistant principal job," he said, still looking at the sinks.

"Oh. A bit young isn't he?"

"A rising star, though. I think there's going to be quite a few in for it. Funny. Not the nicest of jobs, dealing with all Sicko's discipline cases for him. You just had to see what it did to old Murdoch to see what a nightmare it is."

"Good money though," said Jane, nursing her sense of power.

Jim sniffed and then ruined the effect by having to cough straight afterwards.

The bell rang. Suddenly the building seemed to be under siege. From every angle, the roar of children's voices approached them like an advancing army. Doors slammed. There were screams. A child with a deep voice ran along the corridor outside, chanting, "Celt-ic, Celt-ic, Celt-ic." As he did, he ran a ruler or a stick over the radiators so that they emanated a strange off-key xylophone sound. The floor in the art room shook as he ran past the door and the draft he created made a thin pile of coloured tissue paper on the table in the centre of the room rise and then fall as if a clutch of invisible faeries had rushed under it for cover.

"You're not going in for it?"

Time was running out but Jane knew that wasn't the only reason he asked the question then. It was because he was cowardly and the noise of the pupils coming in from their break helped him to appear casual.

Neither the fact that Jim wanted to know if she was going for the APT job, nor the way he tried to find out, bothered Jane. She already knew her former lover now saw her as little more than work rival. It was Jim's tone of voice that reignited some of the pain she'd felt when she'd been dropped by him.

"*You're* not going in for it," he'd said, the emphasis on "you're" implying a vehement contempt for her very essence.

It was an unnecessary and cheap intimidation tactic, and its effect was so profound that at that very moment Jane Ellingham for the first time in many years made the decision to bow to her lower self.

"Och, yes, of course," she said, lining up Jim Beetham between narrowed eyes. "*I'm* going in for it."

15

LOVE cast a spell over me.

"Hey, blondie, looking good..." workmen shouted as I walked down Craigie High Street.

My husband paid me compliments. Our daughter smiled again. It was as if the sun had suddenly come out in a landscape that had known nothing but dark cloud.

In the summer of 1998 I sat in the middle of this warmth with only one thought on my mind, that Ruaridh would be getting in touch. It was like being back at college again, waiting for his letters to arrive during the long summer break. When I felt any guilt about my affair, which was rare, I invited Susan round and opened a bottle of wine. Susan who had left her freelance publishing job in London for a few months to be with her mother following her father's death, was only too delighted to recreate a little of the capital's wine bar culture in dullest Craigie.

"To the return of the old Corinne," she would say, clinking her glass noisily against mine.

From Susan there was no fear of the judgement my Craigie friends would have meted out if they had known about Ruaridh. Twice divorced, Susan had given up 'proper relationships' for flings with married men. She joked that it was a matter of principle. No point being the taken-for-granted main course when you can be the savoured dessert, she said. I listened to her with a heart lighter than I had known in years. But every so often I would notice my eleven-year-old daughter, her presence like the steady ticking of a clock in the corner of a room. A quiet watchfulness began to intersperse her smiles.

To rid myself of the discomfort this brought I began opening bottles without inviting Susan round.

And when Ruaridh wrote to tell me there was to be no "us" again (it was "madness" to have thought we could be what we once were) I began to drink so heavily I felt the need to bury the evidence.

A farm is a good place for an alcoholic to live. Acres of fields. Plenty of spades. Very few people around.

Actually, I've no idea how those of you who live in a town flat did it.

16

"HELLO is that Katy Clemmy, the one with the big tits? I just want you to know I'm watching you."

```
                                Big Tits I want to
                                shag u Ill phone U
                                again 2nite.
```

```
Hi Katy. Dan from
RockFrendz      forum
here. Thanx 4 ur mob
no. Just got tckts
for me and pal Seth
4 Bel&Seb at Brixton
Ac April. Cant wait.
How u? Lking fwd to
meeting u Fri nite.
Dx
```

26th April, 2002.

Dear Sir/Madam,

I am emailing you concerning your adverts in Misty magazine. I am interested in breast reduction surgery and have made an appointment for a free consultation this Friday. I was sent a brochure about your clinic and it said I should fill in an information form and post it back to you before my appointment. However, I haven't received any form. Please could you tell me what to do about this.

Yours truly,
Katy Clemmy.

Best Not Mist

You can't accentuate your positives until you've eliminated your negatives. Our revealing quiz will help you uncover each and every one of your flaws so you need never look your worst again.

1. Where are you most likely to put on weight? A. Your hips ... B. Your bust ... C. Your stomach ...

2. Do you put on weight? A. Constantly ... B. Only when you eat the wrong things ... C. Never ...

3. Do you find it difficult to find clothes that fit you? A. Only for your bottom half... B. Only because they don't make clothes for real women nowadays ... C. Never ...

4. What 'type' would you say you most resemble? A. Jennifer Lopez ... B. Sophia Loren ... C. Calista Flockhart ...

5. Who is your mother most like? A. Dawn French ... B. Madonna ... C. Courtney Cox ...

6. What is your worst fear about growing old? A. Not being able to eat as much ... B. Being like your mother ... C. Being spoon-fed Complan ...

7. Under stress what are you most likely to do? A. Reach for the biscuits ... B. Seduce the first acceptable man you kind find ... C. Forget to eat ...

8. Which most appeals to you? A. Chocolate profiteroles with cream and ice-cream ... B. Baked trout with almonds, served with duchesse potatoes and French beans ... C. Carrot sticks and low-fat hummus ...

9. Which has the least calories? A. A bag of crisps ... B. A Mars Bar ... C. An avocado pear ...

10. Do you exercise? A. Never ... B. Once or twice a week ... C. Constantly ...

With the exception of question 9, score 3 points for each time you answered A, 2 for each B and 1 for each C. If you answered C for question 9, score 3 points. B scores 2 points and A 1 point. Now add up your score and write it down ...

25-30 points: You probably don't need us to tell you but you're fat. Put down that bowl of Frosties and start running, preferably to the nearest branch of Weight Watchers.

19-25 points: You like to think you're all woman, Sophia Loren meets Kate Winslet. Sorry to inform you that if you're not careful some of the those 'curves' could morph into blubber. A little less pasta, a little more sex – but be careful not to wear your man out.

Under 19: Sorry, we didn't see you there. You were standing side on. Fat isn't your problem but has anyone told you that you can be too thin? What looks good when you're a Swedish high jumper is about as sexy as a clothes horse when you're a pasty-faced Brit.

Misty Recollections

"She's probably the most feminine woman I've ever known." Ralph Fiennes talking about his inexplicable love for 50-something Francesca Annis.

"You get to realising life's not about what size you are." Thunderous Dawn French fails to explain how she managed to snog George Clooney on national prime-time television.

"Forty didn't bother me. Inside I'm happier than I've ever been." Caroline Quentin reveals how she manages to keep smiling.

To Do

Remember

Tickets
London A-Z
Misty
Phone?
Straighteners
Sponge Bag
Tops and underwear. Socks.
Check map for hostel.

Friday

Rosewood Clinic.
Dan.

Hi Dan,

I love Belle and Sebastian too, and Tori Amos. But Dylan is the best, as you know! I haven't been able to get on RockFrendz for a while. My Dad doesn't like me being on the computer. The other night he started yelling at me because I wanted to go on it after my tea. He's always like that when my Mum's been ill.

Anyway, it's good to email you. I can't wait to meet you for real. Can't stay long on email cos I'll get chucked out the library soon and I've got a music lesson later. At least it means I don't have to go home and make my mum's tea or get yelled at again by my Dad. Mind you, he's not talking to me at all at the moment so he probably wouldn't even shout.

C u sn!

Katy.

--

Hi Katy,

What are you doing in the library? What music do you play? And what instrument?

Yep. See you T Square 6pm tomorrow – if still ok.

Dan

--

Hi again Dan: I am just finishing an essay. I play piano – violin too but not that well. I'm taking my Grade Six (piano) in the summer. I'm getting extra lessons because I've not played properly for a while.

Trafalgar Square is fine – looks close to where I'll be in the afternoon.

I've never been to London so I'm kind of excited.

Katy.

--

Hi Katy. There are some really good music venues in London we could go to tomorrow night but I have a benefit gig I need to be at from around 9pm if poss. You're welcome to come along... can't promise Belle & Seb or Tori Amos but there are some good local groups playing (world music mostly).

What are you studying? Suppose I'm lucky I had flat when I was a student. Difficult living at home – know all about it as currently live with my mum when not abroad.

Dan

--

Hi Dan: Sorry it's taken me a while to get back to you. I'm really tired. It's difficult to sleep at home sometimes because my Mum and Dad shout a lot.

I'd really love to go to music venues in London but the benefit thing sounds good too.

Katy.

--

Hi Katy: Sorry about the music venues but the gig should be good. It's just in a community centre near me but as I said, the bands are worth hearing – local samba and reggae groups, plus some great acoustic acts. And a few of us might go out afterwards anyway. You could always join us!

So what do you look like/wear? I'll need to recognise you. Your forum picture is Tori Amos?!

Dan

--

Hi Dan: I am just over five foot five and have blonde hair. I like wearing all sorts of different things. Sometimes I wear old things of my Mum's from the 1970s. I found them up in our attic.

I'd like to go out after the gig.

What sort of music do you like (apart from Belle and Sebastian)? What do you look like? Your RF picture is kind of dark!
Katy.

--

Hi Katy: That's what my sister says – I'm "dark". LOL. Dunno really. I look like that picture 'cept lighter. LOL. I have no style except non-fashion victim. Music-wise I like... dark!
Dan

--

"Hello. This is a call for Katy Clemmy from Marlene Davis at the Rosewood Clinic. Just to remind Katy that Dr Nanjani is expecting her for her initial consultation at 3.45 pm tomorrow afternoon. We usually prefer our clients to fill out an information form before their first appointment but if Katy can arrive twenty minutes early we can make sure we've got her details down before she sees the doctor. Thank you."

17

JANE Ellingham didn't enjoy parents' nights. In her early days of teaching, perhaps, but not now when the parents were the same age as herself, or younger. It was as if God was re-opening the wound he had inflicted ten years ago when her friends had begun settling down and starting families. Just to remind you, you're still on your own Jane, no family life for you. Too late anyway, isn't it?

This particular parents' evening she was feeling even more irritated by what lay ahead than usual. She had been enjoying planting out her strawberries when she had looked at her watch and realised it was time to return to Craigie Academy. It was a beautiful spring evening, one on which she could have truly forgotten all about school. She didn't even have any marking to do. Several days' hard graft during free periods and intervals had seen to that.

She approached the narrow entrance into the staff car park feeling angry rather than bored, as she usually did in the mornings. The pile of coal next to the doors leading into the assembly hall irritated her. (Why didn't they put it somewhere out of the way where people didn't have to walk round it to get into the school?) And even just the sight of Jock Wilson, the janitor, annoyed her. No doubt he'd tell her she couldn't enter by the assembly hall – Sicko's orders – and that she'd have to walk round to the front of the school like everyone else. Jockie was a man whose greatest pleasure in life came from putting difficulties in the way of others. "I'm sorry, dear, the library's shut for repairs today." "You'll need a note from Mr Dick before I can fix your desk, dear." "I'm afraid the cleaners have asked me to return your bin to you. Health and Safety. They won't empty it with that glass in it." "This is Saturday, doll. You can't get into the school on a Saturday without a special pass. You could be anyone, Miss Ellingham."

She pulled her handbrake up in exactly the way her driving instructor had told her not to twenty years ago – so that it made a horrible grinding sound. Out of the corner of her eye she saw Jockie who had been on his way to his dunnie, hovering by the assembly hall doors. He was watching her like a Collie dog, keen that she came his way so he could chase her off his territory.

Miss Ellingham (for she was already feeling in her handbag for her red pen and union diary, the key props of Jane's alter-ego) sighed. She hadn't even entered the school building and the ache in her shoulder, which accompanied her the whole academic year, was intensifying.

She had just felt one of the brass protective corners on her diary when she became aware of a flicker of movement in her rear-view mirror. A battered red Micra with an engine slightly louder than it should have been pulled up just outside the car park gates. It was an odd place to stop, as Jockie's suddenly raised chin testified. Splendid, thought Miss Ellingham. With a bit of luck Jockie will be too absorbed with the category one crime of stopping on the single-lane route into the car park to find fault with my own entrance.

But within a few minutes her own attention also had been absorbed by the red car. For out of it was stepping Katy Clemmy, and not Katy Clemmy the third-year blazer girl who flushed red when a boy so much as spoke to her but Katy Clemmy, femme fatale, dressed in hipster jeans, platform trainers and a skin-tight midriff top with "Babe" picked out on it in sequins. Her blonde hair was in two pigtails. Make-up around her eyes was glittering in the evening light, and her lips, even from Miss Ellingham's somewhat removed vantage point, were visibly glistening with extremely red lipstick.

There was a pause in proceedings as Katy bent down to look back in the passenger door. She stood up again swiftly, clutching a long navy, V-neck school sweater which she pulled on hastily. After that she took a quick look round and walked off towards Glaisnock Wynd, the narrow street which led away from the 1960s concrete comprehensive to the heart of what remained of old Craigie. Miss Ellingham watched her until she had disappeared from sight, noting with interest that when Katy was a safe distance from the car she pulled out her pigtails and ran her hands through her hair so that it fell in its more usual, untidy fashion.

A puff of black smoke emerged from the exhaust of the red car as it proceeded jerkily into the staff car park. Miss Ellingham found herself waiting to see who it belonged to. As it drew up not far from her she got her answer. Ron Turner the music teacher was in the driving seat.

Miss Ellingham closed her handbag quickly and opened her car door. Without so much as glancing in Ron Turner's direction she hurried towards the assembly hall doors. Jockie stood in front of them, stepping from one foot to another.

"You can't go in this way, dear," he said, as she walked towards him. "They're setting up for the parents' night."

"But that's where I'm going, Mr Wilson, to the parents' night."

"You're a teacher aren't you?"

Miss Ellingham rolled her eyes.

"Well, you'll be going to your classroom won't you?"

Miss Ellingham heard Ron Turner's car door slam shut and turned round. Jockie followed her gaze. He pushed past her.

"Hey," he shouted in Ron Turner's direction. "Was that you who stopped outside the gates a minute ago?"

Miss Ellingham felt a surge of schoolgirl mischief. As Jockie was advancing towards Ron Turner she slipped quietly towards the assembly hall doors and let herself in. Behind her she heard Jockie admonishing Ron Turner.

"What if a fire engine was trying to get in?"

"I'd drive into the car park."

"Now don't you get smart with me. See those double yellow lines? You know what these mean?"

Miss Ellingham closed the doors behind her carefully. Inside, the assembly hall was bustling with senior pupils and tired-looking male teachers, their ties askew, shirt tails falling over their trouser waistbands. A familiar voice could be heard above the others. Jim Beetham was directing both staff and pupils, like a ship's captain overseeing the loading of his boat prior to a long expedition.

"Cups and saucers on the long table at the back, Sophie. Dust cover on the piano please, Miss London. David, put these questionnaires in a pile next to Mr Dick's table, please. Eleanor, could you go to the secretary's office and get me some more of last year's school magazine, please. Gordon, help Kylie with those plates, the damsel looks a little distressed."

Oh, but he was commanding, thought Miss Ellingham. Look how the girls giggled and the boys were keen to carry heavy loads, how Miss London, not long arrived at Craigie Academy and as graceful as a delphinium in a lilac summer dress, flushed as he touched her arm and thanked her for arranging the chocolate biscuits.

The familiar assembly hall smell of boiled cabbage and hot fat reached Miss Ellingham. It came from the school canteen next door but as she never stepped inside there, preferring her own sandwiches or leftovers for lunch, the smell was one which she associated only with parents' nights, school shows, prize givings and morning assembly. She began walking briskly to the other side of the hall, sure that the dark depressed feeling that was creeping over her would go as soon as she reached the fresher air of the corridor.

"Jane – looking lovely as ever."

Jim Beetham had appeared beside her, clutching a large pile of art work.

"Just thought it might be nice to put some of the pupils' work around the hall to brighten things up a bit," he said, noticing that her attention had been grabbed by what was in his arms.

"Yes, it'll reflect well... on you and the school."

Jim glanced out the window. A hint of embarrassment, perhaps?

"Don't you need them for your own walls, to show the parents?"

It was cheap of her to go on like this and she knew it but then Jim had been hard on her when he'd invited her up to his room. The fact that he seemed to have no idea of the wounds he might have re-opened had simply added to the pain of the whole liaison. And what was he thinking, calling her 'lovely'? If I'm so lovely, why did you dump me, she wanted to ask him. But with her usual Miss Ellingham restraint she kept quiet. More than one person had asked Jane herself as much in the months and years following her split from Jim. "You're so gorgeous, Jane," she remembered a French *assistante* called Marie-Claire, who'd lodged briefly in her spare room, saying. "I can't imagine why he let you go." Well, the fact is he did, thought Jane – and Marie-Claire had probably just been trying to make her feel better.

Jim looked over at a prefect who was arranging school magazines in a fan shape on the reception table.

"Just pile them up, Judith," he yelled.

It was his way of dealing with the discomfort her comments had caused. Miss Ellingham took her cue and left. Jim Beetham and boiled cabbage in one breath was quite enough.

In her classroom, she sat down behind her desk and waited for the first of the parents to arrive. Outside, the branches of the blossom trees in the park cut like fissures into the orange-blue evening sky. She could hear bird-song and the distant voices of some boys playing football. There was little traffic. Very little happened in Craigie after the shops and schools had shut for the day.

She opened a window. The smell of freshly cut grass filled the air and the noises of the children playing grew louder, catching in her ears with a resonance that inflamed both her heart and her imagination. What would it be like, she wondered, to go back to a family tonight? In her mind's eye, she saw two red-haired children, rather like she and her brother had looked, playing in the cottage garden. Their excited shrieks mingled with those coming from the park. "Mum, over here," she heard. "Mu-um." Their knees were green from falling on the cut grass. "Look what we've found." "Over he-re."

She stood up to try and spot who the voices belonged to but the light was fading fast. The sun, large and heavy, was sinking down through the darkening sky. The horizon burned orange and red. The bird-song and children's voices disappeared. Miss Ellingham felt herself gripped with an apocalyptic terror.

There was a cough behind her. Miss Ellingham turned round suddenly, half expecting to see a hooded figure holding a scythe but it was only a parent, dressed in a sports jacket and tie, smiling in a way which suggested he wanted their encounter to be friendly.

"Sorry, I didn't mean to give you a fright," he said.

Miss Ellingham found to her annoyance that her heart was pounding. She was aware too that her face was flushed and that her expression was probably anything other than professional and commanding. "You've got your alien look again," Jim used to say to her when he found her dreaming. He said her eyes grew when she was off on one of her "journeys". He'd found it "cute" in the beginning.

"No, no, you didn't," said Miss Ellingham quickly.

"Lovely sunset," said the parent, looking in the direction of the park.

"Yes," said Miss Ellingham, thinking that it hadn't been lovely at all. Quite the reverse.

"I don't get enough time to enjoy things like that these days," said the parent. "Sorry, I'm Alan Clemmy. I should have introduced myself. My daughter Katy's in your English class."

Alan Clemmy extended his hand. Miss Ellingham took it and as she did tried to connect the calloused palm she felt squeezing the life-blood out of her own much smaller hand with the dreamy, confused girl who sat in the desk right in front of her own three times a week for English lessons.

Alan Clemmy was big, about six foot two, and broad shouldered. His face was red and weather beaten, and he moved slowly but purposefully, as if he was used to planning out his time. Before Miss Ellingham had time to offer he had drawn up a chair beside her desk and sat down. Then, before she had time to introduce the subject herself, he began to talk about Katy.

"Katy likes English," he said. "She's quite good at it too. Must be all those magazines she reads. A lot of rubbish most of them, but I suppose they're better than nothing. Better than that computer she's always on. I try to tell her but it's not easy. It's not with teenagers, is it?"

Miss Ellingham opened her mouth to speak, but was cut off again before she could utter a sound.

"She works quite hard at her school work. She's a good girl

really. I just wish she had a few more friends. I suppose being stuck out where we are, it's not so easy. But she could bring some of them home if she wanted."

He looked at her sharply as if waiting for a reaction. Miss Ellingham saw that he had very blue eyes and that they seemed tired and a little sad. She found this hard to reconcile with the overwhelming physical presence of his bulk right next to her. To Miss Ellingham's mind, big, physical men like Alan Clemmy didn't have tortured souls.

"Katy seems, well, you know, quite well integrated into the school."

Alan Clemmy stared at her intensely as she spoke and waited for a moment after she'd finished to see if she was going to add anything else.

"You mean she's quite sociable? She did say she was going to a sleepover at a friend's tonight. Girl called Madeleine. Nice lass. Daughter of our GP as it happens."

Miss Ellingham felt her heart soften at Alan Clemmy's eagerness for his daughter's wellbeing. At the same time she felt mounting confusion about Katy. With a father so direct and down-to-earth it was hard to understand why Katy was so dreamy and sensitive. A girl with a father like Alan Clemmy should be solid and red-cheeked with a robust personality to match. Ron Turner had indicated Mrs Clemmy was very unwell, but even so, thought Miss Ellingham, a man like Alan Clemmy would see to it that life continued and that his daughter wasn't unduly deprived. She found it hard to believe that he would allow Katy to do all the housework, letting it interfere with her school work the way Ron Turner had suggested.

"I mean she's quiet, Katy, not one of the loud ones... not at all but she... you know..."

Alan Clemmy had resumed his eager look. Go on, his eyes seemed to say.

"...she works hard. She's quite good at English, like you say."

Miss Ellingham was glad to be able to say something with sincerity. But Alan Clemmy wasn't going to be easily distracted from his mission to find out more about his daughter's general wellbeing.

"I know she works hard. I'm a bit worried that she works *too* hard. She's always upstairs in her room. The minute she can get away from me, she's off. But I suppose maybe that's normal for teenage girls?"

Miss Ellingham put down her red pen and looked at Alan Clemmy steadily. She had hoped to steer the conversation to Katy's work, to run over a few points she'd written down in a spiral notebook marked "Parents' Night, 3A" and then to move on to another parent. Glancing at her door, she could see there were at least three or four of them already gathered. Just now they were chatting with each other patiently but she knew it wouldn't be too long before they started to become irritated and say things such as, "I took a night off work to come here. I thought they'd at least have worked out a certain amount of time to speak to all of us."

Alan Clemmy was beginning to aggravate her. Not only was he creating potential problems for the smooth running of her parents' evening but he was forcing her to become involved and Miss Ellingham did not become involved in her work. Not since her affair with Jim Beetham had she allowed anything or anyone outside her home and her immediate family affect her sensibilities. It was a matter of survival, as she saw it. Learn by your mistakes, people said. If she so much as stepped briefly into a pupil's shoes she would be contravening that piece of common wisdom.

"Mr Clemmy, Katy is a good pupil. You've got nothing to worry about with her. She's in the top five per cent of her year. She'll pass her Standard Grade at credit level easily. And from what I hear she'll do just as well in her other subjects. I hear she's very musical."

Alan Clemmy dropped his head, took a deep breath and then sat up straight again and clapped his knees with his hands.

"I'm sorry, Miss Ellingham," he said. "I've been going on a bit."

His eyes had lost their intensity. Miss Ellingham suddenly felt overwhelmed with a mixture of guilt and pity. This man had come to her for help and she had denied him the honest communication he had been brave enough to appeal for. She put her red pen in her mouth, chewed it and set it back down on the table again.

"Mr Clemmy, I'm Katy's guidance teacher as well as her English teacher, you know, so if there was anything wrong I'd hear about it. But the last time I had a chat with her, she seemed fine. I did hear..."

As soon as she had said it she wished she hadn't.

"You heard?"

Alan Clemmy's face had resumed its eager expression.

"Well, one of our staff members is giving Katy piano lessons."

"Mr Turner."

"Yes."

"Katy seems very happy with that arrangement."

"I'm sure."

"She's being put forward for another piano exam in the summer."

"Yes."

"Of course it's her mother she gets that from."

Miss Ellingham paused. Alan Clemmy had mentioned his wife himself but this suddenly made Miss Ellingham less confident about broaching the subject of her illness. It must be an extremely sensitive matter or why wouldn't such a frank and straightforward man bring it up?

"Sorry, you were going to say...?"

Miss Ellingham picked up her pen again, then realising how nervous her mannerisms must be making her look, set it down, as out of arm's reach as she could manage.

"I just heard, from Mr Turner, that Katy's mother is ill."

Alan Clemmy frowned and looked out the window.

"What did Katy say?"

Miss Ellingham had an urge to reach out and pat Alan Clemmy's arm but she stayed still and continued what she had started, realising all the while it had probably not been a good idea.

"I don't think she said anything much. Ron... Mr Turner was just concerned that she was maybe having to do a lot of housework. I don't think he thought it was a big deal or anything. He just mentioned it to me because I'm Katy's guidance teacher."

Alan Clemmy kept his gaze fixed on the view from the window. His mouth had narrowed and tightened, and there was a deep furrow between his eyes.

"We've got a home-help coming in now. She just started yesterday in fact. Katy knew that was happening."

"Mr Clemmy, please... I'm sure Mr Turner was only doing what he thought was... Teachers pick things up when they see pupils often enough, especially if it's on a one-to-one basis. Anyway, if everything is sorted out at home there's no problem, is there?"

Alan Clemmy turned back to face her. His eyes were a little moist and had lost their friendly sparkle. He slumped down in his chair and seemed to diminish in bulk before her eyes.

"Corinne... my wife... she's been a bit better recently," he said dully.

Miss Ellingham leant towards him, reaching out across the table. She wanted to take one of Alan Clemmy's calloused hands in her own and squeeze it. But that would have been inappropriate. She felt herself scowl and pull back her hands. She would never understand why life was so clipped, like a well-tended hedge that had been trained to a certain size and height according to a set of standards everyone adhered to but whose originator nobody knew.

"Well, that's good," she said, gently.

The standards dictated that she could not ask what Mrs Clemmy was suffering from. Cancer, perhaps, or Multiple Sclerosis. Whatever it was, it didn't really matter. The palpable pain it was causing Alan Clemmy would be the same.

"Yes, yes it is, I suppose," said Alan Clemmy. "God knows, I've tried everything..."

Clemmy's face suddenly flushed a deep red. A pause followed, in which Miss Ellingham wondered what on earth Katy's father was talking about. He had "*tried everything*"? Was he suggesting he had the power to heal his wife? But there was to be no clarification. Alan Clemmy had decided his meeting with his daughter's English teacher was over. He gave Miss Ellingham a quick, forced smile and stood up.

Miss Ellingham stayed seated and gazed up at him.

"Thank you," said Clemmy.

"Not at all," Miss Ellingham replied and watched him turn slowly like a carthorse and walk towards the door.

18

FOR a long time my drinking was secret, even from me. I hid the bottles, threw them away as soon as I'd emptied them. I never drank heavily in front of other people. At parties I was often sober. I'd start after my daughter was away to school and my husband out in the fields. By the time I saw both of them again I'd have managed to make some food, done a little housework, and drunk a few cans of cider. It made me happier to see them, helped me to love them. If either of them noticed anything they said nothing. We were three planets orbiting the same universe, never meeting but aware of each other's presence.

19

"THIS is a message for Katy big tits Clemmy. We just want to tell you we're watching you and we'll be in touch the same time again tomorrow. By the way, we saw you in your shorts at the playing fields yesterday. Nice fanny."

```
Hi Katy: Gd to have
email  chat.  Guess
u  got  chucked  out
library. Sounds heavy
at  home.  Gd idea to
use hols 2 c Big Smoke
and chill. C u T Sq.
Txt if any prob.
Dx
```

St Paul's Hostel

Ideally situated for the South Bank St Paul's Hostel is one of the YHA's busiest. All-year round it receives visitors from every quarter of the globe. Choose from single rooms with en-suite facilities, single-sex dormitory accommodation for between 4 and 8 people and family rooms capable of holding up to 6 related adults and children. To find us, just click on the multi-map below. Book on-line or by calling us on the number at the bottom of the page. Discounts are available for members of the YHA or its affiliated associations.

Misty Murmurs

What on earth has happened to Martine McCutcheon? Has anyone else noticed those dimpled thighs, blubbery breasts and ballooning hips? She dropped out of *My Fair Lady* because of stress. Someone ought to tell her she won't get that role again unless she puts away the jellied eels. Cockney charm alone don't make the lady fair, ducks.

Misty-rious Truth

Some of the world's most gorgeous women are doing it and finding it rather suits them, writes the *Misty Shrink*. What am I talking about? Think Annette Bening and Catherine Zeta Jones. Yes, you've got it – marrying older men.

But just why would such lovely leading ladies choose to star with old wrinklies like Warren Beattie and Michael Douglas, even if their faces have been propped up by the best plastic surgeons? Could it be, dare I say it, money? Let's assume Bening and Zeta Jones weren't short of a bob or two before

they linked their smooth hands with their wrinklies' gnarled ones. My bet is it's the safety of daddy. He's older, he'll take care of you and he's not about to run off with anyone else.

Curious? Why not give it a whirl yourself? All that experience is bound to have its, ahem, bonuses and what have you got to lose? They can't be called Sugar Daddies for nothing. Sample the sweet taste of a mature vintage and my guess is you will never want to drink from the fountain of youth again.

Is that Katy, the one
with the big tits?
Watchin u. Want to
do it with u. What u
doin Sat?

Rosewood Clinic Client Testimonies

"Thank you Rosewood. My breast enhancement has
made both me and my husband so much happier. Our
relationship is better than ever!"
Cheryl, Edinburgh.

"I can't thank you enough for my daughter's new nose.
Since her treatment she has been a different girl. Last
week she went to her high school prom with the captain
of the football team. It was her dream – and mine –
come true."
Victoria, Chester.

"The staff at Rosewood are so wonderful. I took my
sister for a breast reduction and decided to have an
enhancement there six months later. We're both delighted
with the results. We've even been able to save on
underwear costs by swapping bras."
Lucy, Chelsea.

"My hair started falling out when I was only 35. I wasn't
even married yet. Thanks, Rosewood, for giving me back
my hair – and my marriage prospects."
Charles, Kensington.

Is Rosewood the Best Next Step For You?

Read the statements below and tick any you agree with:

I would like to look different.

I often feel ashamed of my appearance.

I feel my relationships would be improved if my appearance were different.

A good appearance is important to my earning capacity.

When I look good, I feel good.

My appearance makes everyday tasks difficult to perform.

I have suffered ridicule and insults because of my appearance.

I have often been depressed because of my appearance.

My body is great, it just needs a little TLC to make it perfect.

If you ticked one or more of the above, it is possible cosmetic surgery could have a positive impact on your life. At Rosewood we will take time to discuss what cosmetic surgery could do for you before creating an individual treatment plan with you, the client, at its heart.

20

JANE liked her cottage best when dark had fallen, the stair window lit up with stars, owls hooting in the oaks nearby. She kept lighting to a minimum, just a lamp with a pink pleated shade on in the hall and candles and an angle-poise to read by illuminating the living room. The curtains were rarely drawn, except in the bedroom, so that her home felt like a ship afloat in the night. When the wind blew she fancied she could feel the cottage creak and change course, the whirly-gig in the back garden jangling like loose rigging.

Sometimes she wandered through her home like a stowaway, listening for clues to her course. In spring the sounds were warm and brisk, trees rustled with new leaves, the bird song was light. If there was an unexpected bang in the eves or attic it wouldn't send her scurrying, as it did in the depth of winter, back to her den in the living room, her heart hammering.

So it was that now, the grandfather clock on the landing having just struck eleven, Jane was tip-toeing through her own house in her bare feet, stopping at each window to gaze at a smudgy moon. There was a haar creeping in and she could smell the sea in the chill air which slithered under the back door and wound its way round the ill-fitting windows in the upstairs bedrooms. In the distance, where the coastline was, a lighthouse blinked on and off. Jane kept her eyes fixed on it, as if watching her own pulse on a heart-monitoring machine.

A noise rang in her ears and set the ornaments on the landing windowsill rattling. She watched, astonished, as an art deco fruit bowl moved towards a porcelain figure of the same 1930s vintage. It was as if the contents of her house had come alive and were wasting no time in doing what they had always wanted. She imagined the 1930s lady setting off to the nearby village in her fur trimmed coat and skullcap, cheroot dangling from her long white fingers. What a sensation she would cause with Mrs McDuff in the Post Office.

She soon collected herself and rushed down to the hall, almost tripping up in her narrow-fitting nightdress. As she approached it the phone became almost painful to listen to, wailing in her ears like an air raid siren.

"I'm coming, I'm coming," she shouted.

She was a little out of breath by the time she picked up the receiver.

"Hello?"

"Miss Ellingham?"

It was a male voice, but not her father's, or her brother's. Not an emergency then, she thought with relief.

"Yes."

Who was it? It wasn't a familiar voice but she knew instinctively it wasn't one to worry about either. Nuisance callers didn't speak so hesitantly or politely.

"I'm sorry. Sorry for bothering you. I know it's late. Are you okay?"

"Yes, I'm fine. I just got a bit of a fright – the phone ring was on amplify... I'm sorry, who's calling?"

"It's Alan Clemmy, Katy's father."

Jane's head played out a number of different options. Number one, Mr Clemmy was so preoccupied with his daughter's wellbeing that he'd looked up her English teacher in the phonebook so he could continue their conversation where it had left off at parents' night. But it was getting on for midnight. No, thought Jane, that was unlikely. Number two, Mr Clemmy had something really important to say to her which he had been unable to impart earlier in the evening. Jane thought of Mrs Clemmy's illness. Possible. However, couldn't it wait until tomorrow? Number three, Mr Clemmy was a philanderer and was phoning to chat her up. Impossible. Alan Clemmy was clearly not a philanderer.

"Mr Clemmy."

"Yes, look I'm really sorry but I was just wondering if you knew Katy's music teacher's phone number. It's not listed."

"I'm sorry?"

"Mr Turner. His telephone number. I was wondering if you knew it."

"No, I'm sorry," replied Jane, bewildered.

"Katy was supposed to be staying at a friend's tonight – Madeleine McCutcheon's." Clemmy coughed and took a deep breath. "Anyway, she's not there. I just phoned the McCutcheons..."

Before Jane had a chance to think, let alone speak, Alan Clemmy continued. "Katy was meant to have a piano lesson with Mr Turner tonight after school," he said. "I just wanted to know if she went."

"To her piano lesson?"

"Yes." Clemmy sounded embarrassed.

I should put an end to this call right now, thought Jane, sensing she was being drawn into something it would be difficult to get out of later. But just as she was about to repeat that she did not know Turner's number and bring the conversation to a close, her mind flashed to the scene she had witnessed outside the school car park earlier that night – Katy Clemmy in a sequined t-shirt and platform trainers slipping out of Ron Turner's Micra.

Jane wrestled for a moment with not mentioning this but her conscience got the better of her. "She did go to her lesson," she said to Clemmy cautiously. "I saw Ron Turner dropping her off in the school car park on my way into parents' night."

There was a faint grunt at the other end of the line.

"She headed into town," added Jane.

"Katy?"

There was no other option but to finish what she had started.

"She looked like she was going to meet someone," said Jane.

"Meet someone? Who?"

"I don't know... maybe a boyfriend or something?"

"She doesn't have a boyfriend."

Jane bit her lip. She knew she should have kept quiet.

"My daughter isn't dishonest, Miss Ellingham. She's always been reliable. She's a good..." His voice trailed off. When he spoke again it was more quietly. "We've been through a lot Miss Ellingham... Katy... she's really a very vulnerable girl..."

Jane stepped out of the pool of light beneath the lamp and leant against the hall wall in the darkness. She pressed her cheek against its cold surface. A rage rushed through her like a team of black horses. All teenage girls are vulnerable, she found herself wanting to scream at Clemmy. *I was vulnerable and I have been paying the price for that vulnerability all my adult life.*

Her hands and knees had begun to shake.

"Miss Ellingham?"

Jane slid down the wall and sat on the hall floor. Her legs were weak. She must not cry. Not now.

"Have you called the police?" she asked Clemmy at last.

The phone went quiet. Then through the darkness, Jane heard the sound of sobbing.

"Mr Clemmy," she said softly.

The sobs grew louder.

"Mr Clemmy, I'm sure she's okay. Really."

She wanted to reassure him that Katy would probably sneak in the door at any moment but she had lost her confidence in what to say and how to say it.

God, what a deep, dark sound it was, the noise of a grown man sobbing.

"The police?"

What had she mentioned them for? She was useless, she thought. Useless to herself and useless to other people.

She tried, desperately, to think of ways to relieve Alan Clemmy's distress.

"Maybe I could call someone who'll have Ron Turner's number," she said, after a period of silence.

"But you said she went to her lesson."

"Well, yes. It looked like it."

"But you think it's worth checking?" Clemmy's voice sounded brighter again.

"Yes," she lied, ashamed of herself. The best thing Alan Clemmy could do, she thought, was sit tight until his daughter came home. But she did not know how to say that.

"I'll give you my number..."

Jane was just about to reach for a pen when she recalled the cream envelope Turner had given her to pass to Katy, and the teenager's flushed face when she had opened it. She stiffened.

"Actually, I'll have a word with Ron myself if you like," she said hastily. "It might be easier that way."

Clemmy was quiet. "Well, all right," he said eventually. "If you think that would be best. You'll call me back?"

"Yes, of course."

Clemmy dictated his number to her slowly and then repeated it. I did not want to get involved, thought Jane, bearing down heavily on the paper as she wrote.

"Thank you, Miss Ellingham,"

"No, thank you, Mr Clemmy," she said, before realising what a ridiculous thing it was to say in the circumstances.

Alan Clemmy mumbled something incomprehensible and put the phone down.

21

SOMETIMES I hid the bottles in the cistern. My husband found out all my other places, one by one. The washing basket was good for a while. He just opened the lid and put clothes in. Later they'd appear washed and ironed in his wardrobe. It was only ever me who rummaged about in there. But I'd forgotten my daughter was growing up. In the fog of drinking I didn't even notice I'd stopped doing the washing and that my teenage beauty was doing it for me. She must have found the bottles and told him. There was an almighty row and he went about the house like a policeman. I sat in the living room and listened to the rafters shaking, waiting for his return. He put it all in a crate and set it down in front of me. Bottles I'd forgotten I even had. "Everywhere," he said. "In old toy boxes in the attic. Amongst your underwear. In a vase on the landing. Up the chimney in the bedroom." He was covered in soot but there were white marks like drips of sauce down the side of a saucepan where he'd been crying. All I could think was how I could get my hands on the drink before he threw it out.

He said, "Don't you ever think what this is doing to us, Corinne?"

But I didn't. I couldn't. My daughter was standing at the door listening to every word. When she saw me looking she slipped away like a ghost.

22

DR NANJANI crossed his legs and sat back in his leather, swivel chair. Idly, he reached out and picked up the uppermost manila folder from the pile on his desk. Before opening it, he looked at his watch. Almost three forty-five. He had hoped to leave the office at five sharp for once. It was Good Friday after all. Not that this meant anything to him but every other clinic would have shut up already – if they had opened for business at all. He would have to be quick with the next patient if he wanted to squeeze in at least a little of the relaxation most of his colleagues seemed to enjoy as a matter of course.

With the end of his pen he flicked open the folder he'd taken off the pile. He could see at a glance that all it contained was a single piece of paper – a patient information form. In other words, Marlene, his secretary (or 'clinic manageress' as he preferred to call her for the purposes of Rosewood publicity material) had booked a new patient into a ten-minute appointment slot. Bloody nuisance, he thought, flinging the folder back down again without reading its contents. He was now in the position of having to choose between losing a possible client or, once again, working later than he would have liked. At one time the choice would have been easy – ditch the client and head to golf course – but as Marlene had pointed out to him back in January when he'd complained that the demand for surgery at Rosewood seemed to be dropping, he could not afford to be that blasé anymore. The days of waiting lists and L.A. prices were over, apparently. According to Marlene, cosmetic surgery was becoming as commonplace as hair tints and teeth whitening. If Rosewood was to survive it was time to take the "bucket shop approach" and pull in the masses.

Dr Nanjani cursed under his breath and looked again at the pile of folders on his desk. Its size was a testament to Marlene's business savvy. Most of the folders contained the notes of clients who had opted for treatment as a result of his secretary's idea of an Easter Discount Offer to bring in the hoi polloi. But the size of the pile was also offensive to Dr Nanjani's pride. Had he really trained at the best medical school in the USA and worked at some of the finest cosmetic surgery departments in the world to end up touting for business like an East End hairdresser?

Apparently so, he thought now, with a bitter laugh. As Marlene had said, he was no longer "a big fish in a small pool". Cosmetic surgeons were ten a penny in London now and their prices were falling by the month. More and more women had bought into the concept he had helped propagate through his best selling book, *Rebuild Your Body, Rebuild Your Life* – that by refining their looks they could refine the very essence of their being.

For make no mistake about it, Dr Nanjani liked to tell guests at his dinner parties in Chiswick, women who wanted breast enlargements were rarely seeking simply a more feminine outline. They wanted romance, their youth back, or sometimes a youth they had never had. Dr Nanjani liked to look round his dinner party guests as he told them this and wait for the predictable responses. From the men there would come the inevitable paltry attempts at ironic wit. "Hard life you've got Rajeet." "Yeah, all those breasts to examine." "And feel…" The women were more cautious, hiding curiosity beneath a veil of political correctness. "Don't these women wonder about their husbands instead of their breasts?" "Yes, I mean if I felt I had to spend – what does it cost, *thousands*? – on bigger boobs I'd be questioning the quality of my relationship. It's not as if these women's lives change because their boobs do, is it?"

Dr Nanjani knew fine well, of course, that the women at his dinner parties believed, just as all his female clients did, that bigger breasts could indeed bring bigger happiness. Goodness, *Rebuild Your Body, Rebuild Your Life* was full of examples of the wealth and celebrity enhanced breasts had brought to countless actresses and singers who would otherwise have remained unknown. Women might not want to believe it. They might not acknowledge, even to themselves, that they believed it. But they did. How could they not? As the doctor liked to tell the women at his dinner parties, observing them grow uncomfortable and trying to change the conversation by complimenting the kulfi, "Breast enhancement is often a far better investment for a girl nowadays than a degree, both financially and personally." That the men smirked was hardly comforting and Dr Nanjani knew it. He had sown the seeds of insecurity in his female guests, which had the double bonus of ending further conversation about his work while inflicting emotional pain on a gender he had little respect for.

Whether the conversation was about breast reductions, nose jobs, liposuction, face lifts or rib removal its general shape was much the same. As Dr Nanjani understood only too well, it wasn't the type of surgery *per se* which agitated the women but the general, irrefutable truth that a woman's worth was weighed cosmetically and no amount of intellectual ballast could compensate for a lack of feminine beauty. If a woman had a sagging bottom or a crooked nose, if she heaved with fat or dripped with middle-aged jowls she was of less value than a twenty-year-old whom nature had not yet had time to undo. His sensitivity to the bounds of what was politically correct prevented him from saying it but Dr Nanjani had it on good authority that a twenty-year-old would sell for many more goats and chickens in the remote parts of Africa where women were still bartered for than a sagging forty-year-old, whatever her knowledge of the law or medicine.

Dr Nanjani thought of all this as he pulled the patient information form he had not bothered to read out of its folder and laid it on his desk like a theatrical prop. As he pressed his intercom his mind moved to the woman who would be sitting in front of him in a few minutes. Forty-five or so with dyed blonde hair, boxed into well-cut, casual-smart clothes and expensive shoes. Her watchstrap would clank heavily on his desk as she sat forward to ingratiate herself. Her sleeves would be rolled up a little to reveal tanned skin just faintly crinkled on the surface, like that he removed from glazed roast chicken on the odd occasions he ate it. The teeth, almost certainly whitened, would smile at him and there would be the distraction of earrings and other jewellery that jangled. The whole effect would remind him of Christmas decorations pinned around a dingy room, all the more depressing for its attempt at entering into the expected spirit of hope and cheer.

"Next patient please, Marlene," he said, leaning towards the intercom.

"Right, Dr Nanjani," said Marlene.

Her complete lack of awareness at her error in booking a new patient into a ten-minute appointment slot was evident in the easy, chirpy way she replied. Dr Nanjani felt himself clench his teeth. It was a pity that 38-year-old Marlene, apart from having the occasional astute business observation to make, was so good with the clients. He paid her £25,000 a year to sit there and answer phones, make coffee and tea as necessary. It was a job any 17-year-old could do and he could pay a 17-year-old a lot less to do it, a point which had not been far from the forefront of his mind in the financially difficult past year.

The door opened. Dr Nanjani grabbed the patient information form and set it so that it was facing him on his desk. Its right-hand edge was crumpled where he'd grabbed at it and he made a half-hearted attempt to smooth it with his palm. Beneath his chair he tapped his feet on the floor impatiently. His eye caught the gold strap of his watch beneath a starched cuff. Quickly, he stretched out his left arm so he could see the time. It was almost ten to three. For goodness sake, he thought. He had better get this new patient to sign on the dotted line quickly.

His patient came round the door, rather than opening it and walking in. But perhaps, Dr Nanjani thought, taking an astonished look at the young girl who stood in front of him, this was because she lacked the strength to push it open properly. Dr Nanjani stood up. It was something he usually did when a patient entered the room but in this case the action was more a surprise reflex, like choking on a drink, or stopping mid-sentence. Maybe, he thought, as he looked at the girl again, she was the daughter of a friend of Marlene's, sent in to pick up dirty cups. She certainly couldn't be a prospective patient.

The girl stayed close to the door and looked at him. She could be no older than sixteen, Dr Nanjani decided. Her white-blonde hair and small, pale face gave her an ethereal look which was emphasized by the fact that she stood in the full glare of the light from the surgery window. She seemed almost to be disappearing before him. Her arms were pale too, and thin, and appeared less substantial than the rest of her body which was clad in garish teen fashion; flared jeans, platform trainers and a pink tee-shirt with "Babe" written on it in sequins. Dr Nanjani blinked and stared at the girl again, half expecting her to reassemble as an ageing pop star.

But no, she was definitely young. Dr Nanjani's eye for age was as sharp as the scalpels he used to defy it. In a Kensington supermarket queue he would compare the smooth face of an expensively clad shopper with the hands which passed money to the check-out girl and do the necessary algebra. Face equals twenty-five, hands forty-five, real age fifty – for one had to factor in the five years the rich bought themselves with easier living. It was a mathematical formula he kept to himself since it revealed the limitations of his work but it was one he always relied on.

Dr Nanjani felt excitement begin to replace his initial shock. The form that had angered him a few moments ago now assumed an intriguing quality. He reached out and grabbed it again, but this time hungrily. He had dealt with so much forty-five-year-old meat he had almost forgotten the sheer freshness of the young and tender. For a split second only, he felt a sense of despair at the possibilities of his own work. No amount of stretching, cutting, scraping, sucking, lifting, removing or augmenting could recreate the plumpness of flesh and brightness of eye that was the signature of youth.

Dr Nanjani's eyes latched greedily onto the first box in the girl's patient information form. "Personal Information" read the title at the top. Below, in blue ballpoint pen, the script large and childish, the letter "I's" not dotted but rounded off with large circles, several with smiley faces inside them, lay the bones of the girl in front of him. Name: Katy Clemmy. Date of Birth: 01/03/87. Address: Millhouse Farm, Ayrshire, Scotland. Telephone: Craigie 817352. Occupation: Schoolgirl. Annual salary: N/A. Contact in case of emergency: Alan Clemmy. Telephone: As above. Surgery sought: Breast reduction (Easter Discount Offer).

She was still in the light and the sun filtering through the white, net curtains was brighter than ever. Dr Nanjani coughed and walked to the front of his desk. He should tell her now she might be too young to have surgery, unless she had good reason and parental consent, but he sensed an opportunity. What was it Marlene had said the other day when he had complained about the necessity of the 'bucket shop approach'? "Unless you can tap into some new market then that's what you're stuck with." What, he thought, if this girl represented that market? His mind began to race. A colleague of his in the States had recently begun to give breast enhancements to teenage girls who wanted to star in 'adult movies'. Another in Monte Carlo had refashioned the cheek bones, nose and chin of a well known 'stunning' twenty year old actress. Youth was a growing market, but one as yet untapped in the UK.

Dr Nanjani frowned in the way he always did when he wanted to appear professional and held out his left arm to indicate the girl should sit down on one of the two leather armchairs beside the glass coffee table in the centre of the room. The girl bit her lip and proceeded with her head down in the direction indicated. Dr Nanjani noticed her white skin flush pink, her blue eyes flicker nervously. Her build was slight but she curved gracefully at the hips and generously at the bust. As she sat down, her chest jumped fractionally, like two small beach balls. Dr Nanjani could see in his mind's eye the exact construction of the girl's breasts, their milky whiteness and the small, pale pink nipples shaped like bicycle tyre valves rising out of them.

"Miss eh..." He looked at the girl's information form for effect. "...Clemmy."

"Yes," she said, her face flushing again.

She had high cheekbones and beautiful, almond-shaped eyes. But her nose was crooked. Perhaps, he thought with another surge of excitement, he could suggest a few additional treatments to her while they discussed her breast reduction.

23

PICKETT the Stick-it had sounded angry when she answered the phone. She was even angrier when she found out it was Jane Ellingham speaking. Despite the fact that Jim Beetham had elected to marry her and not Jane, she appeared to view his former girlfriend as a potent threat. The Home Economics teacher's petty self-absorption irritated Jane to a degree that she would like to have put her fist down the phone *Tom and Jerry* fashion and knocked her out. As this was a futile fantasy she made do with secretly calling her the name Jim himself had given her on first seeing her. "That's the new Home Economics teacher, Miss Pickett," Jane had said as a woman who looked as if she spent at least half her day following good grooming tips in women's magazines wiggled past them, leaving a strong scent of musky perfume in her slipstream. "The one all the boys have got a crush on." "Her?" Jim had responded, looking after her. "Stick-it the Pickett, I say." So Pickett the Stick-it was born, although ever since Jim had become involved with her she had been "Sammy" and it was as if their nickname for her had been surgically removed from his brain.

"I wondered if I could speak to Jim, please," Jane said in a tone carefully modulated to indicate both that her call was not personal and that she was not prepared to discuss the reason for it with Pickett the Stick-it.

"Jim's in bed," said Pickett the Stick-it, in the manner of a doctor's receptionist.

"It's an emergency, Sammy," said Jane, letting a little of her irritation filter through. Pickett the Stick-it wasn't the sort to like confrontations.

"Jim," Pickett the Stick-it called out, her tone a reprimand.

Jim would have hell to pay for this phone-call later, thought Jane.

There was a muffled exchange and then Jane heard Pickett the Stick-it's voice again. "For God's sake, Jim."

"I've got it, now put the phone down please, Sammy."

There was a harsh click and a pause.

"Jane?"

His voice was raw and gravely, heavy with sleep, stripped bare of its daytime defences and pretensions. Jane imagined him naked from the waist up, rubbing his eyes with a freckled hand, his golden hair standing on end like a little boy's. A sharp pain cut through her chest. God, please, she cried out in the silence. Don't taunt me with this anymore.

"Yes. Sorry for bothering you," she said.

Appearing not to care was her forte, she thought. It was as if her whole purpose in life had been to learn disinterest.

"No, no, that's okay."

"It's just I was wondering if you had Ron Turner's phone number."

"Ron Turner?"

Jim was waking up now. Jane detected a mocking irony in his tone. What was she up to? Having an affair with the young music teacher? That he could be so light about her love life and think so little of her sexual proclivities brought her back to her senses.

"There's a bit of an emergency with a pupil," she said, her voice full of Miss Ellingham.

"Oh, right. I'll just have a look."

She heard him get out of bed and open what sounded like the catch of his briefcase. Then she heard books being thumped on the floor. "Shit," he said quietly. Next he appeared to go to his desk and start opening the drawers. Jane imagined him, by the drawn floral curtains, pulling open each drawer in turn. Unless he had changed it for some reason, it would be the same pine desk they had constructed together after a trip to Ikea. The memory of the two of them surrounded by screws and pieces of wood veneer, laughing uncontrollably as they attempted to follow the instructions, made her smile. After two hours they had given up, gone downstairs, ordered an Indian take-away and made love on the living-room floor. "The desk is waiting for us," Jim had said when at 2am, or perhaps later, he had taken her hand and led her up to bed.

"Jane?"

"Yeah."

Time had evaporated. Was it the word "emergency" or simply the late hour which made him so warm and familiar, so devoid of his usual sarcasm? It would not have seemed inappropriate if at that moment he had told her loved her. "Come over," he sometimes used to say when they called each other late at night. "Now." And she had done it, sometimes driving in no more than her dressing gown, her body aching and moist with desire. No matter how much they had of each other's bodies it never seemed to be enough. Lust not love, she had told herself when it was all over. But whatever it was it was a lot more vital than her present existence, she thought.

"His number is 812325. Got that?"

"Hang on."

Jane reached for a pen.

"81232 ..."

"Five."

"Right."

"Jane?"

Again the same innocence. She pressed her foot against the wall of her nightdress and looked at the shape it made. Part of her wanted to prolong the conversation but for what? Jim Beetham was married. They had split up four years ago. She officially considered herself over him two years ago.

"Yes?"

"Are you okay?"

Jane stood up straight and stared into the living room at a pile of jotters sitting by her armchair.

"I'm fine."

"This emergency..."

Jane kicked the wall, her foot still locked behind her nightdress. What was she thinking of? Jim was just curious about why she needed Ron Turner's number.

"I'll explain everything when I see you," she said. "I'd better go."

"Oh, right."

He sounded disappointed but, she told herself firmly, it was probably only because his curiosity wasn't satisfied.

"You'd better get back to..."

She thought about saying "the Stick-it" but the Miss Ellingham in her got the upper hand.

"Sammy," she finished.

24

ONE morning – it must have been four years after that heady fortnight with Ruaridh in Deja – my husband told me our daughter was missing. I was in the bathroom being sick. When I stood up and flushed the toilet I saw him in the mirror. His reflection filled the glass so completely there was no room for anything else. He was wearing dark clothes and his face was in shadow. He blocked out all the light from the hallway.

"Katy's disappeared," he said a second time.

He wouldn't move from the doorframe. It was as if he was trying to imprison me. He certainly wanted me to hurt.

I moved towards him, expecting him to move, but he stayed where he was.

"Don't you care?" he asked.

I tried to push him with the palm of my hand but his chest felt like a wall. I turned sideways and tried to shift him with my shoulder but he still wouldn't move. Eventually I butted him with my head like an animal. This time he laughed. But it was a horrible, cruel laugh, full of mockery.

"That's right. Run away," he said. "That's all you ever do, Corinne."

The next time I tried to push past him he simply stood aside and I fell out onto the landing.

I remember I lay where I landed for a long time, expecting him to come and pick me up. But after a moment or two I heard his footsteps disappearing down the stairs. Slow, heavy footsteps, that dropped like tears. I hadn't even noticed him stepping round me.

When I went back into my room the darkness frightened me but I was even more scared to open the curtains. I was afraid of what I would see. I had no idea what day it was or how many days I had lost. I thought our daughter came into my room and shook me. "Mum," she said, with tears in her eyes. "Mum, please wake up, please. I want to talk to you." But maybe I imagined it. I don't need to tell any of you about the blurring of reality and nightmare which is the domain of the active alcoholic.

I went down into the kitchen and rummaged around in the cupboard under the sink, behind the bottles of bleach and kitchen roll. I felt my way across our daughter's old toy watering can, some ugly iron candlesticks we had never used, a cracked teapot my mother had given me and which I had never had the heart to throw out, and a bag of dried dog food. To touch each item was a relief. I was like a blind woman navigating my way along a road by the touch of familiar objects. My destination was an old flowerpot, still filled with compost, in which I had hidden two quarter bottles of vodka.

I felt the rim of the flowerpot and dug my hand into the soil. My heart thumped as I did so. For several years now my husband and I had been playing a silent game of hide-and-seek. Of course we always knew who had won each particular round but we never acknowledged it in as many words. If I won he found me passed out on the sofa or my bed, or sometimes on the kitchen floor. If he won the bottles would have disappeared from their hiding place, whisked away in the night like spies called in from the cold.

This particular time I was the victor. How triumphant I felt as I cracked open the first of the bottles, unable to wait even to get back to my bed. As I glugged down the first gulp I reached up into a cupboard for a teacup and then went into the fridge for some Coke. I liked to pretend to myself and others that I drank black tea, not alcohol.

Two quarter bottles was enough to get me started but it wouldn't last me long. "Katy's disappeared" – is that what Alan had said? I needed to stop that thought turning into an emotion. Feelings were like snakes to me, wicked, silent, slithery creatures that could wind round me like a vine and squeeze me into unbearable pain. I could not confront the fact that something could have happened to my beautiful daughter, that the world was this cruel, my life so hard. Could not, would not. Thank God for the wine rack.

My husband thought this was safe. The bottles were counted but I only drank on the sly. I don't know if he knew about the times I downed several of the bottles and then drove into town to find replacements. I liked to think that was one particular game only I knew about.

This day, though, I had no intentions of replacing the bottles. I felt it was my right to drink as many of them as I needed. After all, something awful had happened. It was excusable.

I went upstairs again with two of them, a corkscrew, the cup, the Coke and the vodka. There was so much to hold I had to put it in a plastic Tesco bag. As I took the steps lightly, two at a time, I felt like an excited schoolgirl carrying an unopened gift. The anticipation of the pleasure was all the greater because I was going to savour the experience myself. It was my little secret and no-one else was allowed a taste of it.

Back in bed, there was a wet patch on the sheet. I leaned down and smelled it. Urine. I stripped off the sheet and then sprayed some perfume round the room. Then I got back under the duvet and, with the curtains still closed, began to drink.

25

"YOU think you'll manage along to the benefit gig tonight?" Dan asked Ryan as they approached Trafalgar Square.

"Do my best, mate," Ryan replied, slapping his old university chum on the back. "It's been great bumping into you anyway. We'll need to have a pint before you head back to Mali. I'll text you."

Dan grinned. "Do that," he said. "But let's keep it at one pint. I'm a real lightweight these days. Never drink when I'm in Africa – too knackered."

The two men stopped at the foot of the National Gallery steps. Trafalgar Square was thronged and fractious commuters jostled them in their hurry to reach Charing Cross tube station. Dan watched as the man who'd once headed up the university's Green Society looked him up and down, taking in his sandals, combat trousers and hemp tee-shirt. He suspected he now appeared to Ryan as he did to his sister Donna who'd accused him on his return home from Mali of looking like a Californian beach bum. ("A Celtic Californian beach bum," she'd qualified her remark later, tugging playfully on the long dark locks he'd since found the time to have trimmed.) Ryan, who had just told him he had given up his job as a campaign manager with a wildlife charity to work for his cousin's new IT business, was wearing a smart, dark suit.

"Well, mate, I'm meeting someone here so I'm not going any further," said Dan.

Ryan lifted his eyes from Dan's sandals and gave him a grin. "Oh yeah? Who's that then? Not that dark-eyed babe you were with when I met you last year?"

Amira, thought Dan, and felt a faint tightness in his chest. "No, not her."

Ryan winked. "Well, I'll leave you to it then."

He held out his hand. Dan took it and felt his hand being grasped warmly. As he stood and watched Ryan's stocky blond figure disappearing into the crowds of tourists and commuters he felt himself overcome by a sudden burst of melancholy. Ryan had been as close as a brother during their years as students together but more recently their meetings, like this one, had been result of accident rather than design. They were gradually growing away from each other, Ryan's suit and his scruffiness merely a symbol of a much deeper parting of outlooks.

It took Dan a moment to regain his usual sense of buoyancy. It had been like this quite a lot recently. He'd be going about his day with a sense of optimism and purpose only to find himself engulfed by a sudden wave of sadness which he could only put down to the realisation that time had not stood still while he'd been working in Mali. He'd returned to London just before Christmas to find Amira had re-established her relationship with her previously estranged husband and his sister Donna had moved in with her boyfriend Josh. Other friends and colleagues from his student days and his periods of work at the Refugee Centre had produced babies, opened cafes, moved to Bristol to take up jobs with the BBC. At his darkest moments it would make him wonder if his own choices had been the right ones. The life of an NGO was an unsettled one, the highs of creating a solar generated water pump and seeing it transform the lives of several villages counterbalanced by the lows of being unable to sustain a relationship or being there for his mother on the anniversary of his father's death.

Still, he thought, taking a sweeping look round Trafalgar Square, he was looking forward to the prospect of meeting Katy. The girl he'd begun chatting to on the RockFrendz forum seemed to share a lot of the same interests as him and she sounded attractive – blonde, slim, preferring vintage clothing to brands or High Street fashion. He liked the fact that she also seemed to read a lot, even if it appeared to be Jane Austen and George Eliot and not the books on globalisation and the environment that he spent most of his spare time devouring. Amira hadn't been much of a reader, preferring to campaign rather than spend time considering what other people had to say about the issues that excited her most. Dan hadn't minded that, in fact he'd been attracted to Amira's fiery passion on all matters of social justice, but he had also found himself intrigued by Katy's quiet reflections on the novels she read and on the lyrics of her favourite songs. It had been Katy's contribution to a forum discussion about Dylan's *Blowin in the Wind* which had first drawn his attention to her. "It's not a protest song," she'd written. "It's a protest song about people who don't protest." Dan had liked both the observation and the way it was expressed enough to post a response, and later to start exchanging personal messages with Katy. Three months later he was still interested enough in the Scottish girl to want to meet her in person.

He looked at his watch. It was well past six and still no sign of anyone who fitted Katy's description of herself. He wondered idly about a few of the gaps in his knowledge about the woman he was about to meet. Physically, he thought he had her pinpointed, but he'd forgotten to find out exactly what age she was, though from the sounds of it she was at least an undergraduate if not doing some sort of masters. He'd never found out what her subject was exactly but judging by her reading matter it had to be English, or perhaps History. But she was also musical, so perhaps she was a music student of some sort, studying for her grade six piano exam as an afterthought to her main discipline of singing. Hadn't she mentioned something recently about auditioning for a choir?

He scanned the square again, beginning to feel excited. He wanted to meet Katy right now and talk to her, to establish enough rapport with her to know what clubs she'd enjoy visiting after the gig that night. In the back of his mind he'd already earmarked a couple of places in Brixton he'd like to take her to but he wanted to be certain she would like the music they played there, the atmosphere in each, before he suggested going to either one of them. Just for a moment he allowed himself to imagine being at one of the clubs, The Roxy, dancing with a beautiful blonde woman he invested with the name of Katy. She was wearing a light, cotton shirt and jeans, her hair hung loosely about her face, she was elegant, her pale skin faintly freckled, as if she spent a lot of time outdoors. The music in the background was a Cuban dance mix.

He was woken out of his reverie by a sudden gust of dusty wind, which blew a crisp bag across his feet. Dan kicked the bag away and grinned. He was letting his imagination run away with him.

Resolving not to let it happen again, he stared resolutely at Lord Nelson who gazed towards the Thames, his sights set on far away places, the slate-grey ground sweeping away from his column like cold sea. Heroes like Nelson weren't given to flights of fancy, Dan told himself. They were strategists, practical men who owed their successes, admire them or loathe them, to their ability to focus on the task in hand. Or were they? Maybe Nelson just like Dan had known moments of loneliness when he was far from home and had indulged in the occasional romantic daydream to see him through the worst of them.

The desolation Dan had felt as he watched Ryan walking away from him was beginning to threaten his mood again. He willed Katy to arrive soon so that he could leave the greyness and anonymity of Trafalgar Square behind and return to the colour and chatter of Walthamstow where he still felt comfortable and needed. He pulled out his phone to see if there were any texts to explain where Katy might have got to for it was getting on for half past six he noted, taking another quick glance at his watch. But there was nothing. Just a quick 'hi' from Amira to tell him she'd managed to upload some of her photographs of Iraq onto a Powerpoint presentation for tonight. "We'll project them against the wall in the hallway," she'd texted with typical Amira resoluteness.

"Hi there," he heard a Scottish voice behind him say.

Dan felt himself start. He'd been so lost in thoughts of his imagined Katy that he'd forgotten the real one would have an unfamiliar accent, or any voice at all for that matter. He turned round. But there had to be some mistake, he thought, dropping his phone on the ground in shock. The girl standing barely a foot away from him did not look much more than fourteen.

26

"WHEREVER she's gone it's got nothing to do with me," Ron Turner said to Jane as she ushered him into her living room and gestured towards an armchair.

But instead of sitting down, the music teacher moved to the window, walking round the dining table to the drawn velvet curtains. With his left hand, as if swatting a fly, he opened one of them a fraction and looked out, his face pressed hard against the window. Jane felt a surge of annoyance at his casual manner. There was a trail of mud on her cream carpet, to indicate everywhere he'd been since arriving at her house. Now there would be marks on her window too.

"What are you looking for?" she asked.

She was gripping the back of the settee so hard her knuckles stood out like miniature ox-tail bones.

"Sit down, will you, Ron."

She gestured a second time at the armchair but Ron was opening the curtains again, peering out into the blackness.

"He'll be here any minute," said Jane. Her voice sounded snappy, but she didn't care.

"I don't see what good it's going to do."

"What's going to do?"

He stared at her from his spot behind the dining table. "Getting me and Katy's father round here like this."

"Mr Clemmy's sick with worry. He asked me to call him back when I'd spoken to you, which I did. But he still wanted to speak to you himself. He sounded a bit..."

"What? Crazy?"

Jane sighed. "I just thought that rather than give him your number it might be better – easier – if you both came here. It's not as if either of you live far away. And Mr Clemmy is climbing the walls. It was just an idea. You didn't have to come."

"I could hardly not, could I? I mean, you're saying Katy is missing and you're suggesting I'm under suspicion or something."

"No, you're not under suspicion," said Jane.

"You could have fooled me," replied Turner in a tone that sounded like a huffy teenager's. Jane reminded herself he was, after all, only 22 and not long out of college.

"Look, Ron, I'm only trying to help. I probably wouldn't have bothered with any of this if it hadn't taken me so long to get in touch with you..."

"Oh, right, so now I'm guilty of staying out late?" Turner blinked at her indignantly behind his thick glasses.

"Don't be ridiculous," said Jane. "What I was about to say was that because you were out when I phoned the first few times it was nearly one by the time I got back to Katy's Dad and by then he was going demented. I was worried if I gave him your number he'd..."

"What? Find out my address and send round the heavy squad?"

Jane paused. If truth be told, she was rather concerned that Alan Clemmy had begun to make a scapegoat of Turner. "What was this Turner doing giving Katy lessons at his house anyway?" Clemmy had asked her when she called him back. His tone was angry and suspicious, almost nasty. He seemed to have completely forgotten that earlier in the evening, at the parents' night, Katy's extra piano lessons and musical talent had been nothing but a source of pride to him.

"He did sound a bit het up," said Jane.

A flash of panic crossed Turner's face.

"But I'm sure that's only because he's worried," she added hastily. "To be honest, I thought Katy would have been home by now and none of this would be necessary."

They stared at each other for a moment. Jane looked away first. I am Katy's guidance teacher, thought Jane. I should have noticed she was unhappy.

An owl hooted outside. In the distance, the church bells in Craigie chimed two. Two o'clock in the morning and still no Katy, thought Jane.

"Please, Ron," she said and nodded at the armchair beside the fireplace. The young music teacher sighed, shook his head and walked over to it, throwing himself down with a heavy thud.

"Well, I hope this does some good," he said a few seconds later, in a tone that suggested he didn't think it would. He removed his glasses and rubbed his eyes.

Jane perched uneasily on an arm of her settee. Turner was right, she thought. It had been a daft idea to have the two men round to her cottage. If only she had told Alan Clemmy she had no idea of Turner's number and rung off at the first available opportunity. Instead, she had let her pity for the farmer get the better of her. Almost forty years old, well practised at being Miss Ellingham and still she was capable of being led by her emotions.

"Have you got no common sense?" her mother had screamed at her when, only two years older than Katy, she had gone to her and told her she was pregnant. Her mother had shaken her so hard that she had fallen on the floor and begun to cry. "Stupid girl. Get up," she was told.

"You all right?"

Jane felt her body jump. Ron Turner was staring over at her.

"I'm fine," she said, and forced a quick smile.

"You look a bit pale, that's all."

"No, I'm fine."

Turner put his elbows on his knees and cupped his face in his hands.

"Well, if Katy's Dad is coming, I wish he'd do it soon," he said.

Me too, thought Jane. Having decided inviting Turner and Clemmy to her house had been nothing but stupidity, she suddenly longed for her bed – or, to be more accurate, oblivion. The two were not necessarily the same thing, as Shakespeare and 3B's Shirley Stapleton had reminded her around fourteen hours ago. "...where unbruised youth with unstuff'd brain/Doth couch his limbs, there golden sleep doth reign" she had written on the board under the heading 'Romeo and Juliet – Useful Quotes'. "That means if you're auld and your heid's spinning you'll no sleep," Shirley had said, looking round her classmates with a smug nod of her head.

"What will Mr Clemmy want to know then?" asked Turner. With his glasses off, his elbows on his knees and his chubby face squashed between his hands he looked like an untidy schoolboy.

"I think he just thought you might know something – about where Katy was," said Jane.

"I've already said – I've got no idea where she is."

"None?"

"No," he said. "Why should I?"

"She seemed to tell you things she didn't tell anyone else."

Turner shifted, put his glasses back on and straightened his back.

"Yeah, well. Maybe that's because all the people who are supposed to listen to her, don't."

Jane bit her lip. He really was a creep. But now wasn't the time to get involved in a personal row with a 22-year-old infant.

"There isn't a boyfriend or anything like that?" she asked.

"I've no idea."

"It's just it would explain a lot."

Turner pressed his hands on the arms of his chair and began to stand up.

"She told her Dad she was staying the night at a girlfriend's," persisted Jane. "She wouldn't have lied unless she had something to hide – like a boyfriend she didn't want her father to know about."

Turner stopped still. He was half sitting, half standing, suddenly lost in thought.

"Ron?"

"Yeah, what?" He shook his head and stood up properly.

"You don't know if there is a boyfriend?"

"I don't know if there is boyfriend. Satisfied?"

"I was only asking..."

"Well, I'm getting fed up with these questions. You saw me dropping Katy off in the school car park. Wherever she is, whoever she's with, it's not me, is it?"

"No," agreed Jane, with a sigh.

Turner stared over at the window. "Do you think she's okay?" he asked, his voice stripped of its usual cockiness. Jane was suddenly aware of her own growing sense of unease. If Katy was out with a boy there was nowhere in Ayr, let alone Craigie, that would be open now, she thought.

She caught Ron Turner watching her and looked away.

"Can I get you a coffee, Ron, or a tea?" she asked briskly and stood up.

Turner gave her a sardonic smile. "Got to keep up the social niceties, even at times like this," he said.

"I was just offering..." She trailed off, feeling confused.

"I wouldn't mind something stronger," said Turner.

"I've got whisky," mumbled Jane. "I'll just get it. Have a seat... if you want."

She was half way to the kitchen when the doorbell rang. Alan Clemmy's broad frame loomed behind the mottled glass of the front door. She hesitated and then walked on to the larder. There, in the cool blackness, she gathered up a bottle of Macallan and two tumblers. She pressed one of the tumblers against her cheek and closed her eyes. If only I could stop everything, she thought, press pause and walk away. Miss Ellingham seemed to have deserted her.

But a few moments later she was opening her door to Katy's father.

"Mr Clemmy," she said.

He gave the whisky a disdainful glance and pushed past her into the hall.

"Where's Turner?" he asked.

Jane put the bottle and glasses down on the telephone table and followed the farmer into the living room. He was already by the fireplace, staring down at a terrified looking Turner.

"So it was you who dropped my daughter off in the car park?"

Turner shrank back in his seat. "Now, hold on a moment," he said.

Jane pressed herself against the door. This is all my fault, she thought. Her mother hissed in her ear. "*No common sense.*"

Ron Turner tried to stand up but as he did Clemmy moved towards him. Turner stumbled back in his chair. His glasses fell onto the tiled fireplace with a clatter.

"Did Katy ask you to drop her off at the school?" asked Clemmy. He reached down and picked up Turner's glasses, then tossed them onto the music teacher's lap.

"I... yes," said Turner. "She did."

Clemmy continued to bear down on Turner. Jane reached behind her back for the living room door handle.

"She said she was going to meet a friend in town," said Turner, his eyes fixed like a frightened animal's on the farmer.

Clemmy stared at Turner blankly and then turned away to face the fireplace. He sighed heavily and pressed his forehead against the mantelpiece. He stood like that for several seconds.

When he looked up again his eyes were less glazed. He glanced at Jane for a moment, and then back at Turner, who immediately clutched the arms of his chair.

"A friend," repeated Clemmy.

"Yes," said Turner.

"Didn't you ask her who?" asked Clemmy.

"No," said Turner.

"Why not?"

"It's not my responsibility to take care of your daughter."

Clemmy took a step towards Turner, grabbed him by the lapels and pulled him to his feet. "How dare you," he said with his face very close to Turner's.

Jane let go of the door handle and rushed across the room. Ornaments rattled all around her. As she stretched out to stop the fruit bowl falling off the edge of the dining table she fell heavily to the floor and heard something crash down beside her. She looked round. The standard lamp was lolling on its side next to her, its flex wound round her ankle. She disentangled herself and moved dizzily towards the two men, now wrestling with each other on the hearth.

"Stop," she yelled.

Ron Turner managed to pull himself out of Clemmy's clutches and wedged himself between the back of the armchair and the wall. He crouched down on the floor and put his hands over his face.

"Stop," yelled Jane again. She rushed over to Clemmy, who was making for the armchair, and pulled at his jacket sleeve. "Leave him alone."

Alan Clemmy stopped for a moment, stared at her with glassy

eyes then turned his head back towards the chair.

"Don't," she screamed at Clemmy.

Clemmy took a step back. Jane peered over the top of the armchair at Turner.

"Go into the bathroom and lock the door," she said to the music teacher.

Turner stared up at her with his mouth open.

"Upstairs... oh for God's sake."

She took his wrist and pulled him out of the living room, up the stairs and into the bathroom. With the door closed behind them, she ran the cold tap and put a sponge under it. Then she lowered the toilet seat and sat Turner down, forcing the wet sponge into his hands.

"Hold that to your head," she said.

Turner looked up at her blankly.

"You've got a big bruise coming up," she said in exasperation.

She was half way down the stairs again when she noticed Alan Clemmy standing in the hall. He looked up at her, his arms by his side, his shoulders hunched. As she looked back at him he inspected his feet and glanced towards the front door.

She wanted to throw him out her house and scream at him, "Your stupid daughter is not my problem." But instead she made do with descending the last of the stairs noisily and pushing past Clemmy into the living room. The scene that greeted her hardly improved her mood. The room looked as if it had been picked up, shaken, then set back down again. Dining chairs lurched at an angle, jotters and pieces of fruit littered the floor beneath the dining table, and a photograph of Jane's parents had fallen off the coffee table and lay face up on the carpet.

Jane suddenly felt very tired. This is the sum of my life, she thought, helping a man to whom I mean absolutely nothing, solve his life's problems. "Are you all right?" Jim had asked her earlier that night. No, I'm bloody well not, she said to him now through the ether. And it's no thanks to you and the Stick-it.

She bent down to pick up the photograph.

"I'll get that."

Jane looked round. Alan Clemmy was standing behind her. Before she'd had time to say anything he'd bent down and retrieved the photograph. He handed it to her without saying anything.

Jane stared at the breadth of his chest. He was wearing a dark green t-shirt beneath a sports jacket. At rest he looked awkward and sad, like a caged bear. A surge of pity rose within her and she was just about to reach out and touch his arm when she noticed something orange sticking out of his jacket pocket. In the dim light it looked almost like a relay baton. She squinted. It was one of her jotters.

"That's mine," she said, reaching out to grab it.

"Katy's," he said, taking a step back.

Jane felt her arm fall. All of a sudden she felt like crying, but about what she wasn't quite sure. Was it Alan Clemmy's muddle-headed concern for his daughter, Katy or herself? Everything is such a mess, she thought. Me, I'm a mess. She felt the dizziness return and grabbed the back of a chair.

"Look, I'm sorry," Alan Clemmy was saying. He touched her lightly on the shoulder and walked her gently round to the settee. "I'm really..."

There were tears in his eyes. Jane sat down on the settee and looked helplessly at her knees. There were wet patches on her jeans where the bathroom sponge had dripped water. Her feet, in strappy sandals, looked like a young girl's.

Everything was silent except for the ticking of the grandfather clock on the landing. Clemmy stayed rooted to the spot, staring down at Jane from what seemed like a great height.

"Is he okay – Turner?" he asked eventually.

Jane felt herself give Clemmy a fleeting smile.

"He's fine. He's got a bit of a shiner over one eye but that's all."

Alan Clemmy frowned.

"He only came over to help, you know," Jane said.

Alan Clemmy looked dolefully at the floor.

"It was hardly a crime to give Katy a lift into Craigie, especially when she seems to have asked."

Alan Clemmy glanced at the door.

"Should I go and see if he's all right?"

Jane thought about it for a moment.

"No, I don't think that's a good idea."

"Really?"

"Yes, really. I'll see to him."

As she stood up she gave Alan Clemmy a smile. His eyes warmed for a moment and then dulled.

"He's sorry about it," Jane said to Turner a few minutes later as she coaxed him back down the stairs.

She was feeling impatient but doing her best to repress it. Nursing the literal and metaphorical bruises of a man-child contravened several of her post-Jim commandments – thou shalt not waste thy energies on the inadequate or weak and thou shalt live out thy days peacefully with the minimum of association with the rest of mankind. The others – thou shalt not kill the Stick-it and thou shalt not commit or regret any relationship – had already been tested that night.

"He started it," said Ron, wincing as he took another step downwards.

"Now, Ron," she said, in the manner she would reserve for a difficult pupil. "Why don't we get downstairs and have that malt."

Turner stopped suddenly, grimaced and clutched his right knee.

"Who does he think he is? Mr bloody Barrett Browning?"

Jane giggled.

"What are you laughing at?"

"You, that was just quite witty, that's all."

Ron groaned, descended another step and stopped again.

"Just because you're an English teacher doesn't mean you're the only person who's read a book."

Jane drew a deep breath.

"Obviously not."

Ron sniffed and looked round at her.

"Sorry."

"No, no," said Jane.

He continued to look at her.

"Mistress of control, aren't you?"

"What?"

He had begun to annoy her again. It was bad enough that he was here in her house, leaving his muddy trail all over her carpet and mopping his brow with her bath sponge but now he was beginning to feel he had the right to comment on her, psychoanalyse her.

"Maybe I just like my privacy," she said sharply and pulled him down another stair. Turner, who had opened his mouth to speak again, squeezed his eyes shut and grimaced.

"Bloody hell," he said, under his breath.

Jane pulled at his wrist again.

"All right. All right," said Turner and tugged his arm free of her grasp. A moment later he was thumping down the remaining stairs, one foot heavier on the ground than the other.

"Keep away from me. I'm warning you, Raging Bull," she heard him say several seconds later as he pushed his way into the living room, opening the door as if he was a wounded John Wayne going into a saloon.

Jane rushed past him and placed herself in the centre of the room, between the two men.

"I'm warning you," Ron Turner said again.

Jane raised her arms and held a palm towards each man. There was a pause as everyone looked at each other.

After a few seconds has passed, Alan Clemmy shifted his feet, stretched out his hand and took a step towards Turner. "I'm sorry," he said and gave the music teacher a quick, sheepish smile.

Turner looked at the outstretched hand without moving.

"For Jane's sake, if not mine?"

Clemmy kept his hand extended. Turner sighed, took a step forwards and gave Clemmy's hand a quick shake. The room went very quiet.

27

THE FIRST step, I don't need to tell anyone here, is to admit you are powerless over alcohol. But you cannot do that when you are powerless over alcohol. It requires a brief moment of sobriety. Clarity. The chronic alcoholic has little of either towards the end.

The last thing I remember about the day I was told my daughter was missing is going upstairs to the bedroom and the bed I had pissed on. I started drinking the vodka. A while later, as its effects began to kick in, I realised I'd better open the wine. Sometimes, when I got too drunk I became incapable of using a corkscrew. I stabbed my hand with it in my fury to extricate the cork, or I ended up pushing it downwards into the bottle with the end of a spoon. I could cry over a thing like that.

I don't remember drinking the wine. When I next woke up lizards and snakes were crawling all over me. They were on my face. I could feel their scales on my skin, the lizards' tales brushing this way and that. The snakes wound themselves round my hair and suddenly Medusa was thrashing in my bed. I looked down and could see her struggling with a bedspread which had become a winding sheet, her face speckled with sweat, her mouth open and gasping for air. Her snake hair kept wriggling and moving, spreading itself across the pillow. I wanted to reach down and help but the reptiles began climbing up the walls. I heard a scream and saw a snake disappearing down Medusa's throat. The room fragmented into a thousand pieces, as if I had been viewing it through a kaleidoscope. My husband appeared out of the fragments of lizards' tails and with him people I had never seen. They left words hanging in my imagination which later reassembled themselves and began rattling at the door of my conscience. Katy. Missing. Teacher. Police.

Katy, Katy, Katy. I tried to shut her out. But the drink was wearing off and it was my only defence. One moment I thought she was right next to me. I could smell her baby smell, warm and milky, although the hand that reached out and rested on my forehead was a young woman's. "Mum," she pleaded. "Mum, won't you come downstairs?" She could not be dead, please God. Not her as well. I could no longer shut out the fear. I could no longer stop it shaping itself into words. The strangers' lexicon began assembling itself into sentences that were more horrific to me than the lizards and snakes. Katy was missing. Alan had contacted the police.

My husband's voice came and went like a noise in the middle of the night. When the reptiles had gone and the sentences crawled back into the dark holes behind my consciousness, I was not sure if I had dreamt it or not. For I found myself all alone in a white room in the clouds. The Allan Glen Addictions Treatment Centre, a woman, also dressed in white, said. She gave me what she said was a sedative ("another one") and told me to rest. I was sure that I was in heaven, or perhaps waiting to descend into hell.

28

AS DAN scrambled around on the National Gallery steps for his phone, his mind ran through some of the email conversations he'd had with the young girl staring down at him. It had never occurred to him her references to libraries and essays could mean she was still at school – which she had to be from the way she looked. Her face was almost childlike in its wide-eyed innocence and there were other hints of her age in the collection of bangles and friendship bands round her wrists, as well as the Hello Kitty luggage tag attached to her holdall. All in all, the girl reminded him of his cousin Florence who had just celebrated her fifteenth birthday.

He stood up feeling rather foolish. What a bloody idiot I am, he thought. He was glad Katy had not appeared while he was still talking to Ryan. How embarrassing would that have been? What would he have said? "This is my cyber friend Katy who I thought I was going on a date with before I realised she was just a kid... No, I forgot to ask her what age she was."

So, the question was what to do now? He couldn't just walk away and leave her, not after setting up the meeting with her and her having travelled all the way from Scotland – even if she had made it clear the real purpose of her visit was not to see him but to attend some sort of appointment. He'd forgotten to ask about that too, he thought now. Mind you, she had always been so guarded about her plans for Friday afternoon that he hadn't felt he could enquire any further about them.

I'll take her for something to eat like I planned, thought Dan. And after that I'll make my excuses and get the hell home. He wondered, idly, what Florence was up to. But that was ridiculous. He couldn't just take an anonymous Scottish girl round to his cousin's home in Leyton and expect them to *play* together as if they were six years old. Anyway, Florence was probably down at the track training. According to Donna and his Aunt Sarah, Florence was now part of an elite squad who were being coached for the 2006 Commonwealth Games. Florence was rarely at home apparently, frequently away at competitions and training camps.

"Are you hungry?" he asked Katy.

"A bit," she replied, her face flushing.

"I thought maybe we could go for a Chinese or something." He paused and then added quickly, "After that I'll have to get back."

He didn't look at Katy while he spoke and she said nothing by way of reply but he thought he sensed disappointment emanating from her. Had she taken the huff because he was quite deliberately cutting her out of any further socialising later in the evening? A sharp stab of self-loathing for his expedient ruthlessness was quickly followed by the soothing balm of self-righteous indignation. What on earth did the girl expect – that a twenty four year old man (and she must have known his age the majority of the time they were corresponding because he had mentioned it more than once) would want a friendship with a girl who'd barely started secondary school?

"I was thinking of a restaurant near The Embankment," he said, to break the heavy silence that had engulfed them.

They were still standing on the National Gallery steps. Dan was beginning to feel increasingly exposed and uncomfortable. He knew he did not look old enough to be Katy's father. On the other hand, the age gap between them was greater than the average one between siblings. Why, oh why, hadn't he thought about this more carefully? Perhaps it's living abroad, he thought absently. I've forgotten the questions to ask, the social mores of my own culture and I've become so desperate for female company that I've begun to romanticise, to a ludicrous degree, any hint of it that comes my way.

"Where's The Embankment?" asked Katy. She looked around Trafalgar Square nervously.

"It's not far from here," said Dan. "We're a bit later than I expected but we should get there by seven, which still leaves us plenty of time."

"I got lost," said the Scottish girl, her face flushing. "Sorry."

Dan felt the sharp edges of his annoyance soften a little. The girl looked as she was about to burst into tears.

"Well, never mind – you made it," he said, touching her elbow gently and attempting to steer her across the square. "And it's nice to meet you," he added awkwardly.

The girl blushed a deep crimson but said nothing.

"I think I suggested going to a benefit gig later on," said Dan cautiously. "But I'm kind of... well I don't think it would be all that interesting for you anyway. It's just a bunch of local bands."

Katy pulled the sleeves of her v-necked jumper down over her hands and looked up at him through her fringe.

"What's a benefit gig?"

There were faint, dark circles round her eyes, noticed Dan. For all her fresh faced, girlish prettiness there was something rather troubled and distracted about her.

"It's a gig where all the money..." He tailed off. He had no sooner begun to talk than the girl's attention had wandered to a glamorous blonde woman walking arm in arm across the square with a man who resembled an ageing 1970s rock star.

"Isn't that Caprice?" asked Katy, looking back round at Dan again and then pointing in the direction of the blonde woman.

"Haven't a clue," murmured Dan, trying to remember if he'd ever known who Caprice was or not.

They continued to the far side of Trafalgar Square in silence. Bloody RockFrendz, thought Dan. In the absence of hard facts about Katy he had painted in the enormous blanks in his canvas with whatever colours he'd wanted and none of them had turned out to be appropriate. He remembered a conversation he'd had with Donna about internet dating. His sister, who'd met Josh through TrueLove.com, was a big fan of the phenomenon but Dan wasn't so convinced. "You never know who you could be talking to," he'd told his sister. "Seems like a good place for charlatans to hang out." He should have listened to his own cautionary advice, he thought, even though he hadn't been looking for a date when he'd starting posting on RockFrendz.

He looked down at Katy and felt a rush of guilt. She looked so young and lost. It wasn't fair to liken her to a charlatan. She hadn't actively deceived him about anything and there had been clues to the girl's essence, if only he'd been sharp eyed enough to spot them. All those rows with her father she'd mentioned, the preoccupation with the state of her parents' marriage. He'd stupidly assumed, or wanted to believe, that these comments signified a student who was finding it irritating but necessary to live at home. He might just have easily come to the more accurate conclusion that they were indicative of a young girl mired in the twin miseries of adolescence and a crumbling family.

"Straight on," he said, nudging Katy, who was about to turn left on to Charing Cross Road, forwards. "Just a bit further down here, and then we turn right."

Katy stumbled. She kept her head down but her shoulders were shaking slightly. Dan wondered suddenly if she might be crying.

"Are you alright?" he asked, touching the girl lightly on the arm.

"Fine," she said, keeping her head down and continuing to walk slightly ahead of him. It was difficult to tell from her voice what sort of state she was in. She sounded in control, tough even, but for all Dan knew that was put on for his benefit.

He forced his voice full of joviality. "Once we get to the restaurant you'll need to tell me all about what you've been doing this afternoon," he said.

"I've not been doing anything," she muttered and quickened her pace down The Strand.

An hour and a half later, staring over a concrete wall into a cold, angry river crawling with glass-topped pleasure boats – "just ahead of you on the right you'll see the Houses of Parliament" – Dan was feeling doubtful about the wisdom of heading off to the benefit gig on his own. Over a stilted dinner he'd asked Katy where she'd been staying. "St Paul's Youth Hostel," she'd said. "I'll walk you back," he'd offered but she'd said "no", that she wanted to "walk about a bit". "You don't really want to be wandering around here on your own," he'd insisted. "Go on, I'll walk round with you. It's no distance." "No," she'd scowled.

The net result was that Katy had ended up walking with Dan

to Embankment tube station and from there was planning to take the walk she was so set on. Dan had agreed to the idea half heartedly but by the time they were within sight of the station he was feeling so torn about abandoning the teenager (as he now saw it) that he'd failed to go any further and had begun to point out London landmarks.

"The Barbican and Tate Modern are over there," he was saying to Katy now. He pointed across the river. "You could go to the Tate tomorrow if you've got time. Not sure what's on but there's usually something interesting."

Katy turned round to look at him, her blue eyes momentarily full of sparkle.

"The Barbican's a theatre, isn't it?" she asked. "Our English teacher has posters from it on her walls. Are there any famous actors on?"

"Not sure," said Dan, suppressing a sigh.

The one thing he had managed to grasp about Katy was that she was obsessed with famous people. He'd tried to get her to talk about the books she read, the music she was playing for her piano exam, anything really that might make the time pass more quickly between them but while she'd answered his questions politely she wouldn't expand much beyond the bare facts. She was playing Beethoven's *Pathétique*, her favourite Jane Austen was *Pride and Prejudice* and her Gran had sent her a copy of *Wuthering Heights* which she'd just started reading and was "quite liking" so far. It was only when the discussion moved to the film of *Romeo and Juliet,* which she was studying for her exams, that she had showed any animation and only then when Dan had admitted to a passing crush on Claire Danes four years ago. "Claire Danes," she'd exclaimed. "You think she's pretty?"

A wind was blowing off the river. Dan saw Katy shiver and rub her arms. The grey sky was darkening, bearing down on the concrete complex of the National and washing away any last traces of colour from the Thames. Distant buildings shrunk back to blank, origami boxes, pigeons flapped menacingly. Dark spaces seemed to open up around them – under the Hungerford Bridge, around the corner from the tube station. Night was reclaiming the city, the picture postcard being replaced by its negative.

I *can't* leave Katy to walk about London on her own, Dan thought suddenly as he watched her slight frame fading back in the gathering darkness. He opened his mouth to suggest that she came with him to Walthamstow for the benefit gig. But before he could say anything they were both distracted by a drunk who had lurched out of a side street.

"Any spare change?" he slurred, weaving towards them.

He had a bottle in the pocket of his ripped, waxed jacket, his trousers were falling down and he stunk of urine. His hair was so matted it had begun to form dreadlocks. His face was weathered and his eyes dull and opaque looking, like glass that had been washed over and over by the sea.

"Hey, wee darlin'..."

He spoke with a thick, Scottish accent. Dan saw Katy give the man a sharp stare. She reached into a back pocket of her jeans and pulled out a handful of receipts and several notes.

"Here," she said, handing the drunk a fiver.

The man stared at it for several minutes and then looked at Katy.

"Thankyouvurrymuch yur a lady..."

He stumbled and then steadied himself. "You could be daen' better than him..." he said, fixing his glassy gaze on Dan.

Dan flinched.

"Didnae mean any harm, son," said the drunk, holding up his hands.

Dan began, carefully, to circumnavigate the man, reaching out to grab Katy by the arm as he did so. "Come on, we'd better be going," he whispered loudly into her ear.

But Katy shook him off and scowled.

"Are you okay?" she asked the man.

The drunk frowned and fell forwards, towards Katy. Dan tugged hard on Katy's arm again but she pulled it free then held out her hands to break the man's fall. As if holding back a concrete slab, she tried, without much success, to push him back to his feet.

Dan rushed to the back of the man and pulled him upright again.

The stink of urine was undercut, close up, by a strong smell of vomit. As soon as Dan was sure the man was steady on his feet again, he turned away and tried to breathe some fresher air. When he turned back round, Katy was standing with her back to him, gazing over the Thames, and the drunk was nowhere to be seen.

Light reflections flickered on the water like fireflies. The commuters had stopped funnelling along the waterside. The traffic was less angry and moved faster. The cars seemed to be full of people on their way out, instead of trying to leave work. He heard a horn toot, music blaring. A crowd of black boys dressed in baggy jeans came out of the nearby tube entrance, their voices full of laughter.

Dan looked at Katy as she stared out over the river. She looked remote and lonely, he thought, like the figure of a woman on the prow of a boat, crashing through the waves unseen.

He walked up behind her and placed a palm on the small of her back.

"Come on, why don't we both go to that gig," he said gently.

29

3B HAD their heads down. Even Billy Neill had taken time out from lewd comments and was chewing thoughtfully on the end of a blue biro. Madeleine McCutcheon was gazing out the window and Kevin McCarra was mumbling to himself, but that was hardly a worry. The pair of them would finish any test she set at least half an hour before the rest. Neither, thankfully, had the social wherewithal to use the spare time to distract less able classmates with mischief.

Jane used the peace to think over the previous evening. It had been a pointless exercise inviting both Alan Clemmy and Ron Turner to her cottage. Pointless and out of character – for it had resulted from an inability to leave Alan Clemmy to deal with his own not inconsiderable problems. I'm not a woman who cares any more, she reminded herself now, taking a dispassionate look at 3B's troubled back row of Billy Neill and his cohorts.

But in the small hours of Friday morning, in a living room wrecked by the playground brawl of two grown men, she had attempted to care by trying to engage Ron Turner and Alan Clemmy in a discussion about Katy. Was there something troubling Katy, she asked them. Was she worried about her school work? Had she fallen out with a friend? Was she being bullied? She had deliberately shied away from the more personal questions that seemed to have caused more harm than good when put to Alan Clemmy on the phone earlier in the evening. (Katy, apparently, did not have a boyfriend and was not the type to conceal anything from her father.) She had avoided, too, the question of Mrs Clemmy, since mention of her during parents' night had caused only tension and awkwardness. (Things were fine at home, now that the Clemmys had a cleaner.)

The result of her inept attempt at helping – *caring* – was that Ron Turner had left her cottage at almost three in the morning with nothing but a black eye and a cut lip to show for his visit and Alan Clemmy had departed with only Katy's English ink exercise jotter. ("I'll give it to her when she gets back," he had said, clutching it like a toddler does a comfort blanket.) Certainly, Alan Clemmy had called the police from her cottage. But as Jane admitted to herself now, it's not as if he wouldn't have done that from his own home – and probably more quickly – if she had not indulged him in his belief that Ron Turner might know where his daughter was.

God but she was useless. A useless guidance teacher and a useless human being. She remembered with a sharp pain in her chest Alan Clemmy standing in her hall, his head just inches below the lampshade. His large hands had hung like weights from the end of his arms, his shoulders had been bowed.

"I'm really so sorry," he had said.

Jane had been hit with a sudden realisation of what it would be like for the farmer to go home without his daughter and with no further information as to where she might be. (It's me who should be sorry, she thought now. Sorry for encouraging the man to think I could help.)

"What did the police say?" she had asked.

"They're going to send out a call – you know, in case she's wandering..."

His voice had broken off. His resignation had made Jane *care*. At the last minute and before Miss Ellingham had got the better of her, she had reached out and grabbed his elbow.

"Can I run you home, or call your wife... or something? I mean she must be worried too."

His eyes were very blue. He seemed not to understand what she had said for a moment. Then he blinked.

"No, that's okay. I've got the car anyway... and my wife, well, she's not in a fit state to worry much about anything."

Her puzzlement must have shown in her eyes because he had attempted a brief smile and touched her arm.

"I'm sorry, Miss Ellingham. I don't expect you to understand. Thank you, anyway, for trying to help us."

Jane turned to look back at the class. Katy's absence from the desk directly in front of her own somehow had the effect of making the teenager more present than usual. Her gaze fell on Shirley Stapleton, who occupied the desk behind Katy's. The hyenas' leader had a worm of chewing gum hanging out the corner of her mouth and her blouse was unbuttoned to her not insubstantial cleavage. She wrote casually, popping her gum every so often, as if to indicate education was incidental to the real thrust of her life. There was, thought Jane, something very visceral about Shirley which made her realise how ungrounded Katy had always seemed. Shirley Stapleton was a girl who already knew how to look after herself while Katy was a girl who might never know.

Jane looked at her watch. It was almost half past eleven. She could be at Alan Clemmy's farm by twelve.

"Time up," she said to 3B.

Billy Neill flung down his pen. There was a scraping of chairs, a murmur of conversation and then screams and shouts. The hyenas began talking about their Saturday night outfits. Madeleine McCutcheon and Kevin McCarra put the jotters that had been flung onto their desks into neat piles and stood beside them, like waiters in a chaotic dining room awaiting instructions from the maitre d'. Jane went over to both and rescued them.

"I'll take these," she said, tucking a pile under each arm.

"Have a good holiday, Miss," said Billy Neill, pushing rather too hard into the back of Shirley Stapleton. "Be good."

Jane, for once, allowed herself to smile.

"You too, Billy," she said and meant it. "Be careful."

Jane took a right turn through a cluster of housing association houses on the outskirts of Craigie. A small child stared at her through a wire mesh gate. Her mother, who could have been little more than twenty, left the front step, where she had been smoking a cigarette, and grabbed the child by her anorak hood. She stood like that, with the child in her grip, until Jane had driven past. Jane tried to tell herself that few cars must drive through this estate and onto the small country road which led out of it. The only other explanation she could think of for the mother's suspicious gaze was that she had taken on the unwholesome appearance of a child snatcher. That's what years of single living have done for me, she thought grimly.

But soon she was away from the white houses with their wire fences and weed-filled gardens and driving through an avenue of gnarled oak trees. Above, tiny snatches of sunlight winked like gold while on the road shadows tumbled past like weird creatures in an abstract cartoon. Glimpses of the landscape beyond the trees revealed green pasture sweeping towards a lazy twist of shallow river. An angler with a tweed hat and waders stood like a garden ornament on a white rock, waves like tiny ribbons of white lace creeping and retreating on a small beach of mud behind him.

The trees disappeared and the road narrowed. To the left a steep grassy bank blocked out the sunlight. On the right, fields filled with grazing cows swept towards the river. Beyond rose the Craigie hills. Jane, who had been up them many times, resisted an urge to stop the car. On a day like today the views would be spectacular – the Ayrshire coastline sharply defined, the sea glittering with a thousand pinpoints of sunlight. The isle of Arran would be at its most dramatic, rising from the cold blue water like a snippet of Switzerland that had somehow been set adrift.

The road began to wind upwards. The bank to the left disappeared and sunlight beat down on the passenger seat window. Jane rolled her own window down and felt the stir of fresh air in her hair. The scent of pine trees filled the car. The map on the car's back shelf flapped like a trapped bird. On both sides of the road, boggy fields stretched into the distance, broken only by angular patches of densely planted fir trees.

At the top of the hill, the road forked. Jane remembered Alan Clemmy telling her his farm lay a few miles out of Craigie, close to Ayr, so she took the right hand turn towards the sea. She was now driving directly towards the coast on a road high enough to reveal the views she had yearned for ten minutes before. On the horizon, a boat with white sails cut across a ribbon of sea while, above, the sun filtered dilute lemon light through a dappling of white cloud. Thick Forestry Commission plantations crowded the road at either side. Jane heard flies buzzing and almost swerved the car as a large gnat flew in through her window and darted across the windscreen.

She drove for a long time without passing another car. The firs were unrelenting, lining the road like army battalions. Jane began to consider turning back. The decision to visit Alan Clemmy had been an impulsive one anyway. What could she do that the police, or indeed the Clemmys themselves, could not? But just as she had decided to look for a suitable place in which to turn the car, she saw ahead a triangle of grass with a signpost in the middle of it. She braked slowly. One arm of the signpost pointed right to Symington. Another signalled that Ayr lay straight ahead. The third, pointing left, read "Millhouse 1 mile".

Jane turned left and drove about half a mile along the road until she saw a hand-painted sign propped up on a whitewashed stone. "Millhouse Farm", it said, above a roughly painted arrow pointing right.

The track leading to the farm rose upwards to a clearly visible whitewashed farmhouse. There was no tarmac, just two grooves of mud worn into a useful track through time. On either side, fields that looked as if they had been reclaimed from moorland spread out towards more Forestry Commission woodland. Brown and white Ayrshire cows stood stupidly in groups of two or three, the majority round old stone troughs filled with mossy water.

Jane pulled into the farm courtyard, neat enough, with one side taken up by the farmhouse itself, the two directly adjoining it comprising of outhouses. The fourth side of the yard was made up of an open barn, piled high with bales of straw, and the gateway she had just driven through.

A collie rushed out of the barn and started lapping the car. Moments later a second sped out of the farmhouse door and joined in. The pair barked and wagged their tails, jumping up at the window and doing another lap of the car before chasing each other in circles. As the dogs barked, cows began mooing. There was a plaintive edge to the noise they made. A faint echo to their lowing suggested these cows were indoors somewhere, yearning for open field.

A tractor rumbled past the gateway and then seemed to stop,

its engine still running. The collies hesitated for a moment and then darted away to investigate. Jane grabbed her chance and opened the car door.

She was greeted by a strong smell of manure. In the far distance some machinery buzzed. Out on the lane the tractor engine ceased and men's voices mingled with the dogs' yapping.

Above, the sky was blue and clear, save for a faint suggestion of cloud high above the horizon but Jane still couldn't shake off the feeling of bleakness that had been with her since she had turned onto the high, forest-lined road that led to the coast. The severity of the concreted courtyard and the whitewashed buildings with black-painted woodwork only exacerbated the feeling.

Jane looked round. The outhouses to the right and left of her looked firmly locked up. There was no movement in the barn. But the farmhouse door was ajar. She walked towards it, looking round as she did so, nervous that she might be caught in the act of apparently trying to enter someone else's property.

A light knock brought no response. She knocked harder, peeping round the side of the door at the same time.

"Hullo?" she said.

The door appeared to open into the kitchen. Jane caught a glimpse of a worn, 1970s carpet with a gold and black hexagonal pattern on it. There was a range and a pine dresser, a large table surrounded by an assortment of dining chairs. Above the table a lit bulb emanated a dull glow. The only natural light came from a small window that looked out onto the courtyard, the bottom half of which was obscured by a kist piled high with old newspapers.

Jane felt her hair catch in something. Turning to her right she saw that it was tangled round the button of a bashed-looking Barbour jacket. The jacket was one among a row of coats and anoraks hanging from a peg rail. Below them lay an assortment of Wellington boots and muddy shoes. Jane noticed a small pair of black school shoes amongst them, one upside down on top of the largest pair of Wellingtons, the other wedged between a pair of woman's hill walking boots. She hadn't ever thought of Katy being harum-scarum before but then, she acknowledged to herself, not for the first time in the past twenty-four hours, she hardly knew the girl at all.

A deep voice rumbled somewhere. Jane leaned her head towards the Barbour jacket so as to untangle her hair without pulling it. She listened again. Silence. She was just about to turn and go when she heard it once more.

"Hullo?" she said.

Still no reply. She pushed the door open and walked into the kitchen. It smelled slightly nauseating, like some of the kitchens she'd worked in as a student. If anything had been cooked in it recently it was boiled cabbage and bacon.

As much to get away from the smell as to search for Alan Clemmy she passed through the kitchen and into a tight hallway. A steep staircase slanted across her line of vision. To her right, at the bottom of the staircase, was the front door and opposite a room which looked like a lounge. Jane wandered to the foot of the stairs and stood wondering what to do.

"For God's sake, Corinne."

It was Alan Clemmy's voice. Jane stood still. It sounded harsher than she'd heard it.

"Won't you ever learn?"

There was some kind of commotion. Jane heard the floor above her thump. An ornament on the telephone table to her right shook. She heard a woman let out a small scream. After a moment there were sobs, deep, gut-wrenching sobs.

Jane ran up the stairs and onto the landing. Straight ahead of her with his back to her stood Alan Clemmy. He stood in a doorway, blocking out all but a thin pencil of golden sunlight. It cut across the landing floor as if trying to escape whatever was in the room behind.

Having run upstairs instinctively, Jane now wondered whether she shouldn't run back down again. But the woman crying in the room beyond sounded so sad that she felt she had to at least talk to her. She found herself clenching her fists as she moved towards Alan Clemmy. As she reached out to tap him on the back she took a step away from him again, as if the touch of him had given her an electric shock.

His face as he turned round was one of amazement, closely followed by anger.

"What the hell...?"

Jane suddenly felt the full force of her impropriety. She looked from left to right nervously.

"I just... the door was open. Then I heard..."

Alan Clemmy moved towards her as if trying to sweep her up.

"Have you heard something about Katy?"

Jane heard another sob.

"No, I just wanted to see if I could help... it was all such a muddle last night. It's a half day..."

"Alan."

The woman sounded distressed. Jane tried to see past Alan Clemmy but his breadth was enough to block any view.

"Al-an."

Now Clemmy himself seemed to be anxious. He took a quick glance over his shoulder.

"Alan. I'm going to be..."

There was a retching sound and then a thump, as if something had hit the ground. Alan Clemmy turned on his heel and rushed back to the room. Jane followed him.

At first it was hard to make out what was going on. The small bedroom was in half-darkness, the curtains being only partially drawn. But as Jane's eyes adjusted to the light she saw that Alan Clemmy was lifting a woman in a stained white nightdress into a bed without sheets. On the floor, at her own feet, lay an abandoned duvet without any cover on it.

Alan Clemmy took a quick glance at Jane before dropping the woman onto the bed. Then he came over and lifted up the duvet without looking at her.

"Right. There you go. You get some sleep," he said, patting the duvet round the woman's body and lifting her head so that she could rest it on one of two slip-less pillows.

The woman's hair was long, her frame slight. From a distance she looked like a child. But as Jane looked more closely at her face, she saw hollows beneath her cheekbones, dark circles below her eyes. There was a smattering of something red across her mouth which at first Jane took to be smeared lipstick but which on closer inspection appeared to be some sort of staining. She looked down where the duvet had been and saw several empty bottles of vodka. Further along the floor lay a cork with the corkscrew still in it and a saucepan which the woman had apparently vomited into.

Alan Clemmy pushed past her roughly. She heard a tap running and a few seconds later he was back again with a cloth and basin in his hands. He bent down at the far side of the bed, beneath the window, and started scrubbing at the floor.

"Let me help," said Jane.

Alan Clemmy kept his head down and scrubbed roughly at the same patch of floor.

"I'd have thought you'd want to get out of here..."

Jane walked round the bed and stood over Clemmy as he rubbed harshly at the floor with a towel. She tapped him gently on the shoulder.

"I can help."

Clemmy looked up. His eyes gleamed and then faded as if the sun had passed over two pools of grey water. Slowly, he stood up. He dropped his cloth into the basin and watched the dirty water splash over its rim.

"Well, don't let me stop you," he said and began picking up the empty vodka bottles and saucepan.

Jane hesitated to say something back and decided against it. She glanced at the bed.

"Don't you have some clean sheets?" she asked.

Clemmy's face reddened.

"I was in the middle of changing them – again," he said. "But then she was sick."

Jane squeezed some water onto the red wine stain on the carpet and scrubbed hard, unsure what to say.

When she looked up again Alan Clemmy had disappeared. Blue bottles, some dead, some half dead, caught in spiders' webs were clinging to the outside window frame. A horse fly bumped off the glass and flew on again. The smell of vomit and drink was oppressive. Jane pulled back the curtains and heaved open the bottom sash of the window. Immediately, as if a switch had been turned on, the room filled with busy sounds – machinery, flies, bees. The breeze caught the faded blue curtains and billowed them sideways. Jane heard a moan and turned round. Alan Clemmy's wife had rolled onto one side and appeared to be sleeping peacefully.

"Sheets."

Alan Clemmy stood in the doorway brandishing an assortment of bed clothes, none of which seemed to match. Jane reached out and took them, rolling them into one manageable bundle.

"I'll just put a cover on the duvet," she said.

She picked up the red basin and dirty towel and carried them back to the bathroom, avoiding Alan Clemmy's eyes as she did so.

"So much for keeping myself to myself," she thought.

30

WHEN I'd been in the Allan Glen about a week I was told I'd spent several nights in the local hospital before I was brought, on my husband's orders, to the treatment centre. Apparently, there had been some sort of incident and I'd been knocked out. I had cuts and bruises everywhere. They took a long time to disappear. Every time I looked at them I'd wonder about the time they represented, the missing days.

As I sobered up I realised that it wasn't just days that had disappeared but weeks, months, even years. Someone asked me how old my daughter was. Ten, I was about to say, and then I remembered that she was 15 and I'd missed her birthday. It was April 2nd a nurse informed me one day when I asked. Where had I been on the March 1st, Katy's birthday? Did she have presents? A cake? Who bought them?

The truth peeked out at me from behind shadows I tried to turn my back on. Its dark presence was patient and terrifying. You have not bought your daughter a cake or had her friends round to the house for years, it told me. Her birthday parties since her ninth have been grudging affairs, initiated by her father. It was he who'd go and buy a cake, find candles to put on the top of it, ask what she'd like for a present and make sure it was wrapped and ready on the kitchen table on the correct day.

I felt my husband like a reproach in every thought. I couldn't remember what he looked like. I could feel him but couldn't imagine his features. That he hadn't visited yet didn't bother me. He was present enough, looming darkly over the snatches of what I could remember of the previous months. Did I imagine it or had he appeared with a woman, leant over my bed, words like, "disgrace" and "filthy" falling from his mouth like bile? Did she, the woman, stroke my hair gently, with a kindness I had not felt in years, a sympathy strong enough to break through the haze I had tried to create with drink? You must have dreamt it, I told myself. I may have longed for a mother's touch but it wasn't something I deserved.

White walls. White beds. Nurses in white. Doctors in white. White towels and chairs. It was as if nothing began or ended, the edges of everything blending into a quiet, timeless world where every day repeated itself.

31

East London CND

Benefit Night

Walthamstow Community Resource Centre,
Friday 29th March, 2002.
5pm – late.

An evening of entertainment to raise funds for the national organisation's campaign against missile defence and Star Wars – work supported by Friends of the Earth and Greenpeace, representatives from which have helped organise tonight's entertainment.

Music from Baghdad Express, Gilgamesh's Sister, Islamic In-Laws, Lost Cause and others. (Bring your own instruments for the late-night jam session.)

Food provided by local Iraqi restaurant Babylon.

Creche facilities available between 5pm and 7pm. Special guest appearance by Walthamstow-based Iraqi storyteller Amira Shihab.

Raffle.

Tickets: £6 full-price, £3 concession. Children free.

Want to take more action? Sign our Don't Start Wars petition and join the London-wide Don't Start Wars march leaving Hyde Park, March 30th, at 1pm. (Speeches in Trafalgar Square from 3pm.) This march is supported by the Stop the War Coalition which endorses CND's opposition to missile defence and Star Wars as well opposing the proposed assault on Iraq.

Affordable Rhinoplasty
At the Rosewood Clinic

What's in a name? Well, quite a lot actually, as these 'before and after' rhinoplasty photographs testify. Now this radical improvement in appearance is available to you for a mere 25% of the usual price when you have any of the following surgeries performed at London's exclusive Rosewood Clinic: tummy tuck, breast augmentation, breast reduction, brow lift, eyelid lift.

A rose by any other name might smell as sweet, but at Rosewood we believe a nose that goes by any other name than ours can always be improved upon.

32

THE PALE pink carpet in the Clemmys' lounge was spotless. The lid of the piano was down, the key in the lock. There were no papers on the coffee table, no stray cups on the floor. The armchairs and settee, carefully angled and positioned, leaned towards each other conspiratorially, as if they were the farmhouse's real occupants.

Alan Clemmy stood with his back to a grey tiled fireplace and stared at Jane as she sat sipping her tea. There was no evidence of there ever having been a fire in the grate and the piece of gold wrapping paper made into a fan which had been propped up in lieu of one was long faded. Jane stared at it past Alan Clemmy's legs and felt a dark misery creeping over her. The Clemmys, like their lounge, seemed to have been petrified.

"I'm sorry," Alan Clemmy said.

He had refused to make a cup of tea for himself and Jane felt like an animal on display at a zoo as she drank hers. What reaction, if any, should she give the farmer? Should she even acknowledge that she knew what he was sorry about?

"If there's anything I can do..." she mumbled eventually.

Alan Clemmy coughed and pressed his shoulders back.

"We manage," he said.

"Yes."

"Katy does... did... I mean I've kept her away from it. She's had every opportunity."

Jane glanced at the piano.

"Is that where she practises?"

"When she can," Clemmy said. He kept his head down. A moment later he gulped and looked up. Jane saw that he was crying.

Jane stood up and went over to him. She put an arm round his waist and guided him to one of his own armchairs. He sat down on the edge of it, like a visitor in his own house.

"Are you sure you won't have some tea?" she asked.

"No. I mean, yes."

He took a deep breath and looked at her.

"The police have been. They've taken away her computer and some notebooks. They think she might have been chatting to someone on the internet. Her savings book is missing and she's withdrawn a lot of money."

A stream of frightening thoughts rushed through Jane's mind, as if a group of racehorses had been let out the stalls and were thundering past her, throwing up turf and showering her with foam.

"If they don't get anywhere soon they say they'll make an announcement to the press, to see if anyone knows anything."

I should have done more, thought Jane. Katy was so quiet, so detached. As her guidance teacher I should have done something about it.

A carriage clock ticked on the mantelpiece and a square of sunlight on the carpet faded into nothingness. The lounge began to feel cold and damp.

"It's not too late," Jane said suddenly.

Alan Clemmy looked at her. His eyes were still red and watery but they shone hopefully for a moment as she spoke.

"There must be something we can do. Have you looked in Katy's room?"

"The police did."

"Do you mind if we go up there? I mean, would the police?"

Alan Clemmy shrugged.

"I don't suppose so, they've done all their finger printing and raking through things."

Jane stood up and put her cup and saucer on the coffee table. As Alan Clemmy leant down to pick them up, she put her hand on his.

"Leave it," she said.

33

THE FIRST time the treatment centre's Dr Browning came into my room, I pulled the sheet up high and pretended to be asleep. The sun was very hot on my forehead but I was scared of turning over to escape its glare in case Dr Browning stayed and began talking to me. Long after I heard his footsteps disappearing down the corridor I kept still, convinced any movement would bring him scurrying back to my bedside.

As a child I tried to master my fears by imagining that I had some control over them. I told myself that I would not die in my sleep as long as the plastic bag that was stuck in the cherry tree outside my bedroom window remained there. For months I never went to sleep before checking it was still present. Then one evening it had gone. I stayed awake most of that night and the next but on the third I was too tired and fell asleep. When I woke up the next morning I was not elated, only mystified. It wasn't long before I thought my destiny was dependent on the survival of a crisp bag stuck into a crack in a wall I passed on the walk home from school.

When I think of my childhood I don't think of sports days and birthdays, visits to the museum or school prize givings. I think of dark fears I could tell no-one about and the obsessions that developed around them. For years I thought I emitted a strange, foul smell that repelled anyone who came near me. Every snigger, every rejection, every unfathomable facial expression was the result of that smell. I scrubbed myself three times a day, bathed in Dettol and bought all the deodorants and soaps my pocket money would allow. But still I imagined that when someone walked away from me it was because of the smell I could not rid myself of.

Why should I want to speak to Dr Browning when I had been able to communicate with no-one else all these years? Other people were the enemy. If I let them in they would colonise me, take from me and hurt my feelings.

He left me alone for a few days and then one day when I asked a nurse if I would be going home soon, he appeared by my bedside and began to talk. I would be here for a while, he said. There would be exercises to do, not physical ones but ones I had to write out on paper. I would have to be honest. If I wanted to get better I would need to change.

My husband still didn't come to visit me. I didn't expect him to but I was told there were no visitors allowed anyway. Later there would be trips home for the day or for a weekend, providing I was good. I could call him if I wanted but I was allowed only two phone calls a week so I should choose them carefully.

I chose to wait. I couldn't distinguish what was real from what I'd imagined. But I was sure my husband had been angry with me and didn't want to hear his, what I can only call *wrath*, on the telephone. Only my daughter bothered me. *"Mum, please get up."* The refrain played over and over again in my head. But for the first week or so I tried to tell myself it was not real. Phoning my daughter would mean phoning home. And there was the other thought, surely a dream, that she was missing. I told Dr Browning about my fear. He said I'd had delirium tremens, the DTs, and I was probably imagining all sorts of things at the moment. I was to rest and not trouble myself with dark imaginings.

After a few days I was moved to a shared room. My roommate was a woman called Isla from the Western Isles. She sat on her bed like a squirrel, with all her possessions in a ring around her. As I put clothes into drawers, my sponge bag in the bathroom, she watched me and kept moving her hands over the items she had tipped from her bag. There was a white plastic alarm clock, an array of plastic beads and gaudy earrings, a hair comb with a blue feather in it, nail polish in several shades of blue, a paper wallet with "Virgin Trains" emblazoned on the front and a half-eaten packet of Rolos. When I turned my back I heard paper rustling. The next time I looked, her mouth was full and her wrinkled cheeks looked as if they had a tiny animal crawling around under them. She kept watching me as she chewed. Her brown eyes were like currants pressed into the face of a gingerbread man.

There was sunlight in the room. Filtered through thick foliage and net curtains it created a wavering, mottled effect on the walls that relieved the room of its deadness. Our beds were covered with quilted bedspreads that had a floral pattern on them and there was a thick, green carpet on the floor. All the furniture was white. Hidden behind the net curtains was a glass door leading onto a balcony but it was locked, as were the windows adjoining it.

"They're worried you'll jump," Isla said, as I re-emerged from under the net curtains. She ran her tongue round her lips, licking up some smeared chocolate.

I sat down on my bed and waited to see what would happen.

34

DONNA was watching a television programme about pine martens in North West Scotland. She had tried sleeping, thinking her old bed might be what was needed to lull her out of her recent insomnia. But the orange glow from the lamppost outside the window had irritated her, as had her mother's snoring. After two hours of tossing and turning, she had given up and tramped downstairs to the lounge. When she found she couldn't concentrate on the book she'd grabbed from her brother's bookcase (typical Dan – by some Russian guy called Kropotkin who seemed to operate under the mistaken belief that people were 'naturally programmed' to be nice and help each other) she had switched on the television and stared at some gyrating pole dancers with the sound turned down. It had given her the chance to ruminate further on the male psyche, although by the time the programme about the pine martens came on she was no wiser than she had been a week, or a month, ago.

The gender male had been a preoccupation of Donna's since she had found her most recent boyfriend, Josh, in bed with the unremarkable and ugly girl who worked in the local library. "I was drunk," he claimed the next day when she returned from a night spent on her friend Hannah's settee to tackle him about his infidelity. That apparently explained both his unfaithfulness and his choice of woman. Entreaties and promises followed, then tentative kisses and a passionate love-making session on the kitchen floor. Donna hoped they'd put it behind them. "It could be the making of your relationship," her friends, well-versed in the articles on infidelity that regularly appeared in women's magazines, said, and Donna wanted to believe them. But the truth was, a month on, she was still suffused with an indignant anger. The more Hannah told her relationships required work, the more Donna felt there were some things that could not be excused and that her brother had been right about internet dating sites. ("Seem like good places for charlatans to hang out," was how Dan had put it.) Eventually, she had packed her bags and returned home.

"It's time you were sorting out your own messes," her mother had said earlier that evening as she arrived back in Walthamstow, her possessions stuffed into two bin liners, a suitcase and a rucksack.

"He was seeing someone else," said Donna, substituting the word "seeing" for "shagging" only because it was her mother she was talking to.

Her mother had rolled her eyes. "He was your choice. You made your bed..."

"Well, I'm not going to lie on it," replied Donna. "Whatever your generation might have done."

Her mother had gone upstairs to bed not long afterwards, telling her daughter she'd find some spaghetti bolognaise in the fridge if she was hungry. So that's all the mother-daughter chat we're going to have, thought Donna huffily. It hadn't been long until her huff had turned to tears. She had returned home seeking sanctuary and all she had found was a weary mother who wished she would get on with her own life. Worse, her brother, the one person she could rely on for support and sympathy, wasn't in. "At one of his environment things," her mother had told her. "Six pounds at the Community Resource Centre. If you ask me it's a lot of money for a few dips and a couple of those dreary guitar players he likes."

The programme about pine martens was over and Donna was flicking through the rest of the channels when she heard the front door open. She swivelled round on her armchair. "Hi Dan," she had begun to say when she noticed that her younger brother was accompanied by a pretty but extremely young-looking girl who had long blonde hair.

"This is Katy," said Dan. "She's visiting from Scotland."

Donna started to smile – her brother deserved a nice girl after that last one he'd been out with (what man needs an impoverished Iraqi storyteller who still has a husband back home?) – but the girl immediately edged behind Dan leaving only her left shoulder and holdall visible.

Donna caught her brother's eye. Who had he got in tow with this time, she wondered. The girl looked normal enough but her behaviour was typically odd. Dan was forever bringing what their mother called 'waifs and strays' back to their house – asylum seekers he'd befriended during his volunteer shifts at the local Refugee Centre, anarchists he'd met at anti-globalisation protests, aid workers he'd got to know during his stints working for NGOs in Africa. Inevitably all of them would end up staying far longer than the night or two they'd been invited for. It was just one of the many reasons Donna had been glad to leave home and move in with Josh.

"I thought you were staying at Josh's these days," said Dan. "I was going to let Katy have your room for the night."

"I can go somewhere else," said Katy from behind Dan.

"No, you're all right, Katy," said Donna, giving Dan a look that was meant to be reassuring. "Have my room. I can't sleep anyway. I'll just go and get you some sheets."

"You sure, Donna?" said Dan. "You have my room then."

"Don't be daft. That means changing another bed. I'll take the settee."

She stood up.

"I can sleep on the settee," said Katy, peeking out from behind Dan.

"No, really," said Donna. "Don't worry about it. I was going to try sleeping downstairs anyway."

She felt Dan's eyes on her. He'll be wondering what's up with Josh, she thought. She dreaded the 'I told you so' when she related the story of how the "warm, steady" man she'd met on TrueLove. com had turned out to be faithless.

"How was the benefit thing?" she asked quickly. Best to distract Dan as soon as possible. "Did Katy go too?"

Dan coughed and looked round at Katy but she remained where she was and said nothing.

"We were both there," said Dan, after a pause. He raised his eyebrows at Donna in a manner that suggested it had not been the best of evenings.

Donna managed a faint smile and headed to the airing cupboard. As she thought – Katy was another of Dan's waifs and strays.

35

KATY'S room, high up in the attic of the farmhouse, smelt of patchouli oil. It reminded Jane of rooms she had lived in as a student, its sloping walls covered in Toulouse Lautrec and Bob Dylan posters, its single bed hidden beneath a variety of cuddly toys and cushions.

For a moment, Jane forgot about policemen and possible press conferences and found herself smiling as she observed a Barbie alarm clock sitting beside a bedside lamp bearing a red bulb.

The rest of the room exhibited the same mixture of adult and child. A pile of *Misty* magazines, a half eaten packet of Starburst and a copy of *Wuthering Heights* lay next to two floor cushions just inside the doorway. A pair of pink, fluffy slippers and an ashtray containing burnt joss sticks poked out from beneath an armchair next to the bed. On Katy's desk, which sat below a window overlooking the farm courtyard, a framed print of a Degas ballerina and a small yellow teddy wearing a red bow-tie were clustered together beside a jam jar filled with a variety of pens and pencils. Pieces of sheet music, *Rosemary Connelly's Hip and Thigh Diet*, a video of Mel Gibson's *Hamlet* and a Tori Amos CD cluttered the floor-space underneath.

Jane stood at the foot of the bed, opposite Katy's desk, scanning the room like a searchlight. She bent down and picked up a copy of *Misty*. The cover bore a photograph of a girl of about Katy's age. "Twenty Top Tips To Make Your Man Beg For It" and "A Guide to Robbie Williams' Kinky Sex History" screamed the tasters. Jane flicked through it idly. Photographs of fresh-faced teenagers pouting beneath headlines like "Loving My Boyfriend Nearly Killed Me (AIDS special)" and "Five Naughty Ways to Make Your Lover Misty-Eyed" flashed past. Jane dropped the magazine back on the floor and sat down on the bed.

The late afternoon sunlight held the room in a weak glow. Jane breathed in the patchouli and smelt beneath it an almost human smell of leather and lavender that reminded her of her grandmother and the days when she herself had been a child. She put her head in her hands. Again she had that urge to cry which had overcome her the day Katy had watched her picking up the jotters from the classroom floor. And yet she could not cry. Everything, including her own misery, seemed to be frozen and she had no idea how to set it free. She was imprisoned by feelings and memories, serving her own life sentence.

If only I hadn't listened to them all, she thought, my mother, the doctor, that ridiculous Head of Maths who was supposed to be my guidance teacher. I was made to feel as if I had a disease when all I was, was pregnant.

She raised her head. Where would she have been now, she wondered, if she had gone ahead and had the child who had seemed, at the time, to belong to everyone but her? They told her she had her whole life ahead of her and not to ruin it but no-one had said what that life might consist of – an endless stream of unsuccessful attempts at emotional compensation.

She looked again round Katy's bedroom. The furry slippers, the eclectic reading matter, the art posters, the half-eaten packet of sweets, even the diet books, all breathed life. Katy was feminine. Katy was neurotic. Katy had a sweet tooth. Katy was clever. Katy was confused. Katy could be amused. Katy wanted a better life but had no idea how to bring it into being. Katy is a lot like I was, thought Jane, and not so much younger than my own child would have been now.

The door creaked and Alan Clemmy came in. He had to bow his head to stand upright in all but the very centre of the room. He spoke to the floor like a priest, in a voice Jane had to strain to hear.

"Well?" he asked. "Find anything in this midden?"

He was trying to be cheerful and the effort moved Jane as much as the sight of Katy's Barbie alarm clock and half-eaten sweets had done. She had a sudden impulse to reach out to this man, hold him in her arms and comfort him. But she stayed where she was, her own head slightly lowered, her emotions as tightly drawn as purse strings.

"Not really," said Jane despondently, realising that all her foray into Katy's room had done was to make her feel more keenly the girl's absence.

"I'll call the police again later, if I haven't heard anything," said Clemmy and coughed, as if doing so helped him pretend their conversation wasn't about a missing child, *his* missing child, but about something humdrum, a lost bankcard or a stolen wallet.

Jane looked about the room again.

"Katy had a mobile, didn't she? I saw her using it."

Alan Clemmy looked at Jane glumly.

"Yes, she did. She took it with her, wherever she... I've tried ringing it, I don't know how many times, but it's switched off."

"Did you tell the police the number?"

Alan Clemmy looked at her as if she was stupid.

"Of course, but it's switched off."

"But the police might be able to trace her last call to somewhere. They can do that, can't they?"

The farmer stared at her for a moment. She saw fear cross his eyes.

"Yes," he said. "But if her last call was made in Craigie yesterday evening... to one of her school friends..."

"She might be switching her phone on and off," persisted Jane.

She meant her comment to be encouraging, to suggest there might be a trail that would lead to Katy but she could see from Alan Clemmy's expression all she had done was create more worry and confusion. Why would Katy make calls and not receive them? Who would she be making them to? God, but I am hopeless at this, she thought.

Alan Clemmy bent down and picked up *Wuthering Heights*. "You don't need to stick around Miss Ellingham," he said without looking at her. "I'm sure you've got plenty of things of your own to be doing."

His sudden coldness was like an electric shock to Jane. She felt herself freeze, the flow of her compassion falter. In her confusion she almost picked up her bag and left. But something about the way the farmer was flicking through the pages of the Bronte novel made her hesitate. Alan Clemmy was feigning indifference towards her, she realised, because he was terrified of what she might make him contemplate.

She stared out the window at some crows wheeling in the dimming light. Perhaps he was right to push her away, she thought. So far, all she had given him was false hope, first by inviting him to meet Ron Turner and now by suggesting she could uncover clues to Katy's disappearance by poking round the teenager's bedroom and asking terrifying questions.

She would tell him she was going home, she decided. But as she turned to tell the farmer this she saw that his expression had changed and he appeared to be studying a page of *Wuthering Heights*. There was a deep vertical furrow between his eyebrows and his mouth twitched as if he was attempting, unsuccessfully, to interpret something.

"What is it?" Jane asked, the words blurted out before she could stop herself.

Alan Clemmy looked up at her for a moment, hesitated and then handed her what appeared to be a page torn from a magazine and which Katy had folded in half to act as a bookmark. Jane opened it out. All she could see was a large photograph of a teenage girl wearing a wide-brimmed straw hat and heart-shaped sunglasses, sucking provocatively on a pink ice lolly: "Misty's Sizzling Summer Passion Tips" read the headline in large, red letters. She looked at Clemmy for some indication of what she was supposed to be thinking.

"Other side," he said gruffly and then coughed and looked at the floor.

Jane turned the page over. She was greeted with a patchwork of black and white classified adverts. Their seedy promises jostled for her attention. The "Love Clinic" offered "discreet understanding" for those who knew "just how much love could hurt". A "prestigious pharmaceutical supplier" with a box number promised "easily swallowed" answers to gender identity questions. The Chelsea Sexual Advice Agency was giving 50 per cent reductions on all aides and videos until the end of September. Initial consultations with the agency's fully trained counsellors, all qualified masseurs, were free and conducted in a "relaxing atmosphere".

Jane felt a surge of sadness as she read the adverts though she was at a loss to know what it was about them exactly that made her feel that way. She was thirty-nine, old enough to know about most perversions of human sexuality. She knew about vibrators and orgasm creams, prostitutes who worked out of "saunas", men who wanted to be women, women who wanted to be men, men who wanted to be women but who wanted to make love to women. Human sexuality was an unending series of doors, although she herself had felt the need to go through only the most obvious and conventional of them.

"Well?"

Alan Clemmy was looking at her. Guilt quickly replacing the peculiar melancholy she had been wallowing in, Jane looked back at the magazine page again, desperately searching for some link between its contents and the missing Katy. With her attention focused outside herself, she soon found what she was looking for. A small advert on the bottom right of the page had been ringed, very gingerly, in faint pencil. It was an advert for a plastic surgery clinic in London, the Rosewood Clinic, specialising in breast surgery.

Jane's mind raced back to the day she had seen Katy's eyes fill with tears in her classroom. Katy Clemmy's "got big tits", Billy Neill had said. She remembered too, how she had felt, when boys had commented on her body when she was a teenager. She had hated the attention, the sudden acquisition of an appearance which was at variance with the little girl within. Boys had suddenly seemed to become hot, sweaty predators, their gaze watchful and hungry. Walking past a group of them became an ordeal. Swimming sessions she had avoided completely, by saying she had a cold, or that it was her period, because she knew the boys got changed quickly and waited in the pool like piranhas to watch the girls as they came in wearing their costumes.

All this was going through Jane's mind as Alan Clemmy stood and watched her in his missing daughter's bedroom. And as she stared back at him, sorting through it all, like a postman trying to order an unexpected deluge of mail, she began to wonder if she had not gone missing too. For a few brief moments she had made contact with a girl she realised she rather liked. A confused girl, an over sensitive girl but one who lived so acutely she was remarkable in that alone. Miss Ellingham had found Jane again.

"What do you think? I mean, you don't think she'd go and do something like that would she?"

Alan Clemmy was too embarrassed to use the words in the classified advert. Breasts. Enhancement. Enlargement. Cup size. It occurred to Jane that perhaps Alan Clemmy's life had been truncated too. Beneath his solid, gentlemanly surface there was an absence of confidence, as if something had withered a long time ago.

"I do, actually," said Jane, and seeing his eyes widen in panic she added quickly, "but maybe that's good... you know... a clue."

Alan Clemmy had just opened his mouth to respond when there was a crash from downstairs as if a piece of furniture had been knocked over. Next, they heard glass breaking, a thud, then nothing. They looked at each other for a moment and then, without saying a word, the two of them ran downstairs, heading instinctively to the bedroom where they'd left Mrs Clemmy. But before they got there they were stopped in their tracks by hundreds of tiny pieces of broken glass scattered across the landing floor. In the evening light from the stair window they glittered almost blindingly so that it was impossible not to be transfixed by them. The rest of the landing, the heavy panelled doors leading to the bedrooms, a peace lily in a copper coal scuttle, a small, semi-circular mahogany table set against the wall, seemed to fade back, as if it was a painted backdrop to the real drama.

Jane's gaze followed the glinting trail to the bathroom door. It was half closed. Cautiously, she nudged it open with her right foot, feeling the glass crunch beneath her left. As she did, she saw a pool of blood, dark red against a white bath mat, spreading out like an ink blot from beneath Mrs Clemmy's naked body.

In a split second Jane was able to see what had happened. Mrs Clemmy must have been about to take a shower, stumbled, hit the shower screen and then fallen out of the bath, onto the floor, taking the shower screen with her.

The result wasn't pretty but Jane was reassured to hear Mrs Clemmy moaning and to see her right hand reaching across the glass-strewn floor. She bent down and touched the woman's head lightly. She could barely see her face but she caught a glimpse of a small, not quite perfectly straight nose which reminded her of Katy. As she spoke to the slight, girlish figure at her side it was as if she was speaking to the daughter not the mother, for they seemed at that point to Jane to be one, the older woman's bleeding body the visible representation of the younger woman's mental confusion.

"We'll get you a doctor. It'll be okay," she said, as much to reassure herself as Mrs Clemmy. "Everything will be fine."

When she looked up Alan Clemmy was standing at the door, his face white, his eyes wide and terrified.

"She needs an ambulance," said Jane.

The farmer remained still.

"An ambulance..."

Alan Clemmy turned on his heel and rushed out the room. She heard his feet crunching against the glass then a steadily quickening, thud, thud, thud as he descended the stairs. She listened until she heard an old-fashioned single ring as he lifted the telephone handset and then turned her attention back to Mrs Clemmy.

Jane had only limited First Aid. She remembered something, vaguely, about not moving anyone who had fallen awkwardly. She was nervous, anyway, about the blood flowing from Mrs Clemmy's head. If she disturbed any of the glass which was embedded there she might increase the flow and worsen matters. It was best to leave the woman as she was until the ambulance arrived, she decided.

"I'll be right back," Jane said, standing up.

She rushed to the bedroom and pulled the duvet off the bed. Two empty wine bottles rolled onto the floor with a clank. It flashed through Jane's mind that Mrs Clemmy must have been able to find, open and drink both bottles since she had helped put her to bed. The tenacity of the alcoholic momentarily aroused in her something which was almost, but not quite, respectful amazement.

No more than a few hours ago Mrs Clemmy had been incapable of little more than a few confused words. How had she managed the complexities of opening a bottle?

Back in the bathroom, she put the duvet over Mrs Clemmy as if she was tucking in a small child, shaping it around her body so that no drafts could reach her. Close to her head, where the pool of blood was growing, she placed a towel.

She took the woman's hand and held it firmly.

"Alan's phoning an ambulance," she said. "Just hang on."

36

WHAT I remember most about the treatment centre is the meal times. When I finally plucked up the courage to go down to breakfast Isla followed my every glance and provided answers before I had even formed the questions.

The young women sitting round the long table furthest away from the serving area were 'the anorexics'. "Always trying to get rid of their food," Isla said in a loud whisper. "The big woman sitting with them watches them and makes sure they eat everything. They've got to sit there for at least half an hour after they've finished, just in case they try and puke it all up in the toilets."

I gazed over at the table as Isla spoke and it seemed to me as if the women were all eating in slow motion. There was a misery that emanated from that table which was hard not to contract. With each spoonful the skeletal figures forced to their mouths they seemed to become less and less substantial. It was as if eating was turning them into wraiths, as if all they existed for was to haunt each other with their thinness.

The overeaters, Isla told me, were over by the canteen toaster. "Sometimes people get bored waiting for the toast to come out and just go away. If the fatties are lucky they can grab it before a nurse sees."

Their food, like the anorexics', was carefully weighed out and prepared separately from everyone else's. Like the anorexics too, most of them were young, late teens or early twenties. I watched as a girl shovelled cereal into a puffy face. Her hips and thighs seeped over the sides of her chair like denim clad bags of blancmange. "They're always saying their boyfriends like them cuddly," said Isla, her tongue darting out the corner of her mouth like a snake's to retrieve a piece of grapefruit. "As if..."

The other tables were similarly distinguished by the category of patient – or 'client' as the staff called us – collected round them. We were sitting with "mostly alkies" but a girl down at the other end was "a druggie too". Isla sniffed as she said this. I was to find out she thought druggies a lower class of addict and those who claimed to be alcoholics as well as drug addicts were "just trying to make themselves more respectable".

Self harmers were usually heavily clothed and sat close to the drug addicts. A pinched looking girl with long dark hair and wide, sad eyes caught my glance and looked down at her plate. She didn't seem to have eaten anything at all. Isla looked at me and then the girl. "Daughter of a famous judge, apparently," she said into my ear. "Taken out of one of the top boarding schools because she kept overdosing and cutting herself. If you ask me it's a crying shame to send kids to those places."

Everyone I looked at had a story. A middle-aged woman with dyed orange hair and pink slippers on had not been able to leave her house for five years. A man sitting next to her who pecked at his food like a hen could not stop combing the fringes on his rugs. He spent up to 12 hours a day doing it, said the knowledgeable Isla. A man sitting with the drug addicts was a Presbyterian minister addicted to cough medicine. "When the chemist wouldn't sell him it anymore he started stealing it from the bathroom cabinets of his parishioners," said Isla. "Coughs a lot just the same. Probably just hamming it up on the off chance."

An ash tree was tapping at the window, a faint spring breeze stirring the garden outside into life. I watched the refectory light up with dappled sunlight and felt my face warming. For a moment everything seemed very clear to me and I imagined everyone in the room as whirring pieces of machinery, broken but still turning, our energy misplaced and misspent. There was something faulty with each and every one of us but it could be fixed, I was certain.

But seconds later, the sky had clouded over and like my own genie I went back into the bottle, unable to see anything outside it. It was to be like that for a while longer.

37

DAN peered over the top of his duvet. As he suspected, Donna was sitting on the edge of his bed watching him.

"Good sleep?"

Dan attempted a smile.

"Not bad."

"Nice morning."

Dan hauled himself upright, reached out for the mug of tea his sister had placed on his bedside table and waited for her to come to her point.

"Your girlfriend's still asleep."

Dan spluttered on his tea. Donna was so predictable.

"What are you laughing at?"

Dan reached out and ruffled his sister's curly hair.

"Nothing."

Donna gave him a quick smile.

"Really?"

"Really."

There was a pause as both of them looked around Dan's bedroom. Dan saw his sister stare at the banner he'd prepared for the march that afternoon: "Keeping Space For Clean Air – UK Environmentalists against Star Wars".

"You off on another protest then?" Donna asked.

"Afraid so," replied Dan. "If this defence policy goes through…"

Donna stared back at him with a blank expression.

Dan opened his mouth and then closed it again. There was no point in saying any more. Donna wasn't interested. Years ago it had bothered him. "Dad believed in the power of protest," he'd said to his sister once when she'd berated him for taking part in a protest about a new motorway development on the weekend of their mother's birthday. "He told us to stand up for what we believed in." His sister had thought for a moment and then shaken her head. "And look where all Dad's protesting got him – the car plant still got closed down. Then he got ill and dropped dead at the age of 47."

"This Katy," he heard his sister say.

Dan smiled. "You don't give up, do you, Donna?"

Donna flashed her wide, gap-toothed grin. "I'm your sister. It's my prerogative to vet your girlfriends."

"Well, she's not my girlfriend, for a start."

"I'm glad."

"Why?"

"She seems a bit, well, young, I suppose."

Dan thought about the gig the previous night. Now that he'd come to terms with the fact that Katy wasn't the prospective girlfriend he'd been hoping for he was less worried about her age (just 15 he'd eventually found out) than what she was doing in London on her own and in such a wretched state. Twice he'd had to get Amira to check she was okay because she had spent so long in the toilets and the second time she'd brought her back she'd been crying. He, Amira, other friends of theirs, had all tried to ask her what was wrong but she wouldn't tell them. "It's nothing," she kept saying. "I'm fine." They'd bought her drinks, encouraged her to eat, tried to get her to join in the jam at the end of the night by handing her a fiddle but she'd retreated from every effort at friendship. "I don't play," she'd told them when Dan had given her the violin. "I thought you said you did," Dan had responded. "I know it's not your favourite instrument but I bet you're tons better than any of us. We can't play anything, can we guys?" "What about your bass guitar solos, Dan?" Amira had quipped back. But Katy had only frowned and looked away. "I can't play," she'd said beginning to cry again. "Please don't make me."

Dan looked at his alarm clock. He'd need to be at Hyde Park within a few hours. A friend of his from Friends of the Earth, Seth, was going to give one of the speeches when they reached Trafalgar Square. Dan had arranged meet him at midday so he could march with him.

Filled with a sudden sense of urgency Dan shifted in his bed, nudging Donna's thighs with his toes.

"You going somewhere?" asked Donna, turning round.

"To the march," said Dan.

Donna looked towards the door.

"What about Katy?" she asked.

Dan bit his lip. He could only hope Katy would agree to take the tube into London with him when he went to meet Seth. But that wasn't a given. It had taken a lot of effort to prevent the teenager from attempting to return to Euston on her own after the benefit gig. (She'd never planned to go back to the hostel a second night, she'd told him after he'd persuaded her to come to Walthamstow with him. She was intending to go home to Ayrshire. It had crossed Dan's mind that she could hardly have gone clubbing with him if she'd wanted to return to Scotland that evening, but he said nothing. The girl didn't seem to have thought anything through properly, and she was confused and upset enough as it was.) "Go on, stay at Dan's," Amira had persuaded Katy when he could not. "You'll not get a train home now – it will mean hanging around the station all night." And so, eventually, Katy had trailed back with him to his mother's house, miserable and distracted, but out of harm's way for a few more hours. "I'll come with you into Euston tomorrow, if you like," Dan had said when he'd shown Katy into Donna's room. But she'd refused to say whether she would consent to this or not, mumbling that she'd "see" in the morning, that she might decide to "stay on in London a bit" anyway.

Dan caught his sister's eye. "I'm not sure what to do about Katy," he said.

Donna gave him an appraising look. "How did you meet her... I mean, why's she here if she's not your girlfriend or a refugee, or something..."

"A refugee or something?"

"You know what I mean."

Dan picked up a cushion and threw it gently in his sister's direction. "I don't actually, Donna, but never mind."

"What I mean is, why did you bring her back?" asked Donna, frowning and placing the cushion on the floor.

Dan sighed. "It just kind of happened – she had nowhere to go."

"Every time I come back here you've brought someone else to stay. You're just a big softie."

She patted her brother's cheek affectionately.

"Hey, paws off," Dan replied, the shock of his sister's cold hands on his warm flesh making him flinch. "You're freezing."

"Cold hands, cold heart."

"I don't think so."

"Josh would say so."

"Josh's a jerk."

"You think?"

"I think. You're too good for him."

Donna giggled. "You sound like Mum," she said.

"Well, as we both know," Dan said. "Mum's always right."

There was a pause in which both of them listened to the ticking of Dan's alarm clock and enjoyed the warmth of the sun as it filtered through the thin curtains at the far end of the room. It was good to have Donna back, thought Dan, even if it was only for a few days. For, whatever had happened between his sister and Josh, he was sure she wouldn't be home for long. When it came to relationships, Donna was quick to move on – and move in. She was a survivor, his sister, which wasn't something he couldn't say with any confidence about Katy, from what little he knew of her.

"I'm going to see if I can persuade Katy to come into London with me," said Dan. "And then try to make sure she gets on a train back home."

He gave Donna a shove with his feet and stood up.

"I'll take her a cup of tea," said Donna.

Dan gave his sister a wink. "You do that, Donna. I'm sure she'll be every bit as delighted at your morning alarm call as I was."

38

JANE lay back on a Royal Stewart travelling rug and stared up at the sky. It was pale blue with a few wisps of white cloud. The sun wasn't fully up yet and the grass was still damp with dew but the day already bore all the hallmarks of fine weather. The haar Jane had seen from the bedroom window as she drew her curtains that morning would burn off, as would the dampness lurking in the shaded parts of the garden. The sun would bore through the sky and every inch of the garden and the fields beyond would be busy with insects and birdsong, the ripening of fruits and vegetable crops. By the day's end nature would have worked hard to deserve the quiet warmth of a spring evening.

It was for days like these that Jane had bought her cottage. For on a fine day it was enough to know that there was a track just beyond the gate which led to a ford and then uphill to small wood filled with bramble bushes and rowan trees where the ground was covered in pine needles and the sun seemed to struggle to make an impression. She felt no need to go there just as she felt no need to go to the tiny lane just a few miles to the west that led down a bumpy hillside to a scrap of beach set among the rocky cliff-faces of the Heads of Ayr. Nor did Craigie Hill, just to the east, from which the lush green Ayrshire countryside spread out like the sea, tempt her. Everything, the whole world as she knew it, was within her grasp and all the easier to leave alone because of it. The demons of darkness which stalked her mind so many days of the year had been vanquished for one day at least, burnt off by the sheer beauty of the day.

Jane had planned her Saturday with the precision she normally reserved for weekdays. A morning in the garden, reading and dreaming, would be followed by a lunch concocted from her own spring vegetables. After a sizeable rest, an afternoon of mowing and weeding would be rewarded by the video of Kenneth Branagh's *Henry V*, watched with the windows open and the smell of grass on the breeze.

She lay back and felt the grass give beneath the rug, her hand touch the dew. High above an airplane drew a white chalk line across the sky, cutting like a tiny ornament that might hang from a necklace through the blue emptiness. The sun, which was just beginning to edge across the garden, had reached her toes and calves and for a moment she sat up and stared at them, as if she had only just realised she possessed them. But when she lay back down again she felt the first worm of discontent she had felt all morning bury its way inside her. She lived the life of a nun, she thought. Her body was foreign to her, unused to touch. It had been a long time since someone had stroked or caressed any part of it, laid lips softly upon hers.

She knew, of course, that this was because her body was mostly occupied by Miss Ellingham and not Jane. But clipped, spinsterly, bitter Miss Ellingham was essential for Jane's survival. While Miss Ellingham was out earning money and fending off the world's harsh realities, Jane was able to wait at home in the cottage, dreaming girlish things and feeling every nip of unkindness for herself and everyone else. It was a good arrangement, a marriage of convenience and all the more effective for that reason.

Jane stretched out her hand for her tumbler and then, when she had found it, sat up to take a sip of her orange juice. In her head she scolded herself for allowing Miss Ellingham even to enter her thoughts. This was Saturday and the start of the Easter holidays. It was for Jane's enjoyment.

She had already primed herself not to think about the Clemmys, other than to make a quick call to the cosmetic surgery clinic featured in the advert Alan Clemmy had spotted. It had been Jane and not Miss Ellingham who had driven out to Millhouse Farm and therefore Jane and not Miss Ellingham who had returned home alone, feeling all too acutely the family's pain. Jane didn't need that. She'd had enough heartache in her own life. Her mission in life was to avoid any more. No more Jim Beethams, for Jim, she reminded herself, was probably at this very moment enjoying a day out at the beach with his young family while she did her best to compensate for the lack of one.

To emphasise her determination to do just that, she rolled over onto one side and switched on her radio. A brutal, crackling sound cut through the garden birdsong. She quickly adjusted the dial in an attempt to re-find Radio Four.

"Police in Ayrshire are hunting for a missing 15-year-old girl. Katy Clemmy was last seen heading for Craigie town centre at around seven o'clock on Thursday evening. Police are appealing for information from anyone who thinks they might have seen Katy, described as five foot five, blonde and of slim build.

"This is WestSound local radio news at eleven o'clock..."

Jane turned off the radio and sat up. The police were hunting for Katy. Was it possible they thought she might have been murdered? Had they heard something? Her mind rushed to Alan Clemmy. When she had left him the day before he had been standing by the ambulance that took away his wife with tears in his eyes. All around him his farm seemed to be crying out for his attention – cows mooing, dogs snapping at his heels, a car with a horse box attached to it just drawn up in the courtyard. He stood in his Wellington boots in the middle of it all like King Canute with the sea lapping round his middle. His combination of fierce pride and helplessness had overwhelmed Jane.

"Cheerio, I'll be in touch then," she'd said as if the pair of them had just met for a coffee in Craigie High Street. Then she'd slammed her car door shut as if she was locking a door in a submarine.

The sun was beating down in the garden. A couple were wandering past the gate, arms round each other, giggling and kissing. Jane saw the man stop for a moment, look into the woman's eyes and stroke her cheek. Then the two of them moved on, over the small rise that dropped down towards the ford.

Jane listened to their voices fade, the sound of the birdsong rise again. She turned round. Everywhere she looked there were thick bushes obscuring her view onto the countryside – a snowberry bush, a rhododendron, a hydrangea, honeysuckle, clematis and jasmine. She'd trained and pruned each over many years, a world within the world for Jane to hide in. But right now the garden felt less like a secluded paradise than Sleeping Beauty's bower, a green cage that kept her removed from the rest of mankind. The difference was that there would be no prince to rescue Jane. I'm as likely to find a prince as a fairy at the bottom of my garden, thought Jane wryly.

The spell of contentment broken, Jane began gathering up her breakfast dishes. She was just about to take them back into the cottage when she heard a car engine. Through the hedgerow at the far end of the garden she could see flashes of lime green and orange. The engine stopped and she heard voices crackle on a radio. Two policemen appeared at the gate and peered over.

"Jane Ellingham?" said one.

He was about thirty, still boyish looking, with dark hair and clear blue eyes. His companion was older, nearer fifty, with grey hair and a handsome but slightly fleshy face.

"Yes," said Jane, suddenly feeling guilty, although about what she had no idea.

"We'd like to have a word with you about Katy Clemmy."

Jane dropped the travelling rug back onto the ground. She suddenly felt very weak and tired. Miss Ellingham had deserted her.

"Come in," she said in a voice so soft she hardly recognised it.

39

ISLA had been to The Allan Glen before and knew all about smuggling drink in. After five days without any alcohol I was ready to learn from her. My hands were shaking, I was irritable and I found it hard to sleep. When I did manage to drop off for an hour or two I had nightmares about things which might or might not have happened when I was drinking. On waking I would be drenched in sweat and the incidents I had dreamt about would jostle for the attention of my conscience. I could bear it no longer and wanted to be free of the torment. Drink was the only exorcist I knew.

Isla told me that each time as we went down to dinner we should clap Beanie, the caretaker's dog. Beanie was an old Golden Retriever who lay at the refectory door like a deformed sheepskin rug. It was only occasionally when I felt a wet snout on my ankle that I remembered she was a sentient being.

"Make a show of her," said Isla.

Her currant eyes revealed nothing except intensity. It was a very bright spring evening and the sunlight lit up her skin. She was yellow and wrinkled, slightly shrivelled looking, like a doll that had been placed accidentally in the oven. Her movements were quick and furtive.

We were walking down the stairs and could see Beanie splayed across the doorway as if she had been shot. To make a fuss of her seemed ridiculous, like spoiling an antique soft toy with the stuffing spilling out of it. My expression must have betrayed to Isla what I was thinking for she dug me sharply in the ribs with an elbow that seemed to have been honed out of granite.

"Do you want a drink or don't you?" she hissed, scuttling beside me like a demented clockwork toy.

I am an alcoholic, of course I did. Although I found it hard to understand how clapping Beanie was going to get me drink I was prepared to go along with it. I went up to Beanie like an eight-year-old, crouched down and began tickling her behind the ears. She raised her head a little and licked my wrist with a long, pink tongue that felt like a sea anemone.

"Oh, you're a lovely dog, aren't you?" I said.

Isla stood and watched me for a moment. The other patients were coming down the stairs now too and they had to push past Isla and step over Beanie to enter the refectory. The taste of vodka now firmly planted in my mouth, I continued to stroke the dog and prolong the inconvenience. One man from the West Wing where the drug addicts lived stepped over me so roughly that I nearly stumbled and fell over.

"You make a better door than a window," he said.

After a short while, a small queue had gathered at the door, my stroking Beanie allowing only a slow rate of entry into the refectory.

Isla seized her moment.

"She's not well," she said to me as if she was reading the first line in a play. "There's something wrong with her. Poor Beanie."

She knelt down and stroked her behind the ears.

A woman dressed entirely in denim with dyed black hair and who looked as if she might have once played in a heavy metal band, folded her arms.

"What's wrong with her?" she asked. "She just looks like an old mutt to me. A bloody inconvenient one at that."

She stepped over Beanie as if she was stepping over a large boulder. Several other residents followed her – a man dressed in a tweed suit and slippers, and another man with carrot red hair, wearing orange football shorts and a blue vest top.

The rest of the queue stayed to hear out Isla's diagnosis.

"She's got arthritis for a start," Isla continued. "You watch her sit down. It's a sin for her, so it is. Poor thing."

There was a murmur from the rest of the residents.

"Who are you to say?"

A middle-aged Glaswegian woman whose name I knew to be Maureen stepped forward. She was wearing a white, studded mini-skirt and matching top. Her skin was the colour of stained pine and she too had dyed black hair but hers was short and spiky. She chewed hard on a piece of gum and spoke with her head at an angle.

"I'm a trained veterinary nurse," said Isla.

This surprised me as much as it did the other residents. Isla hadn't mentioned this to me before. In all our discussions about her life in the Highlands she'd only ever talked about Robert, her crofter husband, and the bed and breakfast business they ran in the summer.

"What's going on?"

Bill the caretaker had pushed through the gathered crowd. He was accompanied by Dr Browning and a nurse called Jill who'd conducted a physical examination on me the first day I'd arrived.

"Yur dug's nae weel, son," said Maureen.

Bill immediately crouched down between me and Isla and lifted Beanie's head up by the chin. Beanie's tongue emerged and licked her master's hand lazily. Her tail swept backwards and forwards across the carpet as if it was separate creature, trying to escape the melee.

"What's wrong darlin'?" asked Bill.

Beanie's tail stepped up a few noughts.

"You not well? What have they been doing to you?"

"She's got arthritis," said Maureen.

She folded her arms and her breasts swelled up over the top of her t-shirt like two loafs of over-risen bread.

Dr Browning looked at Maureen as if he was conducting an assessment of her mental health. His dark eyebrows twitched like two caterpillars and he made tiny steps with his feet, his polished shoes sparkling in the sunlight. I watched his eyes dart towards the dog and then fix first on Isla and then myself.

"Isla's a veterinary nurse," I said, feeling about six years old and as if I'd just been caught out by the teacher.

Isla stood up.

"It's nothing Dr Browning," she said. "I was just saying she's needing a bit of exercise to get her joints going, that's all. Sitting at the refectory door eating up leftovers isn't good for an old dog like that."

Bill turned his head to look up at Isla. His round glasses caught in the sunlight. His face was gripped with worry.

"What can I do?" he asked.

Isla shrugged.

"Cod liver oil. More walks. She's your dog. I don't want to be telling you what to do."

Bill stood up, pressing his hands down on his knees as he did so. He was probably about 45 but he seemed about ten years older. He wore a special uniform made out of navy Crimplene but his stomach was too big for him to fasten the blouson. All that was left of his hair was a thin fringe that ran round the bottom part of his head. His bald pate shone in the light.

"She gets two walks a day," he said.

"Oh well then," said Isla.

There was a note of doubt in her voice.

"Is that not enough?"

"No, no, that should be..."

Bill looked at her expectantly.

"As I say, she's your dog."

By now I had seen where Isla was headed. I looked at Dr Browning. I felt sure he must have known too. He was sharp and precise, his eyes always alert. As he stepped forward and looked down at Beanie, I prepared myself for the worst.

"I think if Mrs MacLeod is so concerned about your dog, Bill, she should take it for an extra walk herself each day. Each and every day. Without fail. Responsibility is at the heart of recovery."

Isla rolled her eyes theatrically.

"Aw, Dr Browning. That's a bit harsh isn't it?"

Dr Browning began to walk off, Nurse Jill following.

"Not at all, Mrs MacLeod. You've spotted something that needs doing, now do it. I'll look forward to hearing all about it next time we meet. Bill, in the meantime, get the dog out of the doorway."

Bill looked down at Beanie and then up at Isla.

"She won't need much," he said, apologetically. "I'll give you some biscuits for her and you won't have any trouble. You sure you don't mind?"

Isla sighed.

"No. Might as well keep busy while I'm stuck in here."

As we walked into the refectory she stuck her granite elbow into my side again.

"Party time," she whispered.

40

DONNA stood outside her bedroom door holding the cup of tea she had made for Katy. There was no noise from the room. From the way light was smeared like melted butter round the door's edges Donna could tell the curtains were open. But perhaps Katy had never closed them in the first place, she thought, forgetting she herself had drawn them when she'd first gone to bed.

She put her ear to the door so that she could listen more closely. Nothing. All she could hear was the noise of the street outside – someone, somewhere, mowing their lawn, a child crying, a car engine being forced into life, Mr Hussein next door talking loudly in Arabic to one of his children.

Her mother's bedroom door, further along the landing, was wide open. Mrs Lees had already left for the hospital where she worked as an auxiliary. Donna knew her well enough to know that she would not question why her daughter had slept the night on the settee, just as she had not wanted to discuss Josh, or, a few months ago, Dan's split from Amira. Mrs Lees' modus operandi was to be busy. To Donna it seemed she had stopped talking about anything that had any real meaning when their father had died eight years ago.

She looked at the clock on the stair wall. Ten o'clock and still this girl from Scotland wasn't up yet. So much for her polite protestations about not wanting to take up someone else's bed. "I can sleep on the settee," she'd kept saying. Well, she can bloody well sleep in my bed, that's for sure, thought Donna.

"Katy," said Donna, knocking the door. "You awake?"

No response. Mr Hussein next door had switched to English: "Don't stand on the plants. Go round the path to get your ball, Khalid."

"Right, that's it," thought Donna.

She kicked the door open with her foot and walked into her bedroom, pausing to put the mug of tea down on her old desk before proceeding to the bed. It was then that she realised the bed was empty, the duvet she'd put a fresh cover on last night, folded back, the pillows piled on top of it. Donna felt her cheeks burn from a mixture of alarm and indignation. She looked round the room. There was no trace of the girl or her belongings anywhere. Gone was the black sports bag with the Hello Kitty luggage tag, the blue v-necked jumper she had watched the girl throw over the back of a chair, the pink hair grip she'd released her ponytail from and tossed onto the desk.

"Oh, God," said Donna and rushed downstairs to the front door, suddenly ashamed of herself for thinking so badly of the Scottish girl. As she stepped outside she recalled Katy the previous evening, too shy to do much more than hide behind Dan and pink in the face any time either of them asked her a question. I've probably frightened the girl off with my loud mouth, thought Donna, the colour flooding to her own cheeks. And as she thought about her own brashness it only made her feel all the more acutely Katy's vulnerability.

As Donna rushed out into the street and scoured it in both directions, Dan laid out his banner in the back garden and prepared to roll it up neatly. A football had just bounced over the back wall. Several minutes later, on cue, a small face appeared over the same wall. It was Jason, one of three Riley children who lived in the house that backed onto the Lees'.

"Dan, give us the ball," he said.

Dan grinned. He picked up Jason's muddy ball, held it close to his chest and turned round.

"Aw, come on, Dan. Give us the ball."

Dan turned back round. Jason was scrambling onto the top of the wall.

"Oh, is it yours?"

"Ye-es."

"Finders, keepers."

"Aw, Dan."

"Losers, weepers."

Jason grinned. His two front teeth were missing and there was a dirty mark on his nose. He stretched out his arms.

"Oh all right. I suppose," said Dan and threw the ball in Jason's direction. Jason caught it neatly, despite being poised precariously on top of the wall. Boy's a sportsman thought Dan, just a little jealously. He had watched Jason play. He was thin and lithe, and ran gracefully. Dan hadn't been a bad footballer himself but when their father had died, he'd stopped playing. In fact, he'd given up pretty much everything for a few years.

"Thanks," said Jason and jumped back down into his own garden again. Dan was left standing in the middle of what remained of his father's vegetable patch, feeling suddenly very lonely.

He looked up at Donna's bedroom window, the noise of Jason's football thumping off the wall resounding in his head. The curtains were open which presumably meant Katy was up. Perhaps Donna would be able to speak to her, he thought, find out why she was so unhappy, what had made her so reluctant to mix with his friends and enjoy herself. He picked up his banner and walked towards the kitchen door. If she would agree to take the train back into London with him he'd try to persuade her to have brunch before he saw her onto a train. He felt guilty that yesterday he'd been too annoyed with her for being ten years younger than he'd expected to find out what was upsetting her.

He had got as far as the second of the steps leading to the kitchen door when his head cracked against something hard. He felt himself stumble against the railing. He clutched its cold metal and forced himself to stand up straight and focus. Donna was directly in front of him clutching her forehead.

"Donna?"

"Bloody hell, Dan…"

She bent over, cupped her head in her hands and then straightened up again.

"You okay?"

His sister stared at him with glazed eyes.

"Donna?"

Donna's face was chalk white.

"Donna!"

He shook her gently by the shoulders.

"Yes, yes," she said after a moment. "I'm fine."

She shook her head and looked at him with a startled expression.

"I'm okay but Dan..."

"Oh, no, don't tell me – Katy's gone," said Dan, tearing past his sister into the house, his heart pounding loudly.

41

JANE hadn't liked either of the policemen. They had walked into her kitchen as if it belonged to them and then they'd had the cheek to make comments about the décor. "Yellow's supposed to make you cheerful," said the older one. "Bit much first thing in the morning if you ask me," replied his companion. "You're needing to get someone to fix that tap," the older one had said when she filled the kettle to make them a cup of tea (one they had requested before she'd had time to offer). "That noise is a disaster."

Perhaps it was because it was so long since she'd had male company in her kitchen but she felt squeezed out of her own life. The older one who said his name was Dyer sat with his fleshy legs wide apart, one knee under the kitchen table, the other jutting into the space directly in front of the sink. As Jane squeezed past it, the sight of navy Crimplene stretched to its limit across a fat knee filled her with revulsion. "Oop-la, needing to cut down on the biscuits a bit, aren't we?" was Dyer's comment as she bumped against him while setting down a plate of Rich Teas to accompany the tea.

"You're a teacher, aren't you, Miss Ellingham?" said the younger one who introduced himself as Robinson. ("Like the gollywog jam – you'll remember that. My Dad's got all the badges.")

"Yes," said Jane wearily.

She was stuck between the two of them, one at either end of her kitchen table. It was like being a small child forced to take tea with judgmental elderly relatives who'd never had children themselves but felt they knew how to raise them for the best. Their height and dark clothing had the effect of dimming the light and before long she felt as if she had been consigned to a cell. Her back was to the window so she couldn't even distract herself by looking at the garden.

"So, em, let's see," said Dyer, wiping his hand on his hips and pulling out a notebook from his right pocket.

"You've got a crumb on your nose, sir," said Robinson.

When Dyer failed to remove the particle of Rich Tea from his nose himself, Robinson leaned over the table and did it for him, like an indulgent wife who looked after her husband as if he were another of her children.

"Thank you, Robinson. It's a long time since I had a Rich Tea," said Dyer, as if that explained his messy eating habits.

"Don't get them very often myself," said Robinson.

"I prefer Digestives," said Dyer, flicking through his notebook. "Chocolate...?"

Jane rolled her eyes. "Mr, er, Sergeant..."

"Ah, now, here we are," said Dyer.

He flicked a page of his notebook over with a dramatic movement of his hand and tapped the page loudly with his pen.

"You're Jane Ellingham."

"Yes," sighed Jane.

"Miss?"

"Yes."

Dyer coughed.

"Still time."

Jane stared at him. He was winking at Robinson. The pair of them smirked.

"I beg your pardon?"

"Still time for us to get through everything, Miss Ellingham," said Dyer.

"Is that right?" said Jane.

If only she had the quick responses, the silver tongue that men like Dyer and, for that matter, Jim Beetham, seemed to have been born with. It was always much later, when she was lying in bed at night, she thought of the perfect put-down. She had lost count of the number of times the Dyers of this world had been able to reduce her to tears, leaving her speechless in the wake of some clever comment designed to impress their friends.

But she was forgetting Miss Ellingham. Jane was a pushover but Miss Ellingham handled upwards of thirty kids hour after hour, day after day, in the jungle of the comprehensive classroom. What tender hearted Jane could not manage, Miss Ellingham would take on for her. These bumptious policemen were small fry for a woman who, on her better days, could silence a roomful of Billy Neills with just one cold glance round a classroom.

"You want to know what I know about Katy Clemmy?" asked Miss Ellingham.

Both policemen gave her a sharp glance. Dyer even moved his left leg in a fraction.

"I don't know very much," said Miss Ellingham before Dyer had a chance to speak. "The last time I saw her was two days ago, on Thursday evening, heading into the town centre. Haven't seen her since."

Dyer coughed and nodded at Robinson who took out a notebook of his own.

"Let's go over this, will we, Miss Ellingham?"

Jane smiled to herself. Notebooks out, small talk over, Miss Ellingham had the policemen where she wanted them – out of Jane's personal life.

"Can we start with Mr Ron Turner," said Dyer. "It was his car Katy got out of to walk into town. What do you know of Katy's, er, relationship to this man? What kind of man would you say he was?"

Miss Ellingham sat back, took a bite out of a Rich Tea biscuit and considered the quality of the cream envelope Ron Turner had passed her to give Katy, setting it against her own not inconsiderable knowledge of man's basic instinct. She had told Alan Clemmy that she did not believe Ron Turner had anything directly to do with Katy's disappearance and she had believed that. But what if he had contributed indirectly to Katy's decision to run away? Perhaps he had made advances to Katy which had upset her. Perhaps they had been having a relationship, of sorts, and rowed. Perhaps, she thought, remembering the advert for the Rosewood Clinic, he had added to Katy's confusion about her appearance with a thoughtless comment. "You're a big girl for 15" a man had once said to Jane when, as a self-conscious teenager, she'd inadvertently worn a tight t-shirt to a school sports day. From that moment onwards, until her early twenties, she had worn only baggy jumpers and loose fitting shirts. The sudden advance of womanhood was too much for some girls to handle. It was possible Katy was no different from the young Jane in this respect.

"Miss Ellingham?"

Dyer was staring at her, waiting for an answer.

"Ron Turner... he's just an ordinary young man," said Miss Ellingham.

Apart from being a firm woman, Miss Ellingham was a fair one. She would delve into the truth of Katy's disappearance herself before insinuating half-truths to the police. It also rather pleased her that she was several steps ahead of the patronising men who sat in her kitchen commenting on her workmanship while drinking her tea and eating her biscuits. She made a mental note to phone the Rosewood Clinic straight after they had left. Men like Dyer could never understand a case like Katy's, she decided. For it wasn't, she felt, about facts, but feelings.

The Rosewood Clinic would give her no information about Katy. "It's our policy to protect the privacy of all our clients," a haughty voice had informed her. So be it, thought Jane. If you won't come to me then I will come to you. She took out her *Yellow Pages* and flicked through it until she came to Travel Agents. GlobalSpan was the first name listed.

The girl at the end of the line was an ex-pupil, Karen McNaughton. "You'll be going to the Big Smoke to see some shows," she said, trying to ingratiate herself to the English teacher she had given nothing but cheek to six years ago. "Nice way to spend the Easter holidays."

Jane decided to agree pleasantly with whatever Karen said, sensing her need to atone for her lack of respect as a school pupil. Anyway, how on earth could she explain to anyone what she was about to do? She was going to London to try and find Katy Clemmy. But why? She was just looking out for a young girl no-one else was taking responsibility for, she told herself. But at the back of her mind lurked the thought that something about Katy resonated with her own life.

42

I WAS probably in the treatment centre a fortnight before I had a drink. Isla was walking Beanie regularly and allowed out of the grounds when doing so. At first she was cautious and brought back packets of Minstrels and Revels, not an offence in themselves, but as they had to be acquired by going into a shop, still against the rules of the treatment centre.

"If I can get away with it, I'll know I can bring back the whisky," she said, her eyes darting from side to side like dots on a radar screen. "If I get caught, well, it's only sweeties... and a rethink."

Isla enjoyed sweeties as much as she claimed to enjoy whisky. One day when the nurses came round to sweep search our rooms they asked us to empty our pockets. Isla took her cardigan off with a flourish and shook it out over her bed. Out of the pockets came purple Dairy Milk wrappers, the tin foil from several Kit Kats, a crushed Smarties tube, the sticky remains of a Chomp bar and three little plastic toys constructed from the kits found inside Kinder Eggs.

The older of the two nurses, a large girl with purple-streaked hair, deposited it all into the waste bin with one sweep of her sturdy arm.

"Must be why you're so sweet natured, Isla," she said in a thick southern Irish accent.

"Sugar, sugar," Isla sang. "Honey, honey... you are my golden girl..."

The nurse sniffed and looked her straight in the eye.

"Interesting that you manage to buy so many sweets when the tuck shop only sells biscuits and drinks."

"My family know what I need," said Isla quickly. "Don't they Corinne? Aw, poor Corinne, nobody sends her anything."

Both the nurses looked at me, as if noticing my existence for the first time. The younger one, small and nervous with straight brown hair, a white, rather plain face and bitten finger nails, looked as if she might cry on my behalf. The older one looked embarrassed.

"Well, Isla, now, I hope you appreciate what you've got then," she said.

A moment later, the pair of them were gone.

The remark, and the nurses' hasty departure following it, left me unsettled. The doctors had told me I was not ready for trips home yet or visitors under supervision but why had no-one sent me as much as a card? Isla's dressing table was strewn with flowers and cards. Earlier in the week she had received a box of homemade shortbread. "From my sister in Inverness," she informed me, crumbs escaping down her chin. "Want some?"

That evening I went to the common room on my own after dinner. It was an *EastEnders* night and most of the other residents were in the TV lounge. I picked up a copy of the *Craigie Standard*. It was probably several weeks old but I didn't realise at the time. I was just *compos mentis* enough to have some curiosity about my home town again.

A parrot called Sandy had escaped from a house in the New Holm housing estate. If anyone spotted it in their garden they were to phone the RSPB. I continued flicking from back to front through the pages of garage adverts, reports of swimming galas, Brownie good deeds, and drug offences. It was only as I put the paper back on the table that I noticed the headline on the bottom of the front page, 'Craigie Schoolgirl Missing'.

That night I told Isla to buy me drink. As much of it as she could. When she delivered it the next day, I went into the bathroom and locked the door. I remember unscrewing the top of a cider bottle wrapped in brown paper and pouring it down my throat as fast as I could. It tasted warm and sickly sweet but I didn't care. I was seeking complete oblivion, death if it would have me. But two days later I woke up. I was on a drip in a single room in some sort of hospital. I had no memory of the previous 48 hours. All I could recall was the taste of cider and reading that my only child was missing.

43

DR NANJANI kicked the nearest leg of his mahogany desk in frustration. If it had not been for Marlene's incompetence he wouldn't be sitting in his office on a Sunday morning, desperately trying to catch up with his paperwork. He was furious with her and had become even angrier after spilling his coffee and then knocking his pen to the floor.

The hot, damp patch on his right trouser leg met his skin as he stretched downwards to pick up his gold-plated Parker, a "gift" from a drugs company which had flown him to Dubai several weeks ago for a seminar on "Botox and Non-surgical Cosmetic Enhancement in post-Menopausal Women".

The doctor grimaced as he thought about the conference subject matter. Right at this moment he felt he had met all the post-menopausal women he would ever want to in a lifetime. After Katy Clemmy's appointment had, predictably, run over the ten minutes Marlene had allotted for it, he had dealt with a succession of these self-obsessed fifty-something women, their unrealistic demands keeping him back until well after his desired clocking off time of five.

"If you hadn't put a new patient in for a ten-minute appointment slot we'd have been finished hours ago," he had said to Marlene as they locked up the office at seven thirty.

"If you hadn't spent over an hour with said new patient we'd have finished pretty much on time," Marlene had retorted, her dark blue eyes flashing in the dimming light. "You don't normally take more than half an hour with a new client."

They had continued switching on the various alarms and locking doors in silence. But Dr Nanjani found he could not let his rather impertinent secretary go without one carefully worded admonition.

"In future, Marlene, could you make sure new patients send in their information forms at least a week prior to their appointment," he said. "If I'd had that Scottish girl's folder in advance I would have seen you'd made a mistake with the appointment length."

Marlene had dropped her handbag onto the ground heavily and begun locking the outside door with an excessive degree of noise. "The girl wanted an appointment today," she said. "You said we were to see everyone who made contact with us. That is our 'key objective' for 2002, remember? If I'd waited for her form to arrive by post it would have been way past today. I made a mistake with the appointment slot but would you rather I'd let her slip past altogether?"

Bloody Marlene, Dr Nanjani thought to himself. But she had a point. He was glad his secretary had not let Katy Clemmy 'slip past', as it appeared he had not only persuaded the young Scottish woman to sign up for two procedures (subject to parental approval or reaching sixteen) – he had also, through meeting her, tapped into a new source of custom he could not understand having previously overlooked. The beginnings of a new advertising campaign targeted at hundreds more Katy Clemmys had already begun to form in his mind. "Never Too Young" was his currently preferred catchphrase. In his mind's eye he saw a girl not unlike Katy photographed as she ran gracefully against a blue sky. "My life will always be this beautiful," a 'quote' beside her would say, "thanks to Rosewood."

The church bells began chiming further down the road. Eleven bloody o'clock on a Sunday, and I'm stuck in here updating records, preparing for tomorrow, thought the doctor, feeling his earlier irritation at Marlene return. (He preferred *not* to connect his unsociable hours and consequent irritability to any demise in his customer base and the mounting pile of unpaid bills sitting in his Chiswick home.)

"What the hell...?"

Someone was knocking at his office window. He stood up quickly, his mind racing automatically to the two padlocked fridges in the back room, both of them full of drugs.

Dr Nanjani backed away from his desk, and edged his way towards the door that led into the surgery reception – if he had to call the police he should do it quickly and out of sight of whoever was outside.

Just then there was a second round of knocking. Dr Nanjani stopped still and felt his sense of panic decrease. If this was a drugs dealer intending to hold him at gunpoint it was a polite one.

The doctor craned his neck to take a quick peak at the large, latticed window to the right of his mahogany desk. He saw a small, white hand and lemon cuff disappear from view and then nothing, just the dark green leaves of a lilac tree quivering faintly in the spring breeze.

"Hello?" a muffled voice said.

A woman moved across the width of window, waving tentatively at nothing in particular. A moment later Nanjani saw her press her face against the glass, so it completely filled one small pane. She cupped her hands round her eyes to keep the light from them. He saw her gaze fix on him and her hand clench into a fist and hit the glass again.

"Hello? Dr Nanjani?"

This really was ridiculous. The woman knew his name. Was she a patient? He peered at her a little more closely. He didn't recognise her and she didn't look like one of his usual women, dressed as she was in jeans, flat canvas baseball boots and a long-sleeved lemon t-shirt. Not that she couldn't do with a little reconstruction, for she wasn't a spring chicken, as Marlene would have put it. She was just, well, unstudied, natural, the type that didn't bother with appearances.

Dr Nanjani thought of continuing on into the reception area and shutting the door behind him. But the woman had seen him, knew who he was and clearly wanted to speak to him. If he sat in reception long enough she would doubtless start ringing the bell.

He went over to the window. The peculiar woman smiled at him and started saying his name again. He sighed and pointed in the direction of the door.

"The door, go to the door," he said loudly.

"What?"

"Go to the door."

The woman smiled and nodded. He watched her wade through a wall of fuchsia in the direction of the front door.

It was all Marlene's fault, he thought as he walked through reception to open the front door. *Everything* was Marlene's fault. If she hadn't mucked up my Friday appointments I'd never have been here and this demented woman wouldn't be taking up even more of my precious time.

He opened the heavy wooden door and felt the sun warm his skin. It was like stepping into warm water. The scent of the outdoors reached his nostrils. The magnolia was in full bloom and the last of the hyacinths were still making a decent display in the decorative pots Marlene had situated either side of the front steps. (He had to hand it to her for that – Marlene did have a good way with décor, both indoor and outdoor.)

He could barely see the woman because the sunlight was so strong. But as she stepped into the porch and then the reception room her features slowly came to life, as if water colour had been washed over a wax drawing. She was rather Modigliani-like, Dr Nanjani noted – straight, shoulder length, auburn hair falling round serious, fine boned features and a long, white neck. Her frame was slim without being thin. Not his type – rather too unpolished when all was said and done – but not a bad looking woman.

"Dr Nanjani?"

He couldn't quite place her accent yet. It definitely wasn't Home Counties. But as he had already established, she was not a patient. Who then?

"Yes."

"Jane Ellingham."

She held out her hand in a very affable way which rather discomposed him. He was used to making the pleasantries with women, setting up the boundaries of his interaction with them. ("I'm Dr Nanjani. Please take a seat. Now, what would you like? Coffee, tea or perhaps you're a lady who likes to look after yourself and you're caffeine free?")

He took the small, rather childlike hand which was extended towards him. "I'm not open today, I mean for consultations, that is," he said, thinking that the sooner he got her to the point of leaving again, the better.

"No, no, I know that. I'm very sorry for bothering you. It's just I was checking out where your office was and I noticed you in working. I'm just down for a couple of days... I thought I might try and catch you..."

Dr Nanjani stared at her, trying again to get to the root of who she was and why she was here.

"If it is really inconvenient I can come back tomorrow."

God, no, thought Dr Nanjani. Let's get this over with. "How can I help you?" he asked hastily.

He watched the woman taking in the expensive carpet, the re-upholstered antique chesterfields, the mahogany bookcases and sideboard. She looked overawed. He had worked out by now that she was Scottish. He had never been to Scotland other than one visit to the Royal College of Surgeons in Edinburgh. He imagined that the majority of people there were rather like this woman, red haired and unsophisticated.

"I'm, em a school teacher," she said rather abruptly, fixing her gaze once again on the doctor.

She's a nutter, thought Dr Nanjani but in the interest of moving proceedings on he gave the women his best 'meet the patient smile' and nodded.

Jane Ellingham fumbled in her bag and held up a scrap of paper torn from a magazine. It was ripped and dog-eared but Dr Nanjani could just make out a classified advert for the Rosewood Clinic which had been circled in pencil.

"One of my pupils, the daughter of a friend, a kind of a friend anyway, has gone missing. The thing is I was helping this friend, who's her father actually, by trying to find out where she might have gone and I found his advert for your clinic in her bedroom."

Dr Nanjani stood very still and quiet, like an animal sensing an unknown predator in the distance.

"I was just wondering if my friend's daughter had contacted you at all? Her name is Clemmy. Katy Clemmy."

He had done nothing wrong, he told himself. So why was it this schoolteacher had suddenly made him feel like a naughty schoolboy who was about to have something precious confiscated? It was ridiculous – and in his own office.

"We don't give out details of our clients."

"Your secretary said that too, when I phoned her on Friday."

"Well, she's right," he said with a faintly triumphant air.

"The thing is, the police came round to see me yesterday."

"The police?"

"Yes, they are planning to launch a missing person's appeal on national TV – you know the kind of thing where they appeal for anyone who has seen the person to come forward..."

Dr Nanjani had stopped feeling angry with Marlene and begun to feel irate with Jane Ellingham instead. A busybody teacher from Scotland in canvas shoes and carrying a beaten up brown leather shoulder bag that looked as if it belonged to a Left Bank student. Who did she think she was? Miss Marple without the hat?

"If the police are onto this, why are you here?" He felt like a smug schoolboy. Intelligent doctor one, Wannabe Miss Marple zero.

"Because I thought it might be less traumatic for all concerned if it didn't get into the papers and the police were kept out of it as much as possible."

Wannabe Miss Marple's hair shone like polished copper in the sunlight. Her skin was very white and dotted with tiny red freckles. Dr Nanjani found himself feeling oddly off balance. It wasn't often he was faced with a woman who didn't even bother to wear make-up.

"Is it okay?" The Ellingham woman was pointing at one of the chesterfields. Dr Nanjani sighed and nodded. Any control he had hoped for was fast diminishing.

She sat down and put her bashed up bag over her knees. Dr Nanjani felt his shoulders sag and sat down opposite her, on an armchair.

"I did see a Katy Clemmy," he said. "On Friday. She came for an appointment to see about cosmetic surgery. I didn't know that she was missing. First I knew of her was when she came into my office.

My receptionist hadn't got her details in advance – but that was an oversight."

Jane Ellingham raised her hand in a manner reminiscent of the sign policemen use to stop traffic. Dr Nanjani watched her green eyes carefully. They were bright and intelligent. Her lips, he noticed, were full and pink, her teeth even and white. With a bit of lifting here and there she could be quite a beauty.

"I'm not here to cause you problems Dr Nanjani, just to solve them, if I can."

Normally he would have given a sharp, acerbic reply, taken command of the situation again. He didn't like the fact that this stranger had turned his waiting room into her interview room. But his energy and spark had deserted him.

"Oh. Fine then. Fine." His tone was as flat as his mood. He inspected the palms of his hands as he spoke.

"Can you tell me what Katy said – where she might have been going?"

Dr Nanjani shifted uncomfortably in his armchair. He was feeling guilty again and it annoyed him. He hadn't done anything wrong. Not really. Maybe he should not have persuaded the girl to sign up for the rhinoplasty as well as the breast reduction but that wasn't a crime was it? After all, she was practically getting the second treatment for free when the Easter discount offer was taken into consideration.

"She said she was meeting someone. A friend."

"Did she give you a name?"

She was peering at him as if he was a child whose honesty she was undecided about. I am being examined in my own consulting rooms, he thought peevishly.

"Yes."

Her eyes opened wide and she raised her brows. Dr Nanjani was reminded of two question marks.

"She mentioned a Dan," he said.

"Dan," she repeated.

"Yes."

"Did she give you a phone number?"

"She gave me a mobile number. It's in her notes. But she said it was just a temporary one. She was going to phone back, she said, with a different number."

"Could I have a look?"

The question mark eyes again. Dr Nanjani stood up slowly and went into his office. He pulled out Katy Clemmy's folder from his filing cabinet and went back into the reception again.

He handed the schoolteacher the file without looking at her.

"Thank you," he heard her say.

It took him a while to gather the courage to look at her again. When he did he saw that her green eyes were fixed directly on him. He scanned them for disapproval but their brilliance only reflected back a dark image of a large man in a winged back chair who looked remote and lonely.

"She's signed up for a breast reduction and rhinoplasty," said the schoolteacher, keeping her gaze on him.

"Yes," he said. He was tempted to add "So what?" but refrained.

"I presume you won't be encouraging her to follow this up?"

"As you can see, she has signed a contract, like any new patient."

"But she's *fifteen*," said the teacher.

"She can be scheduled in for treatment sometime after her sixteenth birthday and still take advantage of our 2002 Easter discount," said Dr Nanjani.

The teacher stared at him.

"Something wrong, Miss…?"

"Ellingham," said the teacher.

"Miss Ellingham," said the doctor.

"I'm just wondering why on earth you would think a fifteen year old girl needs cosmetic surgery. I can tell you now, she won't be having it."

The woman appeared to be shaking. What on earth was wrong with her, wondered Dr Nanjani. And who on earth was she to say whether his client went ahead with treatment or not?

"I don't think that's any of your business, Miss Ellingham," he said and drew back his lips in an effort to smile.

They stared at each other for a moment. The schoolteacher

opened her mouth to say something and then appeared to think better of it. Dr Nanjani was pleased to feel his sense of control return.

"I'll take that back, if you don't mind," he said, stretching out his hand in the direction of Katy Clemmy's folder.

Miss Ellingham looked at him for a moment and then shook her head.

"You really would give a lovely young girl like Katy cosmetic surgery?"

Dr Nanjani suddenly understood. The woman was a feminist. That's why she was getting so wound up. He felt almost sorry for her. "Rebuild Your Body, Rebuild Your Life," he wanted to tell her but what was the point? He had seen her type before. She would carry on using her ageing physique to make a political point and end up by scoring an own goal with an embittered and lonely old age.

The woman stood up. "I'm just going to take that number down," she said, pulling a pen out of her bag.

Dr Nanjani watched as she scribbled Katy's number down in a diary saying 'Scottish Secondary Teachers' Association' in gold lettering on the front of it. Her biro was leaking and there was a piece of tissue stuck to it. These feminists really did themselves no favours, he thought.

"There you are," she said, holding out Katy Clemmy's folder. "Though I don't think you'll need it."

Dr Nanjani smirked by way of reply. "Good luck finding her," he said.

Jane Ellingham gave him a hard stare.

"That's kind of you," she said, her green eyes glinting. "I've written my number on Katy's form just in case you remember anything that might be important."

She left the surgery without saying goodbye.

"Poor woman," thought Dr Nanjani.

44

JANE hesitated outside a cafe. She needed time to think. How should she approach this phone call? If the number she had copied down in the cosmetic surgeon's office was the one Katy's father had been trying, it was unlikely there would be any answer. But what if it was someone else's number? This Dan's perhaps? Would he try to protect Katy by pretending he did not know her? For a brief moment, overwhelmed by the complexity of all these possibilities, Jane found herself wishing she had never got involved in the Clemmys' affairs at all. But she had, she reprimanded herself, and she owed it to Katy not to give up now.

She pushed open the café's glass and chrome door and found herself in a large Victorian parlour dominated by a glistening, stainless steel counter. Posters advertising poetry readings, a print makers' workshop and "a daring new production of *A Midsummer's Night Dream*" covered the walls. Behind the counter an attractive Mediterranean-looking man was working busily at a vintage, pink Italian coffee machine which hissed like a steam engine. The air smelled of coffee and cinnamon.

Jane chose a sunny spot next to an open window and sat down. The waiter looked over at her.

"Coffee?" he mouthed.

Jane nodded.

"Croissant? Pastry? Eggs Benedict?"

Jane shook her head and looked away.

"You need food," the waiter persisted. "Not good to have coffee on an empty stomach."

He smiled and Jane found herself smiling back. "Ok, a croissant," she said, feeling unable to resist the waiter's flirtatious concern for her wellbeing.

The man winked at her, a heavy lid closing momentarily over a large, brown eye like a taut blind. Jane felt her face colour and stared down at the table. She was so out of practice at this sort of thing. A taster from the cover of one of Katy's *Misty* magazines crossed her mind. *Mistyfy Your Man With Our Fabulous Seduction Tips*, it had screamed in baby pink, bubble writing. Perhaps I should take out a subscription to *Misty* thought Jane with a smile.

But this was ridiculous. She was forgetting her real purpose, to find Katy before any harm came to her. I don't do boho or romance anymore, she scolded herself. All those years in my twenties I spent at peace camps and music festivals, volunteering on art therapy projects, dating dangerous-looking Palestinian men, are over. I am an armour-plated schoolmarm with a past that is firmly in the past. I am Miss Ellingham. Jane, that blundering bag of nerves that was stupid enough to be seduced by the likes of Jim Beetham is as good as dead.

As if to reinforce this point to herself she scowled and kept her gaze firmly on the view outside the window when the waiter delivered her coffee and croissant. After he had gone – following a few moments of hopeful hovering – Jane hauled her bag onto her knees and pulled out her mobile, her SSTA diary and her purse. From her purse she took a scrap of paper containing Katy's mobile number and quickly compared it with the one she had taken down in Dr Nanjani's office. The two were completely different. She picked up her phone and began pressing in the number she had written in the back of her diary.

It took a few minutes, but eventually a female voice answered. "Hello?"

"Who am I speaking to?" asked Jane.

"Donna," said the voice, suspiciously. "Who's this?"

"It's Jane," said Miss Ellingham, doing her best to sound familiar. "I'm looking for Dan. Is he there?"

The voice that was 'Donna' softened.

"I'll just go and get him. He's upstairs. Sorry – I answered his phone."

Jane heard footsteps and muffled voices, then a gruff, male "Hello?"

"Is that Dan? My name's Jane Ellingham." There was no reply so Jane continued. "I'm a teacher at Craigie Academy, a school in Scotland. I'm looking for one of my pupils. Her name's Katy Clemmy."

"Katy?" 'Dan' sounded shocked.

"Yes. Someone gave me your number as a contact for her."

There was silence at the end of the line. Jane's mind raced for the best way to keep the conversation going. This Dan seemed to know Katy. But who was he? What was he?

"Is Katy there?" she asked. The sudden realisation that the teenager might be standing right next to the man she was speaking to filled her with elation, closely followed by panic.

"No, she's gone."

"Gone?"

"She left yesterday morning."

"*Left* yesterday morning?" Jane's hands began to tremble. "You mean she was staying with you?"

"Yes – kind of."

Jane felt a wave of nausea wash through her body. What did he mean, "kind of"?

"The boy at the tennis courts?" her mother had shouted at her after finding out who the father of her unborn child was. "What were you doing spending the weekend with him – a boy without a job or a proper qualification? You told us you'd gone camping with your friends. We trusted you." The rain had beaten against the living room window, competing with her mother's screeching. She had watched the drops form rivulets and hurry across the glass, chased by a gathering wind. Eventually, her mother told her they would 'discuss it' when her father came in but her fate, and that of her child, were already sealed, and she knew it.

"Hello?" said the voice at the end of the line.

Jane felt her body jolt, the sounds of the café return. She was crying, she noticed, with alarm. Out of the corner of her eye she was sure she could see the waiter staring over at her. She ran her hand under her nose and took a deep breath. Katy is all that matters now, she told herself. I cannot save the seventeen-year-old girl that stood speechless in her parents' living room all these years ago, but I can, perhaps, help Katy.

~ 180 ~

She forced herself to concentrate. The man she'd been speaking to *sounded* okay. But what did that mean? "You've got no common sense, Jane, you never did have," her mother's voice reminded her. Just because this Dan didn't sound crazy, or cruel, did not mean he had Katy's best intentions at heart. Jim had the loveliest smile, and look how he behaved, she thought. 'The father', as he was called forever after, scruffy, socially awkward and in and out of care most of his childhood, had shown her more tenderness than any of the Jims she had known since.

She tried to pick up her coffee cup but her hands were trembling so much she was forced to put it down again. I need to think of something, she thought to herself, feeling a rising sense of panic. I need to be sensible.

"Where are you, Dan?" she asked eventually.

"Walthamstow."

"Would it be okay if I came and met you there?"

"I'm... not sure. Why?"

He sounds shifty, thought Jane, her knees beginning to feel weak.

"Look, if you don't help me the police..."

"The *police*?"

"Katy's missing," she said, after a pause in which each of them appeared to be waiting for the other to speak.

"I don't see what that's got to do with me," said Dan.

"She was with you – on Friday night?"

"Yes. But I don't know where she is now. I'm sorry." There was a pause and then he added, "What do you mean 'she's missing'? Like in something's happened to her? Am I supposed to be mixed up in this?"

You *are* mixed up in this, thought Jane, but she said nothing. Keep calm, don't react, she told herself. She stood up and walked out onto the street, scanning it for Underground signs. "I'm coming to Walthamstow, Dan, and I think you'd better agree to see me if you don't want the police knocking on your door. Tell me the name of somewhere we can meet."

It was only when she was on a tube, turning the pages of her A to Z to locate more precisely Walthamstow High Street, home to the Regal Coffee House, that she realised she had forgotten to pay for her croissant and coffee.

45

THE NURSES in the local psychiatric hospital's Alcohol Problems Unit politely referred to my illicit drink in the treatment centre as "a slip", which implied I had been going somewhere. The truth was I had been put in the Allan Glen by my husband and had about as much sense of purpose there as I'd had at home. It is only recently it has occurred to me that I was expected to try and give up my addiction. But like the anorexics I had seen avoiding their food and the over-eaters I had watched funnelling extra pieces of toast into their mouths, my one goal was to continue as I had been – in my case deadening my existence through the abuse of alcohol. You could say I was successful on that count. Whatever the institution – my marriage, someone else's, a treatment centre – I will always do my utmost to subvert its confines.

46

Your Contribution Can Make a Difference

NUMBER 16 is a secure hostel for vulnerable young women who are homeless. A small number of our girls are with us for only one or two nights before being moved onto other accommodation or returned to their families, but the majority stay with us for several years while they recover from traumatic events which have contributed to their homelessness. These can include sexual and/or physical abuse at home, addiction and self harm.

Our aim is to give the girls who stay with us the stability and protection to build an independent life free from exploitation and abuse. Our hostel, funded by the charity FourSquare, can house only 10 long-term residents at any one time. A vast range of service workers are employed in the rehabilitation of the girls who stay at Number 16, including drugs workers, psychologists, nutritionists, counsellors, art therapists, literacy workers and sexual health advisers. We also have close links with the medical profession, particularly specialists in the areas of eating disorders, self harm, addiction and sexual health.

Our service is expensive to run but vital. The majority of girls who spend time at Number 16 are able to put their lives on track, finding their way eventually into jobs and homes. Sarah's story, below, is just one of many similar ones.

If you would like to make a donation to Number 16 or one of five similar hostels we run throughout London, please fill in the attached form.

Christine Baxter.
Director. FourSquare (a registered charity).

Sarah's Story

"I was 12 when I ran away from home the first time but they found me and took me back again. Nobody knew why but I kept doing it – running away. I just couldn't stand the fights at home. My Dad used to hit my Mum and then he started doing it to me and my younger sister. Eventually, I went to London and ended up using. Some girl told me I could make money if I slept with men so I did that too. I hated it. I spent two years like that. But then a StreetWorks worker found me and I went to Number 16 hostel for about a year and a half. They helped get me off drugs and I learned to read properly too. Now I like reading magazines and things. I've started a job now, working in a café. Eventually I want to get a Housing Association house. I'm on the lists. Until that happens I can stay in another FourSquare hostel, one that's not so controlled. I'm a lot happier now. I feel as if I've got a future."

47

WATERLOO Police Station was lit by a mean, yellow light. The wooden doors and floors were coated in layers of cheerless, dark brown varnish. There was nothing pleasant to rest the eye on, to take Jane's mind off what might have happened to Katy between leaving Dan's home early on Saturday and being picked up wandering along the Embankment at three o'clock on Sunday morning.

"Number seventy-five," said a boy with gelled hair and acne from behind the reception desk. He looks as if he's dressed up as a policeman for a fancy-dress party, thought Jane.

She looked down at the ticket in her hand. Number eighty-two. Only when her number was called could she approach the desk. "That's how we work," the policeman on reception had said when she had first arrived and protested at having to wait to find out what had happened to "a vulnerable young Scottish girl" who'd been "missing from home for three days now".

She shifted in her seat, trying to unpeel the backs of her thighs from the plastic-coated cushioning on the bench she had chosen to sit on. What had she been thinking of buying shorts, she wondered. Worse – what had she been thinking of putting them on? It had been years since she had worn anything as revealing. But then again, London had been hot, and she had packed in a hurry. Shorts were a sensible move. She preferred not to dwell on the fact that there was something about being free of Craigie which made flirtations with waiters and experiments with new clothes suddenly rather interesting again. "I'm here only to find Katy and take her home," she reprimanded herself.

The sounds of male bonhomie filtered through to the main waiting area. Jane had yet to catch sight of a policewoman, despite posters on the walls exhorting victims of rape to talk to one of the station's 'many specially trained female officers'.

She had just closed her eyes in an attempt to shut out the ugly waiting room when a heavy crash behind her forced her to open them again. She looked up to see two officers bundling a girl who could not have been more than eighteen into the waiting room. The girl's head lolled like a rag doll's and her feet dragged along the floor. But despite her semi-conscious state, her hair fell over her pale face in a glossy sheet and her frilly mini-skirt and cropped denim jacket looked clean.

"Right, sit her down over there," said one of the officers, nodding in Jane's direction.

"She'll fall over," replied his companion.

"No room in the cells right now. Nothing else we can do, mate. I'll go and see Davy round the back and see if we can sort something out."

The older and brawnier of the two officers went to the reception and lifted the desk up. He had to turn sideways to ease himself through. Jane watched as he opened a second door behind the small reception space. Male laughter rose and fell and Jane caught a glimpse of steam rising from a kettle, the corner of computer screen, a Kylie poster.

The officer who was left had earnest blue eyes. He glanced at Jane and then at the girl he was propping up.

"Do you mind? I mean, I'm just going to sit her down here a moment. She's okay... just a bit... spaced out. She'll not bother you."

Always the sensible looking schoolteacher, thought Jane, but she nodded and shifted slightly to create more space.

"Shouldn't she be taken to A and E?" Jane asked, noting the girl's glazed eyes.

The officer looked at the girl and eased her down onto the bench beside Jane.

"Well, she's in and out there like a jack-in-the-box. The paramedics refused to take her this time. Said she just needed to rest up. The StreetWorks girls will take her to a hostel. Anyway, we'll need to charge her first... for possession."

Jane felt a stab of panic in her stomach.

"StreetWorks?" she asked. The policeman who had called her to say they had found Katy said StreetWorks had picked her up.

"Yeah. They work with the girls – you know the street workers

– pick them up and take them in for medical care, food, sometimes a bed. Run a hostel and day centre near here. Jodie here's well known to them. Anyway…"

"Street workers," Jane mumbled. What state would she find Katy in? What had happened to her? She thought of Alan Clemmy clutching his daughter's English jotter as he left her cottage. The police had wanted her to attend their interview with Katy. Only after that was complete and she had verified Katy's identity would they phone Alan. She had been looking forward to following up their call, sharing in his excitement but what if the news wasn't good, if Katy had been harmed in some way? She was already regretting having called Alan Clemmy the previous evening. "I'm in London," she'd told him. "I'm going to visit that surgery Katy circled in the magazine cutting – I think it might lead somewhere. And I've phoned the police here too – they've got a description of Katy and my number." When Clemmy had got over his shock he'd kept phoning her every few hours to ask if she'd found anything out – and, of course, she hadn't. "I'll come down too," he'd said. But Jane had managed to convince him that he'd be better off staying at the farm in case Katy returned and to be there for Corinne who doctors had suggested should be transferred to an addiction clinic as soon the worst of her cuts and bruises had healed. "Someone will need to pack a case for her," Jane had pointed out. "Anyway, I'll keep you informed if I find anything out about Katy."

She was about to ask the officer more questions but he seemed to have decided he'd said enough. He shifted his shoulders and then bent down to straighten up his charge. With difficulty he positioned her so that she remained upright, her head slightly tilted backwards. Then, with a quick nod at Jane, he absented himself, disappearing through reception and into the back office.

Jodie stirred. Her head rolled from left to right as if she was in the middle of a bad dream. Or is it me who is in the bad dream, Jane wondered. She stared down at her bare legs and tried to remember how she had felt earlier that day, as she had rushed back to her hotel from Walthamstow, put on fresh clothes and walked out into the sunshine, filled with joy at the news that Katy appeared to have been found – and that she would be seeing her later. Katy is nothing to do with me, she thought suddenly. When all this over she will go back home and I will be left with Miss Ellingham.

"Martin," said Jodie. "Mar-tin."

Her hands slapped against the plastic and her head dropped forwards. Jane smelt perfume cut with the stench of vomit.

"Number eighty-two," said the fancy-dress policeman at reception.

Jane took a hurried glance at Jodie and stood up. She needs help, she thought. But the enormity of the situation that had brought Jodie to this point was too overwhelming for Jane to contemplate. "I came here to find Katy and take her home," she reminded herself again. "Someone else will have to take care of Jodie."

48

IT WAS a long time before I could properly appraise my life, the way I'm trying to do for you all now, in this dingy church hall. I was told later I spent six weeks in the psychiatric hospital but all I remember from the first fortnight's detox is a jumble of hallucinations. There were moments of clarity, when I was sure I was awake and not dreaming, that the world I sensed around me was the one I would now define as 'real'. From what I know, I never left my private room in all my time in the hospital. I remember the room was wider than it was long, from the vantage point of my bed, with a small bathroom in the far right hand corner. When I looked in the cabinet next to my bed I found just my slippers, a change of nightdress and a handbag with my purse and a diary in it. None of the nurses could tell me how these items had got there though one of the more chatty ones, a young girl with blonde hair who giggled a lot, told me the treatment centre must have passed them on.

I was too unwell to think that the sum total of my possessions appeared to be nightclothes and a handbag. No-one I knew came to see me and nobody phoned. For most of the time I was in I also had no news about my family and no cards or gifts. The only times I'd been in hospital before had been to give birth to my two children. Back then I'd been showered with bouquets. I couldn't move for relatives and the ever growing piles of presents. Nurses hovered about the clear, plastic cribs which held each of my children and told me how clever I was to give birth to such beautiful babies. They talked to me about their own children's births, helped me paint my toenails, told me to pamper myself. I was special and yet every woman at the same time, the pain and pushing of labour a leveller for all womankind.

Much later, when I was thinking more clearly, I would see the sharp contrast between these periods of my life, how in a few years I had become someone to lock away, whose family no longer wanted to see her. I'd remember the flowers that covered every surface in the maternity ward and compare that with the solitary plastic bottle of water that sat on my bedside cabinet while I detoxed. I'd wonder how I had become this shadow woman. Sometimes, hearing a young girl laugh I'd remember I'd once had friends and family. It came to amaze me that I'd envied the Susan Flockharts of this world, unburdened, as I saw it then, with difficult teenagers and husbands who bored them.

You could ask, why did it take time? Wasn't it immediately shocking to find myself hospitalised in this way, with barely a friend in the world? Well, I suppose I couldn't, *wouldn't,* see what I had become. Plenty of people had already tried to help me stop drinking – my husband, my doctor, my friends, even my daughter in her own childish way. But none of them could do for me what I couldn't do for myself. For all the clinic referrals my husband had got for me, I had found a reason to avoid taking them up. For all the programmes my doctor had suggested to me I found excuses to ignore them. For all the friends who had said "perhaps you should cut down on the booze a bit, Corinne" I had come up with ways of implying that my fondness for a drink was no greater than theirs. And for every time my daughter had asked me to "come and play" instead of nursing my vodka, I had found a way of doing both.

If I'd had it my way I would have stayed in my white cell for a lot longer than six weeks. Better that than face the grey reality of what alcohol had done to my life. In a way, I was right. When I did begin to unpick the destruction, I was left with nothing but pain – something I had been trying to avoid since the death of my son five years before.

49

Waterloo Police Station

Report

Name: ...Katy Clemmy...

Age: ...15...

DOB: ...March 1st 1987...

Parent(s)/Guardian(s):
...Alan Clemmy, Corinne Clemmy...

Address: ...Millhouse Farm...
...Craigie...
...Ayrshire...
...Scotland...

ABOVE subject found wandering on Embankment at approximately 2am on Sunday 31st of March by StreetWorks worker, Stephanie Dooks, who took her to Number 16 Hostel. Brought by Ms Dooks to Waterloo Station 4.30 pm, Sunday 31st March. Answered description of missing person filed by Ayrshire Constabulary. Father informed of daughter's whereabouts following interview with child at 5pm of 31st March. Alan Clemmy to pick daughter up from Number 16 Single Girls' Secure Homeless Hostel on Tuesday 2nd April. Friend and teacher of child, Jane Ellingham, present at interview.

Contacts for child: Alan Clemmy (father), Jane Ellingham (teacher), Stephanie Dooks (StreetWorks), Sue Armitage (Number 16 Hostel). Numbers attached on separate sheet.

Signed: (Police Officer) ....

Signed (Subject) ....

"Hello Katy. Jane here. Just thought I'd give you a call to see how you're getting on but your new phone is switched off, or maybe you don't get a good signal there. Anyway, your Dad is coming for you the day after tomorrow. I've given him your number and he says he will get in touch. Don't be worried about him being angry. I know you are but he's just glad you're safe and well. You've got my number – phone me if you want. Okay then, bye just now."

Hello Katy. You'll be surprised at getting a text from your Dad. Coming to get you on Tuesday. Phone me any time. Keep the phone Jane E bought you on. I'm going to hire a car in L. and drive you home. Love, Dad.

Breathing Space Workbook

Exercise One:

Use Words or Pictures to Show Us How You Are Feeling

Sometimes it is difficult to express what we really feel. But the first step to solving our problems is knowing what these problems are. With your key worker, use words or pictures, or a mixture of both, to express your emotions. Write your name at the top of the space provided. Remember – the Breathing Space Workbook is all about helping YOU to feel better.

KATY

Scared, sad, embarrassed, tired, angry, fat, ugly, depressed, worried.

Now take each of the emotions you have written down or drawn and write beside them why you think you feel that way. Use the lines below. Talk through with your key worker what you write.

Scared: Of going back to school, rude texts, rows with Dad, Mum and Dad arguing.

Sad: Mum drinking, Dad upset, Mum and Dad hating each other, Ben when he was ill, Ben dead.

Embarrassed: Articles in papers and things in the news, everyone at school knowing, Dad and Miss Ellingham knowing about Rosewood, Dan.

Tired: Home.

Angry: Mum. I hate her.

Fat: My chest but my hips too. Over eight and a half stone.

Ugly: Teeth not white. Nose too big. Hair too fine. Freckles. Frog eyes.

Depressed: Mum and Dad. Mum. No boyfriend. Ugly. Never in top five at school. Didn't get merit in last music theory exam. No-one ever mentions Ben. No brother or sister to talk to.

Worried: Mum and Dad. Mum.

Great. You've almost finished Exercise One. Just one more thing to do. Discuss with your key worker whether the reasons you have written down for your emotions are valid or not. Spend a bit of time talking with your key worker about what might be a valid reason for a particular emotion and what might not. Once you have done that, write a few lines about your thoughts and feelings. What are the links between them? Could you think differently about some of the things you have written down? Are your feelings rational?

I'm scared that when I go back home it will all be the same and I'll start getting those texts again. I'm frightened of Dad shouting at me and Mum and Dad shouting at each other. I'm worried and depressed because of Mum and Dad, mainly Mum's drinking but also the way they don't hardly speak, except to argue. I'm sad because Ben died and when he did Mum seemed to hate me even more than she did before.

The key worker says these feelings are normal in these situations. She says a report will be given to my Dad and an educational psychologist and that something will have to be done about my Mum. She says the row with my Dad about the computer was probably because he was stressed and that if my Mum gets help then the rows should stop. I've not to worry about Dad being angry at me running away because he's happy I'm okay. The key worker says Dad's flying down and then hiring a car to take me home because it's more private and that shows how much he loves me. I've to try and explain to him about the appointment at the Rosewood Clinic and how I ended up staying in London because I was too scared to go home. Been told (also by key worker) I'm not seeing myself properly.

She says I'm not fat and ugly and I should think again about that. She says being near the top in school is good, even if it's not the very top. She says sometimes people don't get on with their brothers or sisters if they have them and being an only child can be good. I can't change how I feel about myself right now but been told I can do it with practise.

50

JANE drummed her fingers on the arms of her chair. Once again her own life was on hold as she waited around in someone else's – in this case Dan Lees'. If only she hadn't left the Regal Coffee House in Walthamstow in such a hurry and forgotten her damn jacket. Anything that would have prevented a second meeting with a man she'd hardly hit it off with first time round.

Still, she thought, if her encounter with Dan in the Regal Coffee House had been awkward it wasn't entirely surprising. No sooner had she sat down in the café and begun talking to him than she had received a call from the police to say a girl answering Katy's description had been found wandering along the Embankment in the early hours of Sunday morning. She would "have to dash" she told the bewildered man who'd just bought her a coffee and a piece of carrot cake. Katy had been found and she would phone him later to "explain" – quite what, she wasn't sure.

Where was he anyway – Dan Lees? He had said he would meet her at the National Theatre café at eleven thirty and it was now nearly twelve. Well, she thought, even if he didn't arrive, it didn't matter. All it would mean was that she'd lost a jacket. From what she had been able to gather from her brief meeting with Dan he wasn't liable to be any more trouble to Katy. If anything, it would seem, it was Katy who had been trouble to Dan. What was it he had said to her? "Before you ask, I don't normally put up girls I've chatted to on the internet and certainly not ones who are still at school. The situation just kind of *evolved* and mainly because Katy didn't seem to have any sort of plan. If you're telling me she's run away from home then that would make perfect sense."

It was a defensive start to their meeting but not without reason. I was far too suspicious when I called him after getting his number from Dr Nanjani, thought Jane. Poor man must felt as if he was on trial. Still, she thought, even if he wasn't a malicious predator he was what the kids at school might call 'a loser'. Why else would a man who looked about mid twenties be so idle as to be able to take a trip into central London on a Tuesday morning to return a jacket?

"Hi."

Jane felt her body jolt. She looked up. Dan was standing a foot or so away from her, dressed in jeans, sandals and a denim shirt. He gave her a lopsided smile.

"Sorry I'm late. The tube ..."

Here we go, thought Jane: *"Sorry I'm late Miss Ellingham, the bus broke down."*

"That's okay," she replied, doing her best to supress her impatience.

Dan held out her suede jacket. His arms were very tanned. "There you go – I believe you need these in Scotland."

Jane laughed at the unexpected show of wit, and placed the jacket across her knees. "Thanks," she said.

She watched as the young man glanced at the counter. There was a pause in which both of them listened to the clatter of dropped plates.

"Can I get you a coffee?" asked Jane and immediately regretted it.

Dan paused and then nodded. "Why not?" he said and drew back a chair. God, thought Jane, now I'll have to make conversation with him. *I only wanted my jacket back.* She watched grimly as the young man pulled his chair several feet away from the table. A few moments later he was leaning back in it as if it was an armchair, his legs stretched out in front of him.

"I'm exhausted," he said, with a sigh, running a hand through his long, dark hair.

You don't look it, thought Jane.

"I've spent the last few days running around like a lunatic and suddenly I've got a bleeding briefing session to go to. I wish I'd been given more than twenty-four hours notice."

Jane took a sip of her coffee. A briefing session? What did men, *boys*, like Dan go to briefing sessions about?

She noticed Dan watching her. After a second or two he lifted his canvas haversack off the floor, placed it on his knees and started to rummage around in it, eventually pulling out a small, waterproof wallet.

"Want another?" he said, nodding at Jane's coffee.

Jane stood up. "No, don't. I'll go – it was me who offered to buy you a drink. It's just I thought they'd come and serve us."

Dan grinned. "Hey, no sweat. If it's table service that's cool. I'm in no hurry."

Clearly, thought Jane. She sat back down again. What on earth was she going to talk to this man about? If we don't get served soon, I'll just say I've got to go, she thought.

"So, Katy's okay then?" said Dan after a moment or two had passed. Jane looked up sharply. She felt there was something a little too casual about his tone for her liking. He knew Katy had been found safe and well – she'd told him that during the phone call he'd made to tell her about her jacket.

"She's fine," she said. "Well, as fine as can be expected."

"Meaning?"

Jane found herself looking straight into Dan's eyes. They were more earnest than she expected.

"Meaning her Dad is driving her home today and I think... hope... that things will sort themselves out."

"How come her Dad only made it down today?"

"Katy's mum has just been taken into hospital," Jane replied, wondering how much detail she should go into. "Alan – Katy's Dad – wanted to come down as soon as he heard Katy had been found but I persuaded him to sort out things with the hospital first. He flew down last night and he's hiring a car to drive Katy home this morning. I think he wanted give her the chance to talk... you know, by driving back instead of flying."

Dan had just opened his mouth to reply when there was a loud burst of laughter at the counter. They both looked over. A pretty girl of about twenty, with dark hair pulled into a bouncy ponytail, was pushing an espresso towards a handsome-looking man of thirty or so. He placed the coffee to one side, then leant across the counter and looked straight into the girl's eyes. The girl wound the end of her ponytail round her fingers and giggled. No wonder they hadn't been served yet, thought Jane.

She looked away. There was an ache in her chest. The predictable shape of her day flashed before her in a series of vignettes. A lonely advance into a sea of tube passengers. A solitary dinner in the hotel restaurant. A book lying face down on the pillow next to her as she reached, finally, to switch out the light and sleep.

When she came to her senses again, Dan was staring at her. He smiled and then winked. "You were miles away," he said.

Jane felt her face redden. Billy Neill came to mind. "I think Miss Ellingham's got the hots for pretty boy Leonardo," he'd said with a wink after she'd waxed lyrical to 3B about the Baz Luhrmann version of *Romeo and Juliet*.

"Oh, I almost forgot," Dan said, looking down at his haversack. "Katy left some things."

He leaned down over the arm of his chair and loosened the buckles on his bag. A moment later he plonked a magazine and several flyers onto the table. Jane turned the magazine over to look at its front cover. "Misty – for girls with attitude," she read. Underneath the masthead two girls of about fifteen smiled seductively beneath elaborate hats. "Unleash the Power of an Easter Bonnet," read the text below the picture. "Fashion Tricks to Help You to Pull like a Bunny Girl." Faintly nauseated, Jane pushed the magazine aside and looked at the glossy pink and lilac flyers. Both were from the Rosewood Clinic, one advertising rhinoplasty, the other breast surgery.

"My sister found them down the side of her bed," said Dan, watching as Jane gathered the magazine and flyers up and began stuffing them into her bag. "I thought I might as well bring them along – in case they're important or something."

Across the room, Espresso Man reached out and stroked Ponytail's cheek. Jane felt the ache in her chest intensify. What would her life have been like, she wondered, if she hadn't got herself 'into trouble', as her mother put it? It was not as if she had lacked spark. Perhaps she, like Ponytail, would have lived in

London, worked in theatres, flirted with arty men. Ultimately her pregnancy and the trauma that had resulted from it had left her too scared and too scarred to do much with her young life. It was as much as she could do to leave school as soon as possible and live in 'that squat', throw herself into causes. All when the one cause I should have supported was myself, she thought. It had been too late by then to support her child. Her poor, unborn child.

She turned back to Dan and wondered how she must look to him.

"So you're Katy's English teacher then?" Dan said. He smiled and cocked his head so that she was forced to look him in the eye.

"Yes," said Jane and immediately felt very boring.

"I'm guessing *Misty* magazine isn't on the syllabus," he said.

Jane laughed. "God, no."

"What then?"

"Oh you know – the usual. A bit of Shakespeare, some Ted Hughes, the occasional Bob Dylan song."

Dan sat forwards. "Dylan?"

Jane grinned. "What? Amn't I allowed to teach something that's not in the so-called canon? Bob Dylan wrote some bloody good lyrics."

Dan glanced out the window. "I know," he said.

"People always say *Blowin' in the Wind* is a protest song about Vietnam but to me it's a poem – set to music – and it's about people turning a blind eye... Anyway, it's a good route into metaphor and things," said Jane.

"I don't suppose you taught Dylan to Katy?" asked Dan.

"Probably. I usually give the junior classes a few song lyrics to think about before throwing poetry proper at them."

"I thought you might," said Dan.

"What?"

"Nothing – go on. You were saying..."

Jane had begun to feel self-conscious again. "I wasn't saying anything really. Just that lyrics are a good way to get kids into poetry. It's a bit like feeding a baby – from what I know about feeding babies – if you want them to eat the things that are good for them then you need to mash them up and disguise them."

Dan laughed.

"I probably sound like a complete lunatic," said Jane.

Dan stared at her. "You don't," he said. "You're exactly my kind of woman. And now I'm going to get that coffee before that suit runs off with the waitress."

51

ALTHOUGH I had no visitors who were familiar to me while I was in hospital, I did eventually receive a parcel with a covering letter from Susan. The parcel contained a pile of fashion magazines and a book about clothes design in the twentieth century. In her letter Susan said she remembered how interested in clothes I'd been at school and thought I would enjoy reading about them again. She had been up in Craigie visiting her mother, she said. She'd hoped to meet up with me again (hadn't we had "a blast" when she was up a few years ago?) but had heard from Alan I was in hospital. Unfortunately, she would not have time to come and see me there but she hoped I would "get well soon". I could feel my face burning when I read what she'd written. A visit would have reassured me I had at least one real friend. But the fact that Susan obviously wanted to avoid meeting me face to face told me a lot about how my behaviour would be viewed by the outside world. If it had been possible I would probably have drunk again there and then. Instead I was left to contemplate the emptiness of the white space I now inhabited.

52

Misty Takes on the Sly

1. GET a load of Catherine Zeta Jones at the premiere of her movie *Entrapment* in 1999 – Michael Douglas certainly does. "She has the kind of body which will run to fat before she's fifty," says *Misty*'s Food and Exercise editor, Savannah Goldman. "Think Elizabeth Taylor – beautiful in her prime but these days she needs a season ticket at her local liposuction clinic just to look half presentable in a smock." Move over Liz, Cathy needs room to park her posterior at the clinic too!

2. Renée Zellweger says she blew up like a pumpkin for her role in *Bridget Jones' Diary*. Is that so Renée, love? Strange that you look as large as ever in this snapshot taken in a New York restaurant just two weeks ago. Could Renée's ballooning proportions have less to do with her devotion to her art than misery in her heart? Just three months after moving in with heartthrob George

Clooney it seems the romance is off. Is Renée taking solace in the biscuit tin or did George refuse to live with her unless she cut out the Jaffa Cakes? Whatever! She looks dreadful.

3. Oh dear! If there is one thing Kate Winslet should grab before the Titanic sinks it's her make-up bag. Caught shopping in Knightsbridge without her slap on, Kate's complexion has all the allure of freshly baked pizza. Note to *Misty* readers – if you have spots use a foundation, preferably in quantity. As our Beauty Editor, Jacqui Goodie, puts it: "She may be feted as the archetypal English Rose but Winslet's skin hasn't much of the rose's velveteen flush about it. She needs emergency cosmetic application – quickly!"

4. Cellulite alert. Michelle Pfeiffer once admitted she thought she looked like a duck. It seems to us here at *Misty* there is one thing ducks do which

Michelle should not and that's swim. A *Misty* reader took this photograph of Pfeiffer on the beach at Nice. Lucy Campbell-Redman, *Misty*'s Fashion Editor, says Pfeiffer clearly forgot one essential item when packing her holiday wardrobe – a sarong: "It's light, it protects sensitive skin from the sun and it is ideal for women with dimpled thighs like Pfeiffer's," she says. "I feel like posting her one right now."

53

"YOU OBVIOUSLY like teaching," Dan said to her once he'd returned to their table with a coffee for each of them. He seemed in no hurry to go. Just as he'd seemed in no hurry to arrive, thought Jane.

"What makes you say that?" she asked, feeling obliged to keep the conversation going. Actually, it had never occurred to her that she *liked* teaching. It was just something she had got drawn into through a combination of necessity and a lack of experience in anything very useful.

"Your face lights up when you talk about it," said Dan.

"You're having me on," said Jane, the exclamation out before she'd had time to correct herself.

"I'm not," said Dan. "You've got lovely eyes anyway but when you talk about literature you..."

"Ah," said Jane. "Literature is very different from teaching literature."

Dan laughed faintly and looked down at his coffee. "Well, maybe."

Jane bit her lip. "You've got lovely eyes," he'd said. It had been a long time since anyone had said anything like that to her – and what had she done? Brushed it aside as if it meant nothing to her.

"So this briefing session?" Anything to turn the focus off herself.

"Just a work thing. Nothing that couldn't have been dealt with in an email."

"A *work* thing?"

Dan gave her an appraising look.

"I do work, you know."

"Really? I mean, I'm sure you do but..."

"But what?"

He looks angry, thought Jane, or was it just petulance? He spends all his time surfing music websites and chatting to girls on forums then feels aggrieved when he's not taken seriously because he's got a job in a bar or whatever it was he did.

"I thought maybe you were a student... or something," she lied.

Dan's face warmed again. "I work for an NGO," he said, after a pause.

Jane tore open a sachet of sugar and promptly tipped the contents all over the table.

"Here, have mine," said Dan, tossing her the sachet that had been lying on his own saucer. "I don't take it."

"Neither do I," mumbled Jane. She stared down at the sugar-strewn table. Her face felt hot and extremely pink.

"What do you do... for the NGO?" she asked eventually, stealing a quick glance at his face. The open, friendly expression which greeted her only made her feel worse.

"Environmental stuff," he said. "Last time I was out I helped with a solar power project."

"Out?"

"Oh – Mali mostly but I've been all over."

"You can't get more useful than solar power," said Jane.

"Try telling my mother that, or my sister for that matter," said Dan. "My mother's favourite refrain is that it's time I settled down, by which she means it's time I started wearing a suit and earning some decent money."

Jane smiled. "And your sister?"

"Well, Donna's not so bad about the NGO stuff – it's the 'protesting stuff', as she calls it, that she's down on."

Jane raised her eyebrows. "'Protesting stuff'?"

"Oh you know, things like the missile defence system, anything with an environmental slant – Donna thinks it's a waste of time trying to protest about it because governments do what they want anyway."

Jane looked out at London washed in grey and remembered the squat she had lived in all those years ago. Once she had been like Dan, marching on behalf of the miners, protesting against the Poll Tax. She had written letters in French for Amnesty, signed petitions and protested outside the Israeli embassy. On one occasion she had chained herself to the railings at Faslane. *No Nukes Here. Save Children, Not Weapons. All Submarines are Yellow.* Jim had laughed at her when she told him about her activism. "Idealistic twaddle," he called it. "Grow up, Jane, for heaven's sake. You're not a student now. Live in the real world." And that had been the end of that.

A cold, late winter sun swept across the café. A pale pool of sunlight collected on the aluminium table. Outside, the Thames sloshed against the Embankment. I should go, thought Jane. I have my jacket and I should go back to my hotel. Whatever Dan's family think he should be doing, it surely isn't sitting in a café talking to a thirty-nine-year-old woman.

She looked down at her bag and began putting on her jacket.

"It's been really nice..." she began.

"Don't go," said Dan. "I mean... I'll walk you back to your hotel, if you like."

Their eyes met for a moment.

"If you're sure," said Jane.

"I'm sure," replied Dan.

They talked late into the evening in the foyer of Jane's hotel. Dan asked her if she would recommend some books to take to Mali. He didn't have much spare time, he said, but as there wasn't much to do in any that he did have, he got through books quickly.

"I'll do my best," said Jane. "But that's quite a responsibility you're giving me."

Dan laughed. "Any teacher who gives her students Bob Dylan lyrics to study gets my vote of confidence."

He was sitting opposite her in a purple armchair. A glossy expanse of coffee table lay between them. Suddenly he leant forwards. "I didn't encourage Katy to come to London, you know," he said. "And I spent most of the time I was with her trying to persuade her to go home."

What was it the Number 17 worker had told her? Katy didn't have any plan. She was just terrified of home. When she'd left the Lees' because she was 'embarrassed at making a fuss' she had gone to Euston Station but hadn't been able to bring herself to get on the train. Instead she had wandered the streets into the small hours of Sunday morning until she'd been picked up by StreetWorks.

"Katy was running away from home, not running to you," said Jane. "I know that and so does everyone else."

As she spoke, an image of Alan Clemmy's wife lying on the floor, the shower screen in pieces all around her naked body, flashed across her mind.

Dan stared at her steadily for a moment and leaned across the table again. Suddenly, he held out his hands. Jane looked at them and remained very still.

"Please?" said Dan. He looked straight into her eyes and stretched his hands further towards her.

Jane felt her heart thump, her face grow hot. She glanced across the foyer at a middle-aged man in a business suit taking a large gulp of whisky. What would people think, she wondered, a woman of her age holding hands with someone as young as Dan? She looked again at his outstretched hands and then turned away. Out of the corner of her eye she saw him draw his hands back again, his body slump down in the chair.

"I'm sorry, I shouldn't..."

Jane shot round again. Dan was pushing himself to his feet.

"Don't," she found herself saying. "Please, sit down. Don't go."

Dan stared at her. In the dim light of the foyer his presence was diffuse but brooding, like the heavy air that precedes a thunderstorm.

He came round and sat next to her, studying her for a moment. "What do you want me to stay for?" he asked.

"I don't know, really," said Jane.

Dan leaned back and looked at her. He raised his eyebrows.

"Maybe we could meet up again," said Jane. She felt like a seventeen-year-old schoolgirl.

"Meet up?" said Dan, grinning. "What kind of meeting up?"

Jane thought of Craigie, her miserable life as Miss Ellingham. She was sick of standing on the sidelines as other people lived out fulfilled lives. Jim. The Stick-it. The endless parade of pupils who returned to her classes with their fiancés, a blue baby, a pink baby, a double buggy with one of each.

"Any kind of meeting up," said Jane, feeling flustered. "Any kind at all."

54

THE MAGAZINES Susan sent me were distracting for a time but it wasn't long till I noticed how young the models were, which made me think about Katy. Was she missing? Or was that just part of the delirium I had suffered? The doctors and nurses kept telling me not to worry.

"You've not been thinking straight," said one nurse, a middle-aged woman with grey hair who seemed to work in the Alcohol Problems Clinic on a regular basis. "You've been imagining all sorts of things."

"But..."

"But nothing, love," she said, tucking in my bedclothes as if I was child. "The best thing you can do for everyone right now is rest and get well."

I was tired, I wasn't entirely reassured, but it was easier to think that if something was seriously wrong with Katy I'd be told, so I left it at that. It was less easy, though, to ignore my growing awareness that I hardly knew my daughter.

Would she like the clothes in the magazines? What way was her hair cut? Was she enjoying school? Did she still have the same friends? That girl Madeleine, the GP's daughter? What was she reading? What music did she like? Was she still practising the piano?

I hadn't talked to my daughter in years and she'd certainly stopped trying to speak to me. Sometimes I'd noticed her bedroom door shutting, heard the murmur of her voice on the phone as she talked to... who? A friend? A boyfriend? The rest of the time she had become little more than a phantom to me, a glimpse of long, fair hair disappearing into another room, footsteps on the stairs, the faint smell of an unidentified perfume in the bathroom.

I would see copies of a magazine called *Misty* lying on the kitchen table, an open CD case on the coffee table. Sometimes there would be a hair clip or a bangle next to the sink, a cream for 'troubled teenage skin' in the bathroom cabinet. The wastepaper bin in the hall contained sweetie wrappers, bags advertising the names of shops like Gap, River Island and Monsoon. The local paper was sometimes left open at the "What's On" section. Bands I had never heard of were playing in the Town Hall. The local radio station was hosting a Road Show at Ayr Beach.

Did she go to these events? Who took her? Had somebody talked to her about birth control and internet predators?

At some point after the death of my angel I had forgotten the child who still lived. My own pain had been enough for me, I could not, and did not want to, cope with hers as well.

55

DEAR Katy,

I'm glad to hear from your Dad you got home okay and I hope you enjoy the rest of your Easter holidays. When school starts again I was wondering if you wanted to pop in and see me on Friday afternoons for a bit? I've got a free period last thing and you're in my guidance group anyway.

Your Dad said you were worried about going back to the Academy. Once, when I wasn't much older than you, something happened to me that made me scared to go back to school. Maybe I'll tell you about it some day. Anyway, you know what? Most people weren't interested, or didn't know, and those that did say something soon found something else to interest them. Like they say about the newspapers – today's front page gossip will be wrapping up tomorrow's fish and chips!

A little bird, or two, told me that you'd joined the Junior Girls' Choir recently and that you have a lovely mezzo soprano voice. Are you remembering that the auditions for West Side Story are coming up after the holidays? I think you should go along, maybe with some of your friends from 3B and get yourself a place in the chorus, at the very least. Remember it's just the story of *Romeo and Juliet* but updated to New York in the 1950s and you can't deny that 3B has read the Shakespeare.

Have a think about it anyway. If you're worried about people talking about you then why not get them talking about your wonderful voice?

I'm enclosing a book I bought up in Glasgow. You don't need to read it if you don't want but I thought it might be helpful.

Just call me anytime you want, even during the holidays. (Your Dad has my number.) I'm just a boring English teacher, after all, and will be in Craigie for most of the holidays doing my marking!

Take care,
Jane Ellingham.

The Family Illness

The Family Illness by Steven Epstein, a mental health expert with more than thirty years experience of counselling addicts and their families, is a challenging read. The addict, he claims, cannot exist without enablers, usually family members, who actually facilitate their loved one's addiction through well worn patterns of denial and damage limitation. Epstein has pitched his book at the partners and children of active addicts but his excellent case studies and step by step guide to breaking "the addicted family dynamic" will surely also be of use to all recovering addicts seeking a better relationship with their families.

Dear Dr Nanjani,

Please would you cancel my application for breast surgery
and rhinoplasty. I might like to have the breast surgery
in the future but my Dad has asked me to let you know it
won't be needed this year.

Yours sincerely,
Katy Clemmy.

56

"I HEAR congratulations are in order," Jane said, looking round 3B, with a smile.

New term, new approach, she had decided. Her miserable past was not her pupils' fault, after all.

"Aye, Shirley's having a baby," said Billy Neill.

There was a titter of laughter from the hyenas as Shirley Stapleton turned round and gave Billy a sharp look. "You'll be laughing on the other side of your face when my David gets you, you wee shit," she hissed.

"That's enough," said Jane, already feeling her newfound resolve beginning to fade.

"Maybe you should do something else," Dan had suggested to her on the phone the previous evening. "You could come to London, and get a job in a theatre, or a publishing company. Why not?"

Why not indeed, she wondered again now, as she watched Billy Neill slapping his ruler off his desk. The boy can't sit still, she thought. But maybe the part he had somehow managed to gain himself in the *West Side Story* chorus would absorb some of his energy.

She took a quick look at Katy. At least while Billy and Shirley were bickering the attention was off 'the run-away'. It was her plan to keep it like that.

"What I heard was that some of you have got yourselves parts in the school show..."

There was a murmur of interest as the pupils looked at each other. "Not me," she saw several of the hyenas shrug. We're too cool for stuff like that, their upturned noses implied. But a few embarrassed faces betrayed the students she was talking about – Katy, sitting right in front of her, Madeleine, Kevin McCarra, and that was before she counted those who would be in the chorus, or in more minor parts.

"We've even got our leading lady in our midst," said Jane,

gesturing down at Katy. "Katy Clemmy was offered the role of Maria when the sixth year girl who was going to play the part decided she needed to concentrate on her exams."

This time even the hyenas couldn't hide their interest. All faces turned towards Katy. "Her?" she heard one of the hyenas say to a neighbour. "You couldnae hear her behind a paper bag." "That'll be because she's in London," came the reply. "Hiding from the police."

Jane saw Katy's face flush. "Bet none of you knew Katy here was an excellent singer," she said looking straight at the hyenas. "Mr Turner says he's never heard a voice like Katy's, even in all his days at music college."

Why did she have to go and mention Ron Turner? The school was awash with rumours. What was it Jim Beetham had said to her the other day? "Ron Turner's been in Sicko's office all morning. Apparently he's been winching one of the fifth years and the girl's mother is threatening to take action." She'd wondered at the time if it hadn't been Jim trying to run down the one colleague of his who had also put in for the post of Assistant Principal, but similar stories from gossip queens such as Jeanette Walker had put paid to that idea.

"Ooh, Mr Turner's got a new pet," she heard a hyena say.

Out of the corner of her eye Jane could see Katy glaring at her. "You said people wouldn't talk about me," she could imagine the teenager saying when she finally came to one of the guidance appointments she had asked her to attend.

The noise in the classroom had begun to mount. She saw a ball of crumpled paper fly across the back of the room. A mobile phone rang. I'm losing control, thought Jane, her face growing hot. "There are other people who can take care of Katy now," Dan had said gently when she'd told him how worried she was that her pupil would find the return to school too much. "Let her father deal with that." But still Jane could not shake off the feeling that she had failed Katy and that somehow it was up to her to protect the teenager.

"Enough," she yelled at 3B, in her best Miss Ellingham voice. The class froze. Her fear dissipated. But at what price? She looked at the anxious faces before her. What sort of job was this where she had to frighten her charges in order to do it properly? Dan is right, she thought, with a sudden weariness. I need to stop trying to manage Katy's life and do something about my own. But what? And how? She stared down at the pile of handouts she was about to distribute around the class. "Youth" she had put at the top of her list of "Key Themes in Romeo and Juliet". "Juliet's nurse lacks the 'affections and warm youthful blood' necessary to be as 'swift in motion' as thirteen-year-old Juliet would like her to be while she waits to hear if she and Romeo are to be married," she had written. In other words, thought Jane, middle-aged people like me don't make hasty decisions, if they have any sense.

She began handing out the A4 sheets. Katy snatched at hers angrily, without looking at her or saying "thank you". Billy Neill looked at his briefly and shouted out, "Sex, it says 'sex' here." The hyenas pushed theirs to the far edges of their desks and after a brief, insolent glance at their teacher, began inspecting their nails.

Rain began to hammer against the window. " 'A greater power than we can contradict...' " Jane said to the class. "Can anyone remember who says that and what they mean by it? Which of the themes on your sheet does it relate to?"

She scanned the room for someone willing to answer.

"The friar guy," said Shirley, looking up from her nails. "He means fate, or God, or whatever. But if you ask me that's a cop out. He didn't exactly help matters, did he? If it hadn't been for all his faffing about it wouldn't have ended the way it did."

Jane smiled. "So you don't believe in fate then, Shirley?"

"Naw," said the teenager, pulling at her blouse so it sat more smoothly over her ample bosom. "Fate's for wimps who can't accept responsibility. You make your own fate – that's what my Dad says."

"Load of shite," said Billy Neill.

"Is that right?" said Shirley turning round to face Billy square on. "That'll be why you're always bottom of the class and can't get a girlfriend – because of fate. Nothing to do with being a lazy, spotty chancer who stuffs himself at McDonald's every lunchtime."

"Right that's enough, Shirley," shouted Jane. "And you, Billy.

The pair of you zip it right now or you'll find fate has sent you to Mr Dick's."

The class quietened. Outside, the rain continued to fall, blown sideways by a gathering wind. The cherry trees in the park dipped from side to side under its force. Jane opened up her copy of *Romeo and Juliet* and looked round the class. Queen Mab has been with me, she thought, her eye resting on Mercutio's teasing words to the lovelorn Romeo. If I'm not careful while I'm fantasising about a new life in London with Dan I'll lose the one I do have.

57

IN HOSPITAL my mind dramatised my own life for me. The dramatisation was not linear but all the more difficult to watch as a result. I walked into my past like children sometimes do a plate-glass door and saw it shatter around me. As I looked at them, the fragments of who I was flashed their sharp edges and reflected back at me a disjointed series of scenes so painful I wanted to rip the tubes from my arms and beat my head off the ward walls.

But what was real, and what was not? Even in my delirious state I knew the angelic baby boy who smiled peacefully in my arms wasn't alive. Before the scene had played itself out and I had tucked him into his cot I was filled with a sadness so bottomless that my heart ached and I tasted tears on my lips. The sleeping infant was replaced by a tiny coffin which dropped like a stone into dark water as it was lowered into its grave. "In Loving Memory of Benjamin Joseph Clemmy, born 1992, died 1996. Remembered with undying love by his parents Alan and Corinne, and sister Katy." The inscription on the small marble gravestone was so vivid that I held out my hand and tried to trace it with my index finger. It rested at the engraved form of a sweetpea stem which we had asked to be placed beneath our dedication. Katy's idea. "He liked sweetpeas," she had said. And so he had, holding the ones I picked to his face and then offering them up to me to smell. "Nice, mummy. Nice."

I must have cried out or moaned because I remember a nurse coming in and asking me what the matter was. Did I tell her? I don't think I'd have had the words but my hand must still have been stretched out towards my son's gravestone; I remember the nurse put my arm under the sheets, shushing at me like a mother and telling me to try to sleep.

Once Katy shook me by the shoulders and screamed at me to get out of bed. After she left the room my husband appeared and told me she was missing. "Missing, Corinne," he shouted. "Do you hear me?"

Oh, I heard him all right, I just wasn't sure how true or real his comments were. Alan had become a demon to me, an angry, scathing giant who shouted at me in my dreams as well as my drunken reality. He terrified me as much as I later learnt I terrified him and my daughter. That's the blindness of the active addict, isn't it? The person who doesn't care about anyone or anything but their addiction.

Woven into the other fragments of the drama I couldn't escape were the characters of Ruaridh and Susan. I watched in jealous fear from an ajar door as they wrapped arms around each other and kissed, falling onto a hotel bed and then fading into blackness as if playing out a love scene in a 1950s film. When I woke, covered in sweat, my hair matted, the sterile whiteness of the ward laughed at me more. The passion I craved could not be further out of reach. The fog, *the hallucinatory half-life*, I now existed in screamed of failure but I had nothing to dampen the pain. Stupid and powerless I continued to pick up my life's fragments, their edges cutting ever deeper into what was left of me.

Even in the most surreal of plays or modern of novels there are themes and stories which emerge from their disjointed episodes and narratives, like pictures from a developing black and white photograph. At first they don't make much sense – a hint of black here, a touch of grey in an opposite corner – but slowly they gather certainty, becoming ever clearer in their intent. In that hospital, the story which bound together the episodes I relived or imagined didn't become apparent to me for many months, or years.

What I've learnt is that a life can unravel in a surprisingly short time, at least on the surface. But to glue it back together again could take another lifetime, supposing it's even possible; most people who descend into the abyss which is mental illness will have lost something precious if they resurface into the sunlight again – a spouse, a child, a job, a house.

Though I didn't know it yet, the drama I saw in the hospital was a whole work. Most of the characters in it would leave me, if, like my son, they hadn't already done so. Its backdrops wouldn't be revisited. Fragmentary and terrifying as it was, it was complete. Something new would have to be created.

58

To Do

Go to Madeleine's to practise songs.
Write letter to Miss E.
Write down all the things I like about myself and
a list of good things in my life.
Do some revision.

Teacher Suspended

A SECONDARY school music teacher, believed to have taught at a large comprehensive in the Craigie area, has been suspended pending an investigation into his conduct towards girl pupils. The teacher, who cannot be named for legal purposes, has been accused by a number of female pupils of sexual harassment.

The investigation is due to be completed by the end of July. Bruce Maxwell from South Ayrshire Council's Children and Families Department, which commissioned the investigation following police enquiries, refused to comment when contacted by *The Craigie Standard*.

"We're looking into the matter," he said. "That's all I'm prepared to say just now."

Dear Miss Ellingham,

I am sorry this has taken me so long to write. It was difficult to know whether to try and speak to you at school or to send a letter. I kept trying to speak with you at school but never managed it. Sorry.

It was really good of you, all that you did. Dad says I might not be here if you hadn't come and found me. He says I'm very lucky. I suppose I am. I'm sorry I caused you so much upset. Dad says I have to offer you money for your tickets to London and other things. If you just let us know what it comes to we really want to return it to you.

I am really happy I got the part in West Side Story and Madeleine and me think we would never have gone to the auditions unless you had kept saying we should.

Dad wants me to tell you he has reported the texts I was getting to the police and they are going to try and trace them (but I don't know how as my phone is in the Craigie Water).

Dad and me have some presents for you but they are difficult to carry or post so Dad says you've to come in sometime when you are passing to get them.

I hope you have had a nice day.

Katy.

PS Thank you for your letter. I will try to come to guidance appointments on a Friday afternoon after the exams have finished – got lots of rehearsals just now as well.

Things I like About Myself
For Mrs Blunt, Educational Psychologist

New haircut.
My hands are quite nice now I've stopped biting my nails.

Good things

Mum not here!!! (Can have friends. Not scary. Dad not angry.)
Dad not shouting at me.
No arguments.
Not getting horrid texts.
West Side Story.
Didn't eat any chocolate today or yesterday.

Misty's Top Ten Mist-aches

We all make them but we think it's our duty to help _Misty_ readers learn from the worst offenders. Here's our top ten of recent times:

10. Vanessa Feltz: Mistake: Existence and inflicting that on us by appearing in _Celebrity Big Brother_. It didn't go too well in "The House" for voluminous Vanessa who was voted out on Day Four by 71% of the audience. Lesson: If you're past-it then get over it and put yourself out to graze.

9. Anthea Turner: Mistake: Where to begin? _Blue Peter_ golden girl turned husband snatcher Anthea thought high standards of housework in the _Celebrity Big Brother_ House would endear her to the public. Wrong. Not long after Vanessa, Anthea too was evicted. Lesson: Never a good idea to steal a husband. At least 50% of the population won't like you for it.

8. Princess Margaret: Mistake: Petulance. Never satisfied being in her sister's shadow

Margaret compensated by drinking gin, choosing useless men and squandering her looks, before dying late last year. Lesson: Not everyone can be Queen.

7. Winona Ryder: Mistake: Shoplifting. What on earth was she thinking? She's loaded and people actually pay her to wear their clothes. Winona obviously felt a dress aint worth $5,000 unless it's nicked. Lesson: Only shoplift if you are a nonentity – the humiliation of being caught is less public.

6. Britney Spears: Mistake: Trailer Trash. Known and loved for her squeaky clean image Ms Spears is actually quite the opposite and recently ran up a bar bill of over $11,000 after a night of drinking and smoking with her crew. Lesson: By all means behave like Trailer Trash if you are but don't pretend you are an Ivy League angel to earn your millions. The truth will out!

5. Kate Middleton: Mistake: Prince William. She's 'new money' posh and pretty which is obviously enough for him but what about her? Does she want to make a career out of handshakes and planting trees – all for the sake of becoming a princess? Lesson: She hasn't had it yet but watch out, Kate... like father, like son.

4. Posh Spice: Mistake: Career. The 'refined' Spice Girl has tried to make a go of it alone over the past few months. But who was to know her first album 'Out Of Your Mind' would be her own best advice to herself. Posh's tosh is a crime against music and will doubtless be the end of her. Lesson: If you haven't got it in a crowd you won't find it on your own.

3. Korban: Mistake: Stupid and gay. First off, you are probably wondering 'who's he'? Exactly our point. Remember *Pop Idol*? Yes, it's him. Down to the final ten and then it leaked out that he was gay. Sunk without trace never to be heard of again. Lesson: Probably best not to enter Mr Gay UK if you want to keep your sexuality a secret.

2. Gwyneth Paltrow: Mistake: Have you forgotten that Oscar

speech a few years back? Well, it's not actually that but it could be. No, it's the dress she wore to the ceremony this year. Dear oh dear. Didn't she just look like a banana caught in a fish net? And that hair-do. We think she is the wrong side of 12 to play Heidi. Lesson: Cry all you want Gwynnie but don't make us do it too.

1. The Millennium: Mistake: We should have celebrated it last New Year, not two years ago. Lesson: Misty knows best – but you already know that or you wouldn't reading.

59

"KATY, try looking a bit more excited, please," shouted Jane. "You're in love, remember."

Katy stared down from the fire escape that Jim and his sixth year art and design class had constructed for the balcony scene. Her face looked ghostly in the harsh stage lighting. Jane made a mental note to follow up the local House of Fraser's offer of wigs and make-up in return for an acknowledgement in the show programme. *Au naturel,* Katy Clemmy looked more like a Pre-Raphaelite muse than a Puerto Rican firebrand.

"Can we try *I Feel Pretty* again?" Kay Simpson shouted from the wings. "We've still not rehearsed it with the choreography. I'm not sure we're going to get enough volume at the back of the hall if all the girls are upstage kicking their legs about."

Ellie Littlejohn leaned into Jane and whispered loudly in her ear. "Hear that? That's another way of saying the dancing is interfering with her singing. What does she want – a bunch of teenage girls standing in lines like a male voice choir?"

Jane stood up. The PE teacher's running commentary had set off an irritating buzz in her right ear. "That Madeleine McCutcheon walks like a penguin" and "those Sharks look like a posse of West of Scotland suet puddings" were just two of her most recent observations. Jane wanted to get away from Ellie before she found something derogatory to 'whisper' about Katy. After all, she had encouraged Katy to take part in the show to *feel pretty,* not to add to her feelings of low self worth, which were acute enough already.

She walked to the foot of the stage. God but she was tired. A month of after-school script readings and weekend "character workshops" was beginning to take its toll. And now she was having to use her Friday afternoons, usually an oasis of non-teaching time when she could catch up on her paperwork, to run full rehearsals. All this on top of her relationship with Dan, she thought. Just as well he was willing to do more than his fair share of the travelling. She looked at her watch. Quarter past three. Right at this moment he would be on the train to Glasgow, coming to see her for the second time that month.

"Okay, let's try *I Feel Pretty* again," she said briskly, anxious to fend off the guilty feelings she had been having of late whenever she thought about her own rather half hearted input into her new relationship. "Katy, come down to the stage. Female Sharks, can you come and take your positions behind Maria?"

There was a clattering as Katy began picking her way down the fire escape in red high heels. ("Some actors begin getting into their character with their feet," she had told the cast members early on, which as far as she could make out had only given the girls an excuse to come into school wearing stilettos.) Behind her she felt a swell of energy as the female Sharks hurried towards the stage. "I'm going to wear a rose in my hair," she heard Elise MacDonald say. "I'm putting one between my boobs," Shirley Stapleton replied. She wiggled past Jane in a pencil skirt she had recently taken to wearing to accompany the black patent stilettos which had become her regular school shoes. It's only a matter of time until I get hauled up in front of Sicko for initiating the demise of the school uniform, thought Jane.

Kay Simpson slipped down the steps at the side of the stage and took up her familiar place at the school piano. A minute or two later she was thumping out an improvised version of *I Feel Pretty*, throwing in snippets of the words for good measure. "She can't be looking at herself then," Jane heard Shirley say to Elise as the music teacher sang a line about liking what she saw in the mirror. Elise sniggered. "Unless it's one of those mirrors that makes you look two stone thinner," she said. "Aye, and twenty years younger," rejoined Shirley.

Jane was just about to say something to Shirley and Elise – enough was enough – when there was a commotion at the far side of the hall. The glass doors that led onto the car park flew open, and in a rush of cold air Jim Beetham and Pete Bryce burst in, marching across the hall like Roman centurions with important information to impart from their emperor.

"We need some assistance in the playground, please," said

Jim, puffing slightly. His sandy hair was on end, his eyes wild and alarmed.

"Major fight," explained Pete, who must have seen Jane's expression. (How dare Jim come barging into her rehearsal like this?)

The female Sharks stopped chattering. Mrs Simpson stopped mid-song and Katy Clemmy, just two steps away from stage level (how on earth was she going to move confidently around the stage quickly enough to pick up her cues?) stood still.

Jim clutched Jane's arm and spoke into the ear that was already buzzing.

"Look, I don't want to make a big deal in front of the pupils but Billy Neill has got himself into a fight outside the Old Tech. Apparently he's been calling Shirley Stapleton 'shark face' and now all the boys in the Sharks, which includes that big brute of a boyfriend of hers, David Lafferty, are after Billy. Billy's got the Jets on his side but they're all off getting measured up by Sammy for costumes just now. It's chaos out there. Sicko's trying to break it up with Teddie from CAD but we need more muscle."

Jane scanned the hall. The only man in the room was Lawrence Jones who was playing Tony to Katy's Maria. A gangly six footer who spent most of his time with his nose in maths problems or playing the cello she doubted he'd be of much assistance in a playground brawl.

"Those Jets stink," said a voice behind her. It was Shirley Stapleton, who had been hovering nearby in an effort to pick up what Jim had been saying.

Elise MacDonald nodded and folded her arms. "Aye. They're always singing about giving us Sharks a battering," she said "We'll see about that."

Jane and Jim stared at each other. Jane noticed a faint twitch at the corner of Jim's mouth and felt herself begin to laugh too. She grabbed Jim's sleeve and nudged him away from Shirley and Elise.

"Not sure I can help you, Jim," she said. "I've got a hall full of female Sharks here. Katy Clemmy can't even manage her shoes let alone break up a fight."

Jim looked up at Katy who stood blinking in the light like an albino rabbit.

"Is she really any good?" he asked.

"I know it's hard to believe," said Jane, "but wait until you see her in action. She completely transforms into Maria, and she's got a voice like Judy Garland."

"Just as well," said Jim. He sounded doubtful.

Jane took a second look round the room, desperate to find someone she could send to help in the playground. She had found it easier to be with Jim since meeting Dan but it bothered her that they could still have an easy rapport with each other after all these years. She had spent far too much of her life forcing herself to grow away from Jim Beetham to start relaxing in his company again now.

Ellie Littlejohn was still sitting in the second row, her arms folded across her Fred Perry polo shirt, chewing hard on her gum. Every so often she picked up a bottle of Gatorade and took a large swig of the electric blue liquid contained within it.

"Ellie will lend you a hand, Jim," said Jane loudly enough for the PE teacher to hear.

Ellie looked over her shoulder. She must have been the only person in the room not to notice Jim and Pete's dramatic entrance through the Assembly Hall doors. (Always hears her own name, though, thought Jane.)

"Ellie, didn't realise you were here," said Pete. "Excellent. Get your karate suit on."

"Yes, come over here, Ellie," said Jane. "Jim and Pete need your help."

Ellie zipped up her terry towelling hooded top and stuffed her Gatorade into her handbag. A moment later she was rushing towards them.

Jane patted Jim on the back and pushed him gently in the direction of the doors he had burst through a few minutes before. "There you go," she said. "Ellie will sort you out."

Jim made a face but he smiled and nodded as Ellie jiggled towards them.

"Jim will explain everything," said Jane and opened the hall doors to usher first Jim and Pete, and then Ellie, into the car park.

She turned back round to address the hall. "Right, what's got into you all? Take up your positions for *I Feel Pretty* please. Mrs Simpson..."

Kay Simpson began thumping out the song's opening chords and Katy teetered across the stage in her heels. Elise and Shirley took up their positions beside the other female Sharks, behind Katy. At the far side of the hall, a breeze blew the assembly hall doors shut with a bang.

"A plague on both your houses," shouted Shirley Stapleton in the direction of the doors.

"And Mrs Littlejohn's," added Elise.

Jane shook her head. The pupils were losing their grip on reality. But so am I, she thought, or at the very least my reality is changing. For it occurred to her that only a few months ago she had wanted nothing more to do with men and now she was involved with a man of twenty four who spent more than half the year in Africa. She watched Katy draw a deep breath and heard her belt out the opening lines of *I Feel Pretty*. All because I went searching for a lost 15-year-old pupil, she thought.

"I've got my date for going back out to Mali," Dan told her the next day as they lay in bed together.

Jane felt her body stiffen. This is what she had been dreading. Confirmation that once again she was involved in a relationship that could not, or would not, last. I've got a genius for it, she thought, her mind running through her boyfriends from the age of 17 to the present day. Not a single one of the men I have managed to get myself involved with has ever been truly available.

"No need to worry," said Dan, propping himself up on his elbows so he could stare into her eyes.

"I'm not worried," Jane snapped.

She saw a hurt expression cross her lover's face and felt ashamed.

"Sorry," she said, looking away.

Dan gave her a quick smile. "That's okay," he said quietly.

"It's just quite a thought," said Jane. "Mali – it's a long way away."

Dan's eyes brightened. He sat up. "We'll keep in touch," he said. "And you can come out if you want. You've never been to Africa. Anyway, it's just for six months."

Jane stared up at the ceiling. She felt as if the whole room was closing in on her – ceiling, walls, furniture. How can I go to Mali, she thought. I'm a 39-year-old schoolteacher with a mortgage, ageing parents, and a loan for a fitted kitchen for God's sake. She felt her eyes well up with tears. Always the same bloody story. Whatever I'm given with one hand gets taken away by the other.

She pushed herself up and swung her legs round so that she was sitting on the edge of the bed next to Dan. Neither of them spoke. For the rest of the day Mali hung over them like an unacknowledged storm cloud.

On Sunday Dan woke Jane early and told her they should take a walk.

"You were so down yesterday," he said. "Some fresh air and exercise is what you need. You work too hard."

Jane did her best to smile. This man has travelled four hundred miles to see me, she thought. He's kind, he's considerate, he says he loves me, he wants to continue our relationship – it's a lot more than Jim ever offered. But as she pulled on her jeans and boots and stepped out into the sunshine with him the doubts that had assailed her the day before began to gather again. Ten, maybe even five years ago, I could have done this, she thought – backpacked to Africa, kept up a long distance romance and found it exciting. Now it just seems like hard work.

They strolled along the muddy paths that wound their way through the edges of fields and scraggy woods, under the railway bridge and on up to the top of Craigie Hill. After ten minutes of concerted effort, Jane felt her mood start to lighten. Dan held her hand tightly and they stopped to kiss from time to time at the foot of a stile or on the bank of a burn. The air was warm and fresh and smelt of manure and pine trees. Before long both of them had removed their jackets and tied them round their waists. Dan laughed and skimmed stones in the river.

It was only when they were running down the other side of the hill that Jane realised they were not far from Millhouse Farm. She was just about to point out to Dan the pine forest and the road up from the town that led to the Clemmys' when she saw Alan Clemmy striding up the hill, a collie scampering by his side.

He was walking quickly, with his head down, as if he were being timed. Instead of his usual tweed jacket he had on a denim shirt and jeans. Jane noticed he looked less tired and that the deep frown line between his eyebrows seemed to have disappeared.

"Alan," she said.

The farmer looked up and then from Jane to Dan. There was a look of astonishment on his face.

"Jane," he said. His eyes kept darting to Dan and back to Jane again.

"This is Dan," said Jane.

Dan stepped forward and held out his hand. Clemmy hesitated for a moment and then shook it. There was a short silence interrupted by the cooing of a wood pigeon.

"Dan's up for the weekend," said Jane.

Dan smiled and put his arm round her shoulders.

Clemmy nodded. "Come far?"

"From London."

"A long way."

It's time to go, thought Jane. She hadn't reckoned on much more than a quick hello. Now she was beginning to feel increasingly panicked by the thought that the subject of Katy might come up. Alan's daughter was a connection between all of them that Jane felt was best left undisclosed.

"Time we were making tracks," said Jane, tugging Dan's sleeve. "Dan's got a train to catch later today."

"Unfortunately," said Dan, making a face.

"Can't be helped," said Jane, pulling at Dan's sleeve again.

"I'll be back again before she knows it," said Dan. He gave

Clemmy a broad smile, then looked at Jane proudly and kissed her on the cheek.

Alan Clemmy stared at one then the other in silence.

Jane seized her opportunity. "Bye then, Alan. Love to... the family."

She took Dan's hand and began running down the hill.

"Hey, hold on a minute will you?" said Dan and pulled Jane to a stop.

He cupped her face in his hands and kissed her. "What's the rush?" he asked.

Jane rested her face against his chest and felt its warmth.

"It's just you've got to catch your train," she said, feeling a return of the misery that had greeted her when she'd first woken up.

Dan ran the palm of his hand across her hair and pinned a stray lock behind her ear. "I don't have to go, you know," he said.

Jane sighed. "I've got work tomorrow and you've got... Mali," she said.

Dan smiled but his eyes looked sad.

"Mali's five weeks away, Jane," he said. "And it doesn't mean everything's over."

Jane opened her mouth to try and say something but she couldn't find the words.

When they parted at the railway station Jane wondered if Dan had already guessed it would be the last time they spent together as anything more than friends. Nothing was said but he was quiet, less excited than he had been. He kissed her very tenderly before he got on the train and she stroked his fingers as she held his hands. She tried to push away the thought that for her romance seemed as elusive as ever. Never the right person at the right time, her mother had a habit of telling nosey relatives in her hearing. The annoying fact was that her mother appeared to be correct.

She walked back to the car slowly, feeling Dan's loss as an almost visceral pain in her heart. Her arms and legs were heavy and the dimming light made the grey stone cottages in the centre of

Craigie look bleak and unwelcoming. She felt a sudden charge of hate for the town and its smallness. Dan was going back to London and then to Africa. He was going to make a difference in the world while she remained imprisoned in the stifling small-mindedness of Craigie. As a place it had brought her nothing, except the brief fire of a love with Jim and the day-to-day security of a schoolteacher's life.

As she reached her car she dug her hand into her bag for her keys. Angered because she could not find them she emptied the contents of her bag onto the ground. Just as she did, a car stopped and the driver rolled down the window. It was Alan Clemmy – again – with Katy in the passenger seat.

"You okay?" he asked, his eyes drifting to the pile of used handkerchiefs, tampons, pens, loose change and keys lying on the pavement.

Jane took a breath. "Fine," she said.

"Lost something?"

Jane sighed. "No, just trying to find my keys."

"You've lost your keys?"

"No, I haven't lost my keys," Jane snapped.

"Can I help?"

Alan Clemmy switched the engine off and opened his door a fraction.

"Dad."

Katy was nudging her father in the side.

"We've got plenty of time, love," he said.

Katy rolled her eyes.

Jane spotted an opportunity. She wished to God Alan Clemmy would just go.

"Yes, you get on. I'm okay."

Alan looked round at Katy. "I'm just dropping Katy off at the church hall for youth club," he said.

Katy folded her arms and looked straight ahead.

"It's only two minutes from here. She can walk – can't she?" He looked at his daughter as he spoke. There was a pause and she opened the passenger door.

"You could of told me that was what you wanted," she mumbled.

"What?"

"Nothing," she said.

"I'll be back to pick you up, okay?"

"Okay."

Katy slid down the side of her seat and out the car. She closed the door quietly, then paused and looked across at Jane.

"Hi," she said shyly.

"Hello, Katy," said Jane. "Everything okay?"

"Fine thanks."

She looked down at her feet and then back up at Jane again.

"Thanks for your letter," said Jane. "I kept meaning to say…"

Katy turned her head and looked along the street in the direction of the church. "That's okay," she said kicking at something on the road.

"You'd better get going," said Jane, finding a little piece of Miss Ellingham from the debris around her.

"Yeah," said Katy, with obvious relief. "Bye then."

"Bye."

With Katy off down the road, Jane started to pick up the items she had strewn across the ground. First to go back in her bag were the tampons. Bloody Alan Clemmy, she thought as she stuffed them into the zip compartment, why can't he just leave me alone. But Clemmy was now out of his car and had bent down to try and help.

"Look, I'm fine. There's my keys," said Jane holding them up and rattling them in front of Clemmy's eyes in a somewhat childish fashion.

"Oh," said Clemmy.

He stood up again. Jane bundled the rest of her possessions back into her bag and stood up as well.

"Right. Well thanks," said Jane.

Alan Clemmy took a step towards her. "Did you have a nice walk?" he asked.

Jane examined his face. He was a little flushed, she thought. No wonder, nosey so-and-so.

"Yes," she said. "It was a lovely afternoon."

She glanced towards the railway station and felt again the sadness of Dan leaving.

"He gone home then?" asked Clemmy. "Your... friend."

"Yes," said Jane, feeling a grimness re-enter her heart.

She heard Clemmy take a breath. "Who is he?" he asked.

"What?"

Her voice sounded like someone else's. She hadn't intended the note of astonishment and anger it betrayed.

"I was just thinking...?"

"You were just thinking what, exactly, Mr Clemmy?"

"Alan," he mumbled.

Jane shook her head. "Alan."

"I suppose I was just concerned..."

"Concerned?"

"Yes."

"You were concerned about what? The fact that I was with a man, taking a walk on a Sunday afternoon? Is it any of your business? Haven't you got enough to be worrying about with your own relationships?"

She had begun to shout and the last remark was probably unnecessary but she didn't care. She was tired. She was missing Dan. She was sad about Dan – and here was Katy Clemmy's father, a man with whom she had selflessly shared rather too much over the past months, making her talk about the source of her melancholy.

But rather than being cowed by Jane's anger, Alan Clemmy seemed to have been riled by it.

"Actually, I do think this has something to do with me," he said.

"Oh yes. What?"

Jane could feel herself trembling. Just what could this man possibly think her romantic life had to do with him?

"I think if my daughter is being taught by a woman who sees men as young as..."

For the first time in her life Jane actually felt violent. She wanted kick Alan Clemmy where it hurt most and shove a fist into his sanctimonious face. She steadied herself.

"First of all, you have no idea what age Dan is..."

"He looks..."

She held up her hand.

" ...you have no idea what age he is and even if he is younger than me there is no harm in me having a relationship with him."

Alan Clemmy stared at her with big, somewhat sad eyes. I'm not going to stop because of your puppy-dog expression, thought Jane.

"Dan is a loving and very kind man; intelligent, fair, good hearted. I don't see what his age has to do with anything. OK, I teach young people... but I'm not having an affair with one of them. Dan is well over the... school age and he lives in London, for God's sake."

She had a good mind to add that the only reason she had met him was because his daughter had been so miserable living with the 'appropriate' middle-aged couple that were Alan and Corinne Clemmy that she'd run away from home, but she stopped herself.

"You really are not in a position to judge," she said instead, her voice quiet.

Alan Clemmy looked at her as if he had just realised something – about himself or her, Jane was not quite sure.

"You brought Katy up in house with an alcoholic mother... you didn't ask for help, you didn't leave, you let Katy flounder until it became too much for her. Do you think that puts you in a position to say anything about me and my personal life?"

Maybe she said it because she had wanted to ever since she had been to the Clemmys' farm. Or maybe she just wanted to inflict pain on the man who had exacerbated her own. Either way, she resolved not to take it back. It was the truth and she was tired of being drawn into the Clemmys' web of secrecy.

Alan Clemmy turned and got back into his car and Jane got into hers. Their doors slammed at the same time. Before Jane had got home it was dark. Her cottage felt as empty as an ocean. Arran and the horizon were nowhere to be seen.

60

ONE day I woke up in the hospital to find a woman sitting in a chair watching me. Hettie, she said her name was. She was in her fifties or sixties with grey hair scraped into an elegant French roll. Her face was still pretty, her blue eyes lively as a girl's. For some reason she started to tell me that she had been in this hospital too, but a long time ago. She had drunk so much and taken so many prescription drugs she had nearly died. She had wanted to die. But she didn't die because she'd stopped drinking. Now she couldn't imagine why she ever wanted to give up on life.

I listened as best I could. I'd spent days and nights half delirious; meeting my daughter and my husband in a place I call hell. They shouted at me and told me I'd ruined their lives. They cried with misery. They watched me drink when I thought they couldn't see me. They saw me reduced to my most basic and were powerless to help me. When I tried to reach out and hold my daughter she turned her back and walked away from me while my husband looked on in silence.

Hettie told me my mind would settle. "Don't drink and things will improve," she kept saying. She was kind and held my hand as I sobbed. "There, there, lass," she said as my grief for all three of our lives flooded me. "Let time do its work."

We talked in a way I had never done with anyone before. I told her about my son. It was the first time I had been able to mention him to anyone since his funeral. I raged at the cruelty of the illness that had robbed such a sweet-tempered, happy boy of a life that would surely have brought joy to all who met him. Hettie responded by encouraging me to think how less rich my life would have been for never having had Ben at all. "Do you know what it is to lose a child?" I screamed at her. "To have to stand by and watch as the tiny boy you gave birth to wastes away in pain?" I cried, and Hettie cried with me. "I don't know what it's like, Corinne," she admitted. "But I do know that if you want to live a sober, decent life you will have to find some peace within yourself."

Hettie continued to encourage me to remember the good times I'd had with Ben, before he was ill and eventually I was able to tell her about how he loved the toy xylophone my mother had given him on his second birthday and how he sang along to the notes as he made them. I told her I thought he would have been musical. I told her quite a lot. But it wasn't easy. Even with Hettie there to comfort me I was scared that by speaking about my son I was giving life to him again and I would be plunged back into grief over his absence.

"He was musical like his mother, then?" Hettie said.

"And his sister..." I replied.

I was going to say more but I couldn't. Hettie noticed it.

"Katy?" she asked.

I nodded. I couldn't speak. I'd remembered with shame an exchange Alan and I had had about a year after Ben's death.

We were in the living room and Katy was in the car, waiting for Alan to take her to a piano lesson.

"You should be doing this," Alan said after he'd found whatever it was he had been looking for.

"Doing what?" I asked. I wasn't really listening. You know what it's like, my mind was full of the drink I would consume the moment both my daughter and my husband were gone from the house.

"Taking Katy to her piano lesson," my husband said.

He was standing at the living room door, staring at me as if he hardly knew me.

"She gets it from you, the music," he said, stammering a little as he tried to find words I wouldn't snap at. (My favourite refrain to my husband any time he tried to speak to me after our son died was that he had "no idea how I felt", a cue that he needn't bother to try and should leave me alone.)

"And?"

"And... I just thought it might be something you'd want to share with her. I don't know the questions to ask her about half the things she's playing or these exams they want her to sit."

Perhaps there was a brief moment of guilt but it didn't last long. I had drink on my mind and – as everyone here in this room knows – nothing will come between a practising drunkard and her booze. Not even her blameless child.

"Katy can look after herself," I said, looking my husband straight in the eye and then heading to the bureau in a pretence of having important things to do.

I can still feel his gaze boring into me as he replied: "She's *ten*, Corinne. Is our daughter to take the punishment for our son's death?"

How dare Alan suggest I was neglecting Katy? How dare he mention our son's death? Had he no idea how I felt? Whether I actually uttered my favourite refrain I don't know but whatever I said by way of reply, his remarks had only helped me to justify my decision – *need* – to drink all the harder and faster once he left.

When I told Hettie of this incident she listened without judgement, patting me through the bedclothes when I started to cry. Her husband had left her because of her drinking and never returned she said. "I was a right little flirt with the drink in me," she added. "I don't blame him."

Perhaps that was her way of telling me I could not expect Alan to accept me as his wife again. At any rate, I look back at it now as an omen. For days I went on at her that he had never phoned, visited or written. "I'm sure he's checking up on you," was all she would say. "He'll be in touch when he's ready."

61

Craigie Academy

presents

West Side Story

Music by Leonard Bernstein
Words by Stephen Sondheim

Thursday 28th June – Saturday 29th June

Cast

Maria...Katy Clemmy, 3rd year

Tony..Lawrence Jones, 6th year

Bernardo...........................Graham Copeland, 5th year

Anita......................Madeleine McCutcheon, 3rd year

Riff...Kevin McCarra, 3rd year

Schrank.................................Scott Murdoch, 5th year

Doc..Alistair Cook 5th year

Krupke...Eric Bryce, 6th year

Ice..Billy Trevor, 6th year

Action.......................................John Lamont, 5th year

A-rab...Joe Simpson, 6th year

Baby John.....................................Alan Baird, 3rd year

Chorus

Jets – Billy Neill, members of the senior and junior choirs (listed overleaf).

Sharks – David Lafferty, Saul Weinstein, Elise MacDonald, Shirley Stapleton, members of the senior and junior choirs.

Orchestra

Craigie Academy School Orchestra, Ayrshire Area School Orchestra (strings section).

Special Thanks to:

Jim Beetham
and his team of budding artists for the scenery.

Jane Ellingham
in her multi-tasking role of director, producer and nagger (we don't mean it Miss Ellingham, honest).

All the staff of the Music Department, especially Mrs Simpson who stepped in at the last minute to fill an unexpected vacancy.

Miss Littlejohn for the choreography.

Mist-understanding

Will she ever stop whining about her love life?

Actress Helena Bonham-Carter just can't seem to make any relationship last more than a month. Or is that a week? The so-called English Rose puts her non-existent love life down to a dearth of decent men. But judging by this photo of the aristocratic luvvy, her lack of suitors may well be down to her clothes sense. Doc Marten Boots with a lacy Prada number, topped with hair like a distressed birds' nest and make-up fit for a part in Adams Family just isn't appealing Helena, darling. Try using a comb and putting on your slap when you're sober.

Katy Clemmy's Autograph Book

Katy,
When you are married and have twins, don't
come to me for safety pins.
Madeleine – that's one of my Gran's ;o
honest!

Hi Hot Lips (just how much lipstick did you have on –
I spent hours trying to scrub it off...)
Seriously, you were fab and deserve to 'feel pretty'.
Maybe see you in Glasgow if you decide to apply for uni
there too!
Lawrence/Tony.

Katy – you did really well. Kevin.

To Katy
You may search for richest blessings
Search until the world may end,
But you'll find nothing half as precious
As the love of a loyal friend.
(Shirley Stapleton, June 2002.)

Hope we can bury the hatchette
(not sure how u spell it). Billy.

What a girl! Proud Dad – June 2002.

Grandpa and I thought you did very well indeed. Love,
Grandma.

You set off the scenery beautifully. Jim Beetham.

You asked me to write.
What will it be?
Just two little words,
Remember me.

Gordon the Shark!

Well done Katy.
By hook or by crook I'm the last in this book.
(The old ones are the best – and I don't mean me.)
Jane Ellingham.

62

"BETTER than a professional production," the *Craigie Standard* had said. "Great fun", "cool", "wicked" the kids had remarked. Even the troublemakers like Billy Neill had gained in confidence and maturity from the experience of being in the show – *her* show – as some of the staff were calling it.

Jane stood in the middle of the Assembly Hall and drank in the happiness of the post-show party. On the far side, Katy Clemmy and her father were chatting to Jim Beetham. She watched as Jim clutched Katy on the shoulder and imagined him telling Alan Clemmy how well his daughter had done: "You should be proud. Quite a girl you've got there." Such was her own happiness at that particular moment that she felt no hint of cynicism. That was Jim. He liked to be liked. But didn't we all when it came down to it? The world needed people like Jim. They greased the wheels of social interaction, made people feel good about themselves. The trick was not to take them too seriously. Pity she hadn't learnt that earlier, she thought.

"Miss Ellingham?"

Jane turned round. Madeleine McCutcheon was standing behind her with a parcel wrapped in gold foil.

"For you," she said, taking a step back and looking at the floor.

She had changed into jeans and a green cotton top but her face still bore traces of make-up and her hair remained piled on top of her head, adorned by a red rose. Her cheeks were flushed and her green eyes shone. She looked radiant.

"Thank you, Madeleine," said Jane. "You shouldn't have done that."

Madeleine stared at her intently.

"Yes I should."

Jane smiled.

"Yes?"

"Yes, you got me to try for a part. I'd never have done it if you hadn't..."

"Forced you?"

Madeleine smiled. She had an alert, intelligent face when she lost her adolescent shyness.

Jane looked down at the parcel.

"Well, I'd better open it then," she said, pulling at a piece of Sellotape.

"Oh, don't feel you have to... you know, just now."

Jane patted Madeleine on the arm.

"Madeleine, it's not often you get presents at my age. I'm going to open this right now!"

Madeleine's eyes followed Jane's hands as they busied themselves with the liberal quantities of sticky tape.

"I hope you'll..."

She stopped as Jane tugged off the last of the tape and pulled out a blue, leather-bound copy of *Romeo and Juliet*.

"I know you've probably got it but I thought..."

Madeleine stopped and bit her lip. Her eyes widened with alarm.

"Miss Ellingham?"

Jane gulped but it was no good. Tears had begun to stream down her face.

"I'm sorry, Madeleine. This was the last thing you needed – your English teacher blubbering all over you. It's lovely. The book is lovely. And so thought..."

She had begun to sob again. Madeleine looked round the room in the manner a drowning sailor might look for a life raft. Jane slipped her bag off her shoulder and began rummaging for a hanky, bowing her head so that her hair flopped over her face.

"Jane."

The voice was male and familiar. Jane looked up from her bag with a start. Alan Clemmy and Katy stood little more than a foot away, staring at her. She saw Madeleine and Katy exchange glances. Katy raised her eyebrows.

"Dad, me and Madeleine are just going to get a Coke," said Katy.

"Bye, Miss Ellingham," mumbled Madeleine as Katy pulled her away.

Jane heard Jim Beetham's laugh from the far side of the room. Somewhere else a group of pupils were singing a snatch of *I Want to Be in America*. There was a clatter of feet and a whoop. They were dancing, still caught in the romance of gang-torn New York.

"Jane," said Alan again.

She tried to focus on the party around her, regain her serenity. Mindfulness, the Buddhists called it. For the truth was she was still annoyed with Alan Clemmy for his outburst that day in the town and had hoped to avoid talking to him this evening. She had imagined herself saying many things to Alan Clemmy over the past few days, all of them angry. "I found your daughter." "I helped get your stupid wife into a treatment centre." "How dare you judge me?"

"I've been meaning to come and see you," Alan said.

"Oh?"

"That day I shouted at you in the high street. I'm really very sorry. It was none of my business. I don't know what got into me."

She unclenched her hands. So there was to be no fight, no comment on her morals. What then?

She should say something. She twisted her hanky round her fingers and kept her head bowed. She could smell Clemmy next to her, a mixture of tweed and freshly cut grass. Out the corner of her eye she caught sight of his shoes. They were polished so thoroughly reflections danced in them. In the midst of the squalor and emotional wreckage she knew to be his home life, Alan Clemmy had taken the time to shine his shoes for his daughter's school play.

"Jane?" Alan Clemmy stooped a little so he could look into her eyes. "You're crying."

"Not really."

He'd also had the generosity to apologise for his behaviour, she thought, which is more than she had.

"I shouldn't have mentioned…"

Jane sniffed and ran her hand under her nose, wishing her paper hanky were more respectable.

"I just thought I should say... Here."

He pulled out a cloth handkerchief from his top pocket and handed it to her. It smelt of washing powder.

"Thank you," said Jane, unfolding it and blowing her nose. "I think I should probably go and see some of these budding thespians of mine."

Alan Clemmy stood aside to let her past. Jane took a step and then stopped. Clemmy would think she was still seeing Dan. But so what? Alan Clemmy had his life and she had hers.

63

THE FIRST day I met Hettie all I was able to tell her about was my fear that my daughter was missing. "I didn't dream it, I know I didn't," I said, half hysterical, perhaps still half hallucinating from all the drugs that had been pumped into me. In and out of sleep, I had dreamt of parrots and policemen – the rush of green and blue feathers across my face, uniformed men at the door telling me my daughter was dead. I'd tossed and turned and woken up with tears pouring down my face. Hettie told me to calm myself and a nurse arrived with a drink that would 'soothe' me. I fell into a long, dark blankness where I felt and thought nothing.

But when my hallucinations had stopped, my temper stabilised, Hettie gave me the news I had wanted.

"She's okay," she said. "You were right, she was missing but only for a few days. She was found in London and is doing fine. Back to school, I think."

She gave me a hug.

"How did you...?"

"I've been talking to your husband. He didn't think you knew your daughter had been missing and didn't want to upset you when you were just beginning to get well."

So Hettie began to act as a go-between, relaying information between myself and Alan. He would come and see me in a while, she said. He wanted to give me time to recover. A card arrived apologising for being out of contact: "The business with Katy took over, I'm sorry, and I didn't want to trouble you until you were stronger. The nurses said you weren't really fit for visitors until recently. But I'll phone you or come and see you soon and we can talk about you coming home. Look after yourself, Corinne."

Hettie and I began to discuss what would happen when I left hospital. I could come along to a group, she said, to get support and encouragement, or I could go back to the treatment centre. I told her I would rather attend a support group. After all, it was one of these groups that had sent the proselytising guardian angel

Hettie into my life. And it's because of that decision – perhaps the first sensible one I had made in many years – that I am sitting here now, eight years on, still sober and able to tell my story to everyone here tonight.

64

CASE 214, Ron Turner. DoB - 24/6/1980.
Witness: Katy Clemmy. DoB - 1/03/1987.

Testimony given Friday, June 21ˢᵗ 2002, 4.30pm. Witness accompanied by school guidance teacher, Miss Jane Ellingham. Taped by Detective Spt Caroline Patterson, Craigie Police Station.

I went to Mr Turner, the music teacher, for a piano lesson on March 28th after school. Mr Turner drove me to his house. When I got there he gave me some wine to drink. I said I didn't like wine but I took some sips of it anyway. I played the Pathétique. He said some bits were wrong and we practised them. Then he asked me if I wanted to eat something and he gave me chicken salad and told me to finish my wine. Then I felt a bit dizzy. He put his arm round me and we sat down on the settee. *(Interviewee upset. Break.)*

He didn't really do anything except put his arm round me and kind of pull me towards him. That's when I stood up. I said I thought I should go. He kind of put his arm round me at the door again when we were leaving. Then he got the car out and he drove me back to school like I asked. I'd told my Dad I was going on to a friend's to stay the night but I actually went to the train station and went to London.

When I came back from London I stopped going to choir and orchestra and didn't see Mr Turner much again. I don't know why really. Lots of things, I suppose. I had exams and Miss Ellingham, the English teacher, she's over there, said I should audition for the school show and I ended up getting a part. Mr Turner left around then, I think, and Mrs Simpson took over all the music for the show. Mr Turner just sent me that one letter which he gave Miss Ellingham to give me. It's with the police, I mean you, now, but it's just a letter reminding me about my music lesson. Mr Turner said he thought I could go to music college and he would help me because he'd been there. He was nice to me. It was sometimes difficult for me to practise my piano at home and he let me practise at school. One time I was crying in the practise room when he came in. He asked me what was wrong and when I told him some of it he said he'd see what he could do to help.

(Tape stopped while we asked interviewee if she could comment on other aspects of the case.)

I didn't know about Mr Turner and any other girls until a few days ago. One of the girls at school told me about the fifth year girl whose mum went to the police, I mean you, because she found out Mr Turner was taking the girl out and things. Her friend's mum had told the girl's mum about it, or something. I hadn't heard any rumours. Well, maybe one about a sixth year girl, one of the prefects. Someone once told me she and Mr Turner were going out together but I didn't really believe it.

(Tape stopped. Interviewee asked to comment on anonymous, obscene texts she received between October 2001 and March 2002.)

I didn't tell anyone about the texts, until recently, because they were so rude and used to make me cry. It was mainly texts but there were voicemail messages too sometimes. I couldn't concentrate because of them. I felt as if I was being watched and they made me feel really embarrassed about the way I look and stuff. None of the other girls at school were getting them from what I know.

I got the last one the day I went to London, I think. I threw my phone away that day, in the Craigie Water, and Miss Ellingham bought me a new one in a Carphone Warehouse in London. My Dad was furious he couldn't phone me but I couldn't stand the texts anymore and just wanted them to stop. I wasn't really thinking, I suppose. I can't explain it properly but I wanted everything that was going on then just to go away. Miss Ellingham, the lady over there, is my guidance teacher and she knows about it all.

But, anyway, if you're asking me if Mr Turner would send texts like that, I don't think he would. I think he's quite a nice man really. A girl at school told me the texts were probably from a boy in my class – she says she saw him sending me one once. I said something to him about it but he never properly admitted anything. I ignored him after that and he tried to be all friendly but I couldn't be bothered – even when he wrote in my autograph book that he wanted to bury the hatchet or something. Anyway, I don't want to give his name in case it wasn't him. I don't care so much if you find out who it was or not now, just as long as I never get these messages again. *(Interview ends.)*

Craigie Academy Magazine

ARRAN 2002

Musical Magic

The school's musicians have had a busy year *writes Shirley Stapleton, Arran's intrepid junior reporter.* The senior choir had a fantastic haul at the Scottish School Choir of the Year Competition, picking up a first place in the A Cappella section and a second in the Scottish Traditional Songs section. (For more about this see Madeleine McCutcheon's report on page 7.) There was also a highly commended at the same competition for the Junior Girls' Choir who sang a medley of calypsos. According to one eye witness (who bears a close resemblance to an English teacher by the name of Miss Ellingham) people were crying by the time they finished.

The Junior Girls' Choir highly commended brings me to our 2002 school show, *West Side Story.* The Academy's production starred a new member of the Junior Girls' Choir, Katy Clemmy. Katy stunned audiences for the three nights of her performance as Maria, so much so that *The Craigie Standard*'s critic said she was "better than Natalie Wood" (who starred in the old film).

Katy, who is also a good pianist, has been asked to take part in the local operatic society's Christmas show in 2003. If she does, it will be the first time Craigie Operatics have allowed someone under the age of 16 to join them.

Go Katy and watch this space all musical theatre fans!

The Craigie Standard

Capital's Ad Rage Reaches Ayrshire

As the national press has reported, in the past month a number of adverts for cosmetic surgery placed in tube stations across London have been defaced by a group of women calling themselves Red Mist.

Their leader, Cathy Wiseman, a Cambridge Philosophy undergraduate says Red Mist was formed after the Rosewood Clinic in Harley Street ran a series of adverts featuring real life patients of theirs who had received breast surgery. In one, a woman of 18 called "Sophie" posed in a low cut blouse above the words "Bigger Breasts Enhanced More Than My Cleavage – It's Great To Be Young and Beautiful." Red Mist defaced more than fifty of these adverts with red spray paint, scrawling the words, "All Women Are Beautiful" across them.

Now Red Mist seems to have reached Ayrshire, with adverts for a new cosmetic surgery clinic in Glasgow being defaced in a similar manner. The owners of the Carolina Clinic in Renfrew Street, Glasgow, refused to be interviewed on the matter but issued a statement saying they would follow the lead of the Rosewood Clinic and take legal action if necessary.

Dr Rajeet Nanjani of the Rosewood Clinic in London has been quoted as saying that he thought Red Mist were caught in a bygone era. "Everyone knows feminism is an outdated philosophy and that feminists need to get real," he told *The Guardian*'s Polly Potter. "The women who do things like this just can't accept that looks are as important as brains to any woman who wants to get ahead. Our adverts are based on real life testimonies from young women whose lives have been turned around by a little nipping and tucking. I think you'll find the women in Red Mist are probably just jealous their Oxbridge degrees aren't the passport to success they once were."

So far, no-one in the Craigie area has come forward to admit responsibility for the defacing of the adverts in Ayrshire but it is thought a group of female students from Glasgow University may have kick-started the campaign and recruited women locally.

65

JANE took her flask out her rucksack and leant against the trig point at the top of Craigie Hill. The first day of the summer holidays deserved a toast, she had decided, so instead of her usual hillwalking flask of tea or coffee she had opted for the remains of a bottle of wine opened during an unexpected visit from Ron Turner a few days previously.

People didn't usually visit her cottage unannounced so her doorbell ringing at seven o'clock on a Wednesday evening had been a shock in itself. But to see Ron Turner standing on her doorstep – even now Jane found it hard to know how to react.

"I'm sorry," he had said, looking past her into her hall. "I just wondered if I could have a word?"

Jane opened her flask and poured herself a small quantity of wine. The coconut aroma of the nearby gorse bushes mingled with the faint smell of the sea in the distance. Above, light clouds travelled across a blue sky. It was quiet except for the peeps of a few oyster catchers which had landed beside the peaty tarn tucked in the dip between Craigie Hill and a smaller peak off to the south.

She closed her eyes. At first she had felt insulted that Ron Turner had come to her for help. He only bothers to speak to me when he wants something, she had thought. But later, as he'd poured his heart out about his suspension and asked if she would vouch for him to the disciplinary board she had begun to feel sorry for him. Isolation and censure were matters she knew all about. Who had she had to turn to when she had become pregnant at seventeen?

"You know there was nothing going on between me and Katy," Ron had said to her almost as soon as he had sat down in her kitchen. He was unshaven and had dark circles under his eyes. The hems of his dirty jeans trailed over a pair of formal lace-ups, which looked as if they hadn't been cleaned in weeks.

"The thing is, I don't," Jane had replied. "Katy told me you'd put your arm round her and given her wine..."

"Come on, Jane, that's not fair. You know as well as I do that I was trying to help Katy. For a while, I was the only person trying to help her. There were quite a few times I sat with her for over an hour while she cried about what was going on at home. I just wanted the girl to have a chance. She was letting her piano slip, staying late at school to avoid going home. It was hardly a surprise to me when I heard that night you asked me to come here and speak to her father she'd actually run away. That whole thing was an accident waiting to happen."

Jane gazed across the windswept hilltops, watching hares dashing backwards and forwards, a grouse scuttling into the gorse bushes. Her eye rested on a cluster of sheep grazing in the ruins of an old shieling. Two hundred years ago, she thought, young men and women would have romanced in such a building, free from the rigours of the winter, the restraining eye of the local minister. In those days, any courtship that sprang up between a twenty two year old man and a teenager, even a young one, would have been accepted as a matter of course, and very likely celebrated with a wedding a year or so later.

"I'm sorry Ron," she'd had to say. "I can't testify what I don't know. People are saying you'd been seeing a girl in fifth year. I know that you tried to help Katy but I don't know what your intentions were or what else was going on for that matter."

Ron had left her cottage with his head bowed. "That fifth year girl is seventeen years old, Jane," he mumbled as he stood in her porch. "And there wasn't a lot of chasing on my part, whatever her mother is claiming. Some parents have no idea who their children really are."

Jane slid her back down the trig point and lay flat on the grass, her head resting on her rucksack. *"Some parents have no idea who their children really are."* My parents failed to see me for who I was, she thought. But instead of standing up for myself and my unborn child I took on their shame and lived with it for the next twenty years. "I never want to speak to my mum again as long as I live," Katy had shouted when Jane suggested during one of their guidance meetings she should go and visit her mother in her new flat. "She's ruined my life and it's much better at home now that she's gone." Maybe Katy's defiance was no bad thing, thought Jane. Doing what so-called adults wanted me to do brought me nothing but misery.

66

WHILE I was in hospital my husband found me a flat in Ayr. I moved into it the day I got out. My husband had phoned and told me he'd wanted me to come back to live with him and our daughter but as she would having nothing to do with me he thought it should happen "later" – although when that would be we never did establish.

It was early summer by the time I moved into that flat. I had missed the spring, just as I had missed the autumn, the winter. Time slips through an alcoholic's fingers like sand. With every drink, another few grains.

I liked my new surroundings and Hettie helped me to make them homely. I bought paint and enjoyed the smell of it on my walls enough to buy some canvases and try my hand at still life work again. Alan visited and was complimentary about my efforts. "You shouldn't have stopped," he told me. I hadn't the courage to tell him everything had stopped still when our son died, including me.

For both of us, our own sorrow was always been as much as we could cope with. Neither of us could give the other our son back. The fact that Alan had tried again and again to make me accept treatment for my drinking had only made me more resentful towards him. Did he think a sedative or a 'recovery programme' could make up for the loss of Ben? I drank more and more until my husband left me alone. Eventually everyone I had ever cared for abandoned me and by the time I began to want them back again I had no way of talking to them.

You see, by the time I got well, there was nothing more I wanted than to speak to Katy. The problem was, she didn't want to speak to me. I don't blame her but it hurt. Still does. But I'll come on to that. As everyone here knows as well as me, recovery doesn't necessarily mean a happy ending.

EPILOGUE

~ 2010 ~

67

Mistyfied

We admit she can sing but in all other respects the sudden burst of interest in nonentity Katy Clemmy is truly *Mistyfying*. Rarely seen wearing make-up, her frizzy hair unstraightened and her body more yesterday's Sophia Loren than today's Kate Moss, this woman is hardly a conventional beauty.

Word has it she was a bit of a swot at school and never had a boyfriend until she was 21. Apparently, she's been heard sounding off about the 'destructive and unrealistic standards' set by women's magazines. Yes, Katy. That anger wouldn't have anything to do with the photographs we published last week of the *Alice in Wonderland* after-party would it? How you weasled your way in there we'll never know, but if you had to, it might have been an idea to shave your armpits first. But none of this appears to bother certain male theatre critics – who seem to have mistaken Scotch broth for fantasy dessert. Let's just hope Clemmy sticks with the geeky looking Scots guy she was photographed leaving Blizzard Nightclub with last week.

According to *Misty's* society editor, Beatrice Huffington, the unidentified man on Clemmy's arm is every bit as boring to talk to as he is to look at. We always thought opposites attract – but maybe not in this case. However, fortunately for us, Clemmy's said to be smitten with him and will no doubt disappear into domestic obscurity with him as quickly as she inexplicably found her way onto the West End stage. Bravo, we say.

Kiss Me Katy

SHE'S the young singer-actress from Ayrshire who's been turning a few heads in the West End. *Scottish Student* sent a bedazzled Liam Hannah to meet the 23-year-old lead of Nigel McLellan's updated *Kiss Me Kate*.

Five years ago you were an unknown member of the chorus in a provincial panto. To what do you owe your success?

I've learnt to keep my feet on the ground. My dad and step mum keep me in line. If I've had success it's down to a combination of luck and good guidance. When I left school I thought I'd try acting and singing for a year. I got a few parts in local pantos and musicals, and it just kept growing from there. I always meant to go to music college but somehow it didn't happen.

Is it true you once ran away from home and had an affair with a teacher?

A Scottish newspaper said so, apparently, which means it's half true. Not telling you which half!

When did you first realise you could sing?

At school. A teacher suggested I should audition for the chorus in the school production of *West Side Story* because I liked singing and had just joined the school choir. Anyway, I did, and got in but then the girl who was to play Maria dropped out and I got asked to take on the role. Bit of a baptism of fire but great experience.

How do you like your men?

Scottish.

Anyone special at the moment?

Yes.

Would you like to elaborate?

According to the papers he is called Kevin and we went to the local comprehensive together but I couldn't possibly comment except to say the first time I had a proper conversation with him was two years after I left school. He says we sat next to each other in English but I don't remember it.

If you could have one wish come true, what would it be?

I think you've got to be careful what you wish for.

Meaning?

Let's just say the reality is not always the same as the dream.

You refused to talk about your relationship with your mother in an interview with Footlights. Why?

It's difficult.

To talk about?

That too.

You've had rave reviews for Kiss Me Kate, what's next?

Right now I'm going for a hot bath.

Any advice for aspiring West End stars?

Don't believe what you read. Don't drink. If you read your horoscope do the opposite of what it says. Know that almost any attractive photograph you see of me or anyone else will have been airbrushed. Never reply to classified ads. Audition your leading men thoroughly.

Lots of actresses get asked to do it, would you ever pose naked?

Is that a proposition?

Liam Hannah was talking to Katy Clemmy at the Almeida Theatre on the last night of her role as Kate in Kiss Me Kate. Scottish Student is giving away free copies of "Katy Clemmy, An Angel's Voice" to the first ten readers to text 4444 with the correct answer to the following question: Kiss Me Kate is based on which play by Shakespeare: a. Jerry Springer, The Opera. b. Mamma Mia c. Taming of the Shrew. Texts cost £1 each from all networks.

Bravura
Underwear for the Real Woman

CELEBRATE your curves. Visit Bravura's new shop in Piccadilly and take advantage of our special opening offer – 20% off every purchase over £30.

For 10 years Bravura has been providing support in its purest sense to women who know what it is to be feminine. Our discreet sales staff pride themselves on the close, personal relationships they form with their clients. Whatever your individual requirements, Bravura will be there to provide you with that lift only properly fitted lingerie can give.

Well-figured women know Bravura shapes up. It's the no-padding alternative to underwear that's under par. It's big, it's bold, it's Bravura.

Bravura Piccadilly Opens April 28th 2010. Champagne and canapes will be served between 12 noon and 2pm. Fittings with our specialist lingerie expert Fleur Duval and her team must be booked in advance. Phone 0207 434343 and choose option 4 to be welcomed into the Bravura family bosom.

Bravura – the shape of the future.

Negative thought: *I'm a cold-hearted daughter.*

The Facts: *Threw Mum's birthday present in the bin. Didn't open it, as usual.*

Emotions: *Guilt – 80%; Sadness – 70%; Anger – 80%.*

Evidence for negative thought: *Loving daughters don't ignore their mothers.*

Evidence against: *All those years I spent trying to please her.*

Is there another way of looking at this situation? *Ask Dr Potts at next appointment. Can't see one. Mum didn't care about me so I've stopped caring about her.*

What would you say to a friend in your situation? *Depends who the friend is. (Ask Dr Potts if this is a case of not entering into the spirit of CBT.) Maybe I'd ask why she couldn't forgive and forget. Maybe I'd think she had every reason to ignore her mother.*

Re-evaluate your mood after re-assessing this situation:
Guilt – 80%; Sadness – 70%; Anger 80%; Cynicism about CBT and consequent anger at it – 95%.

Dear Dad,

Thanks for the emails and the texts. I can't believe you have finally started to text! I think I've only ever received one text from you in my life before and that was when I was about fifteen. Jane must be having a good effect on you. You'll be setting up a Facebook page next.

I'm fine, thanks. I was presented with a huge bouquet on my final night as Kate. It takes up most of my room. (Yes, I know I should be thinking about finding somewhere a bit nicer and bigger but I like the bustle of Shepherd's Bush and it's reasonably handy.)

"That man" of mine, as you like to call him, did come down for the last night so that was good. We went out with the rest of the cast for Sushi afterwards (that's Japanese food in case it hasn't reached Craigie yet). I think he was a bit shy. Everyone kept asking him where he was playing and he had to keep reiterating that he was a trainee solicitor in Glasgow! He said he felt very dull but I think he's just great – as you know.

So I've made *The Craigie Standard* – again! Thanks for sending the cutting. I suppose I should start keeping a cuttings book but there isn't much time and I don't like hunting for pieces about myself in case they are bad. Loved the birthday present. The very fact a *Misty* Nostalgia Album exists makes me feel old. It's got bits from all the original Christmas albums I collected in it and I can remember most of them. Oh man! (Did you know I actually featured in *Misty* the other week? A friend in chorus showed me it – she says it was her younger sister's. Anyway, the less said the better. It wasn't very nice.)

Well, got to go and find something clean to wear for a jazz class later on.

Love to you both.
Katy.

PS Am enclosing a clipping from the freebie *London Extra* for Jane. Thought she might be interested!

London Extra

Films to Watch

Green Shoots of Real Beauty

A low-budget documentary about the deforestation of Borneo's rain forest is fast becoming an unexpected hit at the box office. Extra's Jade Oliver talked to its London-born director after the UK premiere and asked him how a working-class lad from Walthamstow ends up filming orang-utans in the jungle.

Dan Lees' film about the deforestation of the Indonesian rainforests to make way for the development of palm oil plantations makes shocking and moving viewing.

Lees, originally from Walthamstow, undertook *Greased Palms* after successfully applying for a Lottery funded Creatively Green award.

"I didn't know much about filmmaking," says Lees, an Environmental Science graduate, who formerly worked as an NGO in Mali as well a voluntary worker with refugees and asylum seekers in London's East End. "But I've always been interested in environmental issues, and what was happening in Borneo and Sumatra was appalling. About the time Greenpeace and other organisations were starting to do a lot a campaigning around palm oil I met my girlfriend Yasmin, a documentary filmmaker. It was really from talking to her that I began to realise film could be a useful campaigning tool. One thing led to another and, eventually, *Greased Palms* was released."

Lees' film was premiered at the Wildlygreen Film Festival in Portland, Oregon, in November of last year, where it won Best Environmental Film Award 2009. Since then it has been screened in a number of cities in Europe as well as the USA. Its run at Shortwave in Bermondsey will be its first UK outing but it is also due to be screened at green film festivals in Cambridge, Glasgow and Cardiff later this year.

Greased Palms is an intelligent film that recognises that the palm oil industry has brought wealth to large sections of Borneo's population. However, it is for its cinematography that many people are queuing up to see it, as much as its message. The scene in which the orang-utan family welcome a new baby into its fold is beautiful and emotional and it is worth seeing the film for this alone.

"The cinematography is all down to my girlfriend," says Lees when the orang-utan footage is mentioned. "She's the real filmmaker and was able to find me all sorts of talented camera men and women I'd never have been able to hire. Her name should be on the credits but she wouldn't have it."

A modest response from a director whose work is sending ripples through the documentary film world. But Lees' mission has never been to become a great director, simply to raise awareness about an issue he feels passionately about.

"The cosmetic industry is destroying the planet," he says. "And it's doing it in an underhand way. Most of us don't even know that palm oil is in our shampoo or sun cream because it's labelled as 'vegetable oil' if it's mentioned at all."

Lees grins. "You see, you've got me started," he says. "I've to learn to let my films do my talking – that's what Yasmin says. I'm sure that's why she persuaded me to make *Greased Palms* in the first place." The young filmmaker laughs, takes a quick look round Shortwave's packed foyer and stands up. "If you excuse me, I'd better go and say hello to a few people. There are a lot of men and women here who've contributed to this film – please make sure you mention them."

Just to please Dan, I will. They include the aforementioned Yasmin Ajamy, camera operators Mo Al-Abani and Chris Wales, and researchers Zahida Parveen and Zoe Jenkins, plus a host of others you will just have watch the film through to the credits to find out about. I guarantee this won't be a chore, or a bore!

Greased Palms (dir Dan Lees) is showing at the Shortwave in Bermondsey until March 30th as part of the 20th London Environmental Film Festival.

Mother's Day Special

Treat the most important woman in your life to a spa day at the Kensington Hilton. Our special rate of £70 per person includes exclusive use of the outdoor heated pool, Jacuzzi and steam room, as well as complementary champagne and snacks, served as you relax on one of our loungers. For an extra £30 we will throw in a three course lunch for that special lady and discounted tickets for the West End hit *Mamma Mia*. She's special and so is our offer. Why not make it an extra-special day by bringing the two together?

This offer expires on March 28th (Mother's Day) and is subject to availability. When phoning to book be sure to have this voucher ready so that you can quote the number on the reverse side.

Corinne's Cabin

Experience the glamour of the past at Ayrshire's only vintage clothing shop. Glasgow School of Art graduate Corinne Clemmy studied fashion design and textiles before becoming a full-time wife and mother. Single again and a little more vintage than she once was, Corinne has rediscovered her eye for beautiful period fashion in a delightful Aladdin's Cave of a shop tucked away in a converted stable building near Craigie. Come and visit. See for yourself the fantastic range of ball gowns, coats, suits, dresses, separates and accessories. From the Victorian era right through to the 1980s, there is no end of choice.

www.corinnecabin.org

"Corinne's Cabin is Ayrshire's best kept secret – shared by those who know style when they see it." Susan Flockhart, publisher, London.

"From the mother of West End star Katy Clemmy comes a vintage revival production that has swept Craigie by storm. Corinne's Cabin has all the glitz and glamour of a show like Kiss Me Kate without the London prices." The Craigie Standard.

London Mercury

Surgeon Mystery Nears End

THE inquest into the death of Rajeet Nanjani, a plastic surgeon who operated a lucrative private practice in London's West End, closes today. Mr Nanjani was found hung in his Chiswick home two years ago by his cleaner, Agata Koslowski. It is thought Nanjani had debts amounting to almost £1 million. It is not yet known when the findings of the inquest will be made public.

To Do

Tesco's

Toothpaste
Condoms
Beans
Bread
Milk
Chocolate muffins

Other Stuff

Think about getting in touch with mum for Mother's Day?
Send congratulations about Corinne's Cabin instead?
Visit that Bravura place in Piccadilly
Appointment with Dr Potts
Think of more stuff to put in CBT diary
Pick up anti-Ds from chemist.

68

JANE glanced around anxiously as she got out the car and made her way across the retail park. It was pouring with rain and most people had their heads down, uninterested in anything but reaching their car or the shelter of a particular shop but she still felt nervous. Of course, she could invent some story if she was pushed ("a friend in London has just had a baby" or "a cousin in Canada is having an unexpected third") but she really did not want to go down this route. She wanted everything about little Catriona's arrival to be pure and unadulterated by deceit of any sort – when the time came.

And it looked now as if that time was imminent. The social workers were happy. The orphanage in China had been paid. Their little girl was waiting for them. It was just a matter of settling the dates, finalising the paperwork.

She allowed herself to smile. Catriona would be one-and-a-half by the time she was theirs. She would need a car seat, cot, toys, a high chair, bibs, babygro's, frilled socks and tiny shoes, cloth books, and plastic ducks for her baths. All that and love, thought Jane. Perhaps more love than I will ever receive back. Jane and Alan had talked at length about the attachment problems Catriona might have already developed spending her first months in an orphanage.

"And that's before she starts resenting us," Alan had added. "What is she going to feel like having two parents who look so different from her? Won't she want to be part of the culture she's been taken from?"

Jane knew all the arguments but somehow she had managed to persuade Alan adoption was right for them, and Catriona. Catriona would have a life, she told him. One she would never have had otherwise. "And I will have a child – one I would never have had otherwise," she added to herself now as she reached the entrance to Mothercare.

The name Catriona had been Alan's final capitulation.

"Shouldn't we at least give her a Chinese name?" he had asked.

"That would be like apologising for what we are doing," Jane had replied. "And we have nothing to apologise for. She will be brought up here by Scottish parents and if she wants to find out about China herself then we will support her in that."

Despite having her hood up, the rain had caught sections of Jane's hair and was now dripping down the side of her face. She caught sight of her reflection in Mothercare's door and felt the familiar doubts creep in. I am twice the age of a lot of the women who come here, she thought. But no, she had to remember what Katy had said to her: "There's always another way of framing things." Katy was full of soothing psychology these days. Alan had spent a fortune buying her Cognitive Behaviour Therapy treatments at a London clinic. Jane was not convinced it had done Katy herself much good but it did make her a reassuring presence for others. When she asked Katy what she meant by "reframing" she was told, "I mean you could see it that you are able to give this baby much more than a much younger or less, you know, stable woman could." Corinne had flashed between them like an unacknowledged bolt of lightning.

"You make your own fate," a fifteen-year-old pupil had once told her. At the time Jane had thought the comment little more than a symptom of youthful arrogance but now she wasn't so sure. Everything she had which was precious – her marriage, her relationship with Katy, the child she and Alan were about to adopt – was the result of determined effort. If fate had had its way with her she would have remained forever imprisoned by the choices that had been forced on her at seventeen.

"So, Jane, found your motherly instincts at last?"

The well-spoken East of Scotland accent was still annoyingly familiar.

"Jim," she said, turning round so quickly that her hood caught on the rough cast wall next to the store door.

"Let me just detach you."

Jim dropped a red and maroon B&Q bag onto the ground and then reached over Jane's head and pulled the hood free.

The rain on her face was cold and dripped uncomfortably down the inside of her polo neck. It occurred to her that she probably looked a complete state – she hadn't even bothered to change out of her farmyard wellies – but the surprising afterthought was that she didn't give a damn. The only thing that bothered her about meeting Jim was that it was outside Mothercare.

"Thanks," she said, as Jim took a rather ceremonious step backwards and smiled at her.

You'd think he'd rescued me from drowning or something, thought Jane.

"Well, I'd better get going," she said, taking a step forwards. But Jim was obviously not for moving.

"So soon?"

He flashed a smile, crossed his arms and cocked his head to one side.

"Well, I'm busy. Aren't you?"

She thought she detected a flash of anger dart across his green eyes.

"It's so long since I've seen you. So now you're a lady who lunches? No more marking – just a care-free life of domestic bliss... Is that right?"

He had now regained any composure he had lost. His voice was full of syrupy charm, mixed with a hint of bitter sarcasm. Jane refrained from rolling her eyes.

"How's life down on the farm?"

He made the word 'farm' sound like squalor which could only be found in the darkest corners of Calcutta.

"Good, actually," Jane replied. "But hard work."

"Yeah?"

"Uh-hu."

There was pause as Jim appeared to think how best to prolong the conversation. Jane wondered how to escape before he returned to the matter of her 'motherly instincts'. He had wedged himself between her and the door.

"Married life?"

What's it to you, she wanted to ask. But instead she sighed and let her arms relax by her sides. What did it matter? He was nothing to her now but an annoying fact of her past. She would wait out the conversation until he had said what he wanted (for he would not be spending his time talking to her unless there was something in it for him) and then move on to her shopping. There was nothing to fear from Jim. The only person he was interested in was Jim. He had clearly forgotten they were standing outside Mothercare.

"Married life is... you know, sort of easy, comfortable," she said. "But you'd know more about it than me. I've only been married a year."

"Yes, right enough."

He sounded disappointed.

"And you? How are you then? Still enjoying life as an assistant principal?"

It was an effort to ask these questions. In the end it was a form of manners that brought the words to her lips. But it seemed to be what he wanted because he smiled and his eyes brightened.

"Och you know. Not so bad. Sammy and I are managing the kids quite well. They seem to have accepted it. I dare say it's for the best in the long run."

Jane, who had been thinking about car seats for Catriona – clowns or trumpets – felt her mind jolt, like the portion of a train between two carriages as the engine starts up.

"What? I mean, what's for the best?"

She saw Jim's eyes dart to the side beneath the orange lashes.

"Oh, didn't you know?" he said, without looking at her. "Sammy and I split up in January."

Jane felt as if she was standing at the bottom of a steep cliff and Jim was throwing boulders down at her. Somehow, he had managed to do what she now realised he had wanted, to dredge up some of that residual feeling he had once been able to manipulate so well.

"Well, that's tough," she said.

Her voice sounded shaky. All that pain, she thought, the standing on the sidelines as he married that woman and had children with her. All that, for it to be over, for it to be nothing in the end.

"Well, at least I'm not in Ron Turner's shoes," he said. "You know, Pete Bryce was telling me the other day Turner's working in the Job Centre these days. Hasn't taken a music lesson in years."

Jane felt a wave of revulsion. He's had an affair, she thought, and was using Ron Turner's weaknesses to mitigate his own. For the first time in her life, Jane felt a wave of sympathy for Sammy. Poor girl thought she'd caught the biggest fish in the pond only to find it was rotten inside.

Jim was staring at her. She took in the freckled skin, the broad frame, the green eyes she had stared into so many times all those years ago. Even the smell of him as he stood in the rain was disconcertingly familiar.

"Fancy a coffee, or something stronger even?"

Jane stared at him. There was no hint of shame, no awkwardness, no sense that she might have other things to do, a husband who might prefer her not to socialise with such a significant ex. Was he serious, she wondered. But of course he was. Jim had always been serious about keeping her dangling.

Her mobile phone vibrated in her pocket.

Jim watched her as she pulled it out and looked at it.

"Alan," she said and felt herself smile.

Thank God for Alan.

"Got to go. It's my husband," she said, holding the phone away from her mouth. "Wants me to get tomato plants at the garden centre."

Jim hesitated then nodded and stood to one side. As she brushed past him he seemed to shrink a few inches.

Safely past her former lover and inside Mothercare, she pressed her phone to her ear.

"Hello, love?"

The sound of Alan's voice made it easy for her to forget she had bumped into Jim at all.

Trumpets, she thought, when she reached the far side of the store and looked at the car seats. Trumpets to herald new beginnings.

69

NOTHING replaces what you have lost. It is eight years now since I left the hospital's Alcohol Problems Clinic and began the long, slow process of healing. The cuts and bruises went eventually but the days which had brought them into being were never reclaimed. My daughter disappeared during them, and returned. But not to me.

I remember her birthday now and because I cannot ask her what she would like, try to imagine myself at that age. She is 23 now. I never saw her turn 21, just as I never saw her turn 15. For her most recent birthday I sent a silk blouse in an electric blue colour. She is still very fair, I believe, and I am sure it will look good on her. She always was a pretty girl.

So now I have two children to mourn, a son and a daughter. But I have the life I once thought I wanted, Susan Flockhart's life. There are no restrictions, few responsibilities – though these days I'd willingly take them on. I own a vintage clothes shop frequented by art college students and boho city dwellers.

Occasionally the bell that rings when the door opens heralds a visit from one of Katy's school friends. If it seems appropriate I ask a little about her, as casually as I can.

A girl called Madeleine McCutcheon came in the other day. I remember her as an awkward, big boned girl with unruly hair and thick spectacles. She is slimmer now and attractive in an earnest, scholarly kind of way – rosy cheeks, bright eyes and a clear complexion. The glasses have gone. She is studying medicine she tells me: "Hard going but should be worth it in the end. Hopefully." As she adds the last word her cheeks flame. She is modest.

"Looking for anything in particular?" I ask, wondering how I might bring the conversation round to Katy.

"Oh, it's one of these wretched balls," she says, biting her bottom lip. "I hate them. All the fuss. The expense. But James, my boyfriend, wants to go. He thinks it's important to do that sort of thing, keep in with the professors and all that."

I glance over in the direction of the ball gowns and Madeleine's eyes follow mine.

"Oh, yes, that's the sort of thing," she says.

She heads over to the rail and then pauses.

"They're cheaper – aren't they? You know, than the new ones?"

I smile.

"Much. And nicer, I think. Try on that green one. It will look lovely on you."

She smiles a huge smile. My heart finds a beat that is almost motherly.

"Katy suited... suits... that colour too," I say.

Madeleine, whose hands are busy pulling out dresses, pauses and looks at the floor. But she looks up again and stares straight into my eyes.

"Katy looks great in everything," she says. "I saw that picture of her in the *The Craigie Standard* the other day. 'Katy's Voice Fills West End Theatre' or something corny like that. She looked amazing."

I nod, hoping she will continue, tell me something I don't already know, but she turns back to the rail and pulls out the green dress. Not yet qualified, she has already worked out how much to say, how involvement can lead to trouble.

You would like a happy ending, I know, and every recovery story has one. Isn't every one of us here, every drunk who gets sober, a prodigal son, or daughter, of sorts – lost and then found, redeemed by God's grace? The losses I've suffered still hurt: "Katy Clemmy, An Angel's Voice," it says on the EP she's just released. "Dedicated to Jane Ellingham, with thanks." But at least now when I hear my daughter's voice, I know that it is real and not imagined, and perhaps, one day, when she's ready, I'll see her again.

Acknowledgements

Thank you to all the team at Cargo for their belief in this novel, their enthusiasm and excellent editing. Thank you, too, to all the other people who read the text, or parts of it, along the way, and provided invaluable feedback and encouragement, including Ron Butlin and Diana Beaumont. I'm especially indebted to the Glasgow gang of Gerrie Fellows, George McQuilkin and Jim Carruth (who knows the correct colours of Ayrshire cows).